Welcome to Garden Valley

Also by Jean Shelby

Winter in July (FREE to my email subscribers)

Coping With Yarn (To be released November, 2024)

Welcome to Garden Valley

Garden Valley Series

BY JEAN SHELBY

JEAN BOOKS, LLC

Welcome to Garden Valley

Copyright © 2024 by Jean Shelby

Contact Info: jeanshelby712@gmail.com

www.jeanshelbybooks.com

Cover design by: Qamber Designs

ISBN: 979-8-9881120-5-1

First Edition: June 2023

Second Edition: August 2024

10 9 8 7 6 5 4 3 2

This book was originally my free short story, but it never felt complete. I have since replaced Welcome to Garden Valley with Winter in July as my free story to my email subscribers. This version of Welcome to Garden Valley feels much more complete with new chapters, new characters, and new fleshed out plot lines. I hope you enjoy!

Chapter 1 A Disconnected Life

I'm not special enough to be in the 'boy's club,' established in 2018 by my two sons. At least, that's the story I've told myself to ease my daily shunning from their lives. I know parents are supposed to raise kids with the goal of them being independent, but did they need to start this in elementary school?

"Have a great day, sweetie," I say, with a touch on Morgan's shoulder.

"Yup, bye," Morgan says with barely a glance my way. He peels off to stand in line with his class since he doesn't like to be seen with me. This behavior has shown up years earlier than I thought, pushing against unprepared emotions, leaving my heart sore.

"Honey, that's gross," I say to Dillon, who has his finger halfway up his nose. I successfully pull Dillon's finger out, much to his dismay.

I use my fingers to brush his straight hair from his forehead, a trait that comes from my Indian heritage. Both my boys have my light brown, wheatish skin color, something my husband, who is as pale as vanilla frosting, adores.

"Stop it!" he yells, forcefully pulling away from me. I look around in embarrassment to see if the other bundled-up moms in the school line are watching this morning's show. A few quick glances away shows judgment of my lack of parenting skills. It's not my style to yell at my kids when there's an audience. What my style is, I haven't figured out yet.

"It's not real school," Dillon says as I mouth his comment. It's a repeat of the exact four words every morning.

"Kindergarten *is* real school," I respond, as usual. "You're right down the hall from your brother."

"Good. I can wipe my boogers on him," Dillon sneers.

Thankfully, his teacher is early, and I relinquish this wild monster of a son to the school's care. I silently pray that he won't climb on his desk, throw snowballs at recess, or dip into his bag of tricks, which is as deep as Mary Poppins's. It's not too much to ask that I won't get a 'Your kids have been naughty' email or a bright yellow slip of paper detailing Dillon's misdemeanors for the day.

"Morning, Joanie," comes a boisterous voice from my left. "Awfully cold, isn't it?"

"Hi, Denise. Yup, nothing out of the norm for this time of year. It wouldn't be all that bad if we had the sun on our backs," I complain. The forecast is a repeat for the foreseeable future: cold and dark, even though we are on the brink of spring. "I swear there are only two seasons here: bitter cold and lukewarm." I clench the hot packs in my jacket pockets, the talk about the weather making it even colder.

"Don't I know it? These scrubs aren't exactly a barrier to the cold." She hugs and kisses her little girl, who has her arms wrapped around Denise's middle. My heart aches with jealousy as they wave a goodbye full of smiles and well wishes for each other's day. "Chad might have a chance to transfer out of Fargo. I keep telling him I'll follow him anywhere as long as it's warmer," she says as we walk to our cars.

"It will take you a year to completely thaw," I say with more envy. Even after ten years, I have yet to grow accustomed to being cold.

The thought of moving and derailing my schedule is terrifying. Besides, my husband, Nick, is living in his dream career, and I could never ask him to move just because I'm perpetually covered in goosebumps.

It was an easy decision to move to North Dakota when my in-laws already lived here and Nick was offered a promotion. They moved to Oregon a few years ago, claiming they could no longer take the harsh winters.

I pull my body deeper into my jacket as a stiff breeze blows right through my fabric, not blaming them one bit.

"Moving sounds like a lot of work. I think my feet are stuck too firmly in my schedule to do something like that," I defend.

"Or is it a rut you're stuck in?" she teases, winking a bright blue eyelid. I've worked with Denise at the nursing home for seven years now. She knows quite a few of my quirks that, as much as I've tried to hide them, are displayed like a poster on my back. This one, she's hit right on the head. "You working this weekend?"

"Saturday, as always." A sigh comes through my voice, an audible sound of the exhaustion my schedule instills. Nick and I haven't had a day off together since Christmas. It isn't like we have plans, but it'd be nice to spend some time together from time to time.

Aside from my feet complaining, working fifty hours a week isn't the worst thing in the world. "It's not like the boys miss me."

"I'm sure they'll come around one day." It's a hollow,

common response from those who aren't invested in my life. I hold no grudges against this 'advice.' After all, our issues keep us busy enough to not wade into the troubled waters others have.

"I guess. They get naughtier every day. I went into the kitchen this morning, and Dillon was swinging on the cabinets! When I asked him to get down, he jumped off the counter and broke two glasses and a plate. I don't know why they still surprise me," I say with a shake of my head.

"Maybe one day he'll be into rock climbing. See you at work," she says with a wave. This is as deep as our conversations go. I've kept a line out there, hoping to reel in helpful advice, but I haven't had a bite in years.

She leaves me on my island of sadness. My tsunami of troubles crashes as it does every time I bring up the disconnect with my boys.

I've reached out to Nick, my mom, my sister, and my sister-in-law. They all have a similar answer to Denise's that brushes my problems from their list: 'Boys will be boys,' or 'They're just independent.' None of it is helpful.

It's a mystery yet to be solved, how to feed the love and attention that I so hungrily crave.

***

I sneak in the side door of the breakroom, as is my usual practice when the big hand is even a smidge past eight o'clock. If my boss, Robert, knew how many times I've done this, my personnel file would need its own drawer.

I won't see this breakroom until my shift ends in nine hours. I reluctantly shrug out of the warmth of my heavy coat and robotically untangle my dark brown ponytail from the hood. As I hang my purse in my locker, the empty hook beside it makes me realize I'm one bag short.

"Nice. I forgot my lunch again," I say to Denise when she joins me. "I swear I've become less responsible now that I'm in my thirties."

"It's called 'mom brain,' hon," Denise responds.

"Maybe today's the day when I actually skip a meal," I say, bouncing my palms against the extra padding permanently glued to my hips. Even though Nick says he loves my bottom half, I wish it would distribute to the rest of my body and even out my pear-shaped frame.

"How's it going?" I ask Rebecca, coming out of the breakroom and threading the white clinical jacket around my shoulders. As the receptionist, she has the worst job in this assisted living facility. I hardly think she notices. She likes the challenge of the arguments that land at this desk.

"Hey, pretty girl! It's slow so far. Gloria is already asking for you," she sings. "She wants a rematch in Pinochle."

"Oh yeah? If you see her, tell her my lunch hour is hers."

Becoming a Certified Nursing Assistant was far from my original plan. I'm in charge of distributing medications, among various other duties, which is quite an undertaking for one hundred residents. It's not my dream job, but it helps pay the endless stream of bills.

The phone barely rings once before Rebecca clicks the button on the headset. "It's colder than the North Pole today. How can I help you?"

Her peppy ways make sense. She graduated high school last year and doesn't yet have the experience of being beaten down by the workforce. I like my patients, but by the end of the day, my chest is typically gripped with the tension of demands.

"Ready to get started, Joanie?" My shoulders flinch at the grate of my boss' voice. Robert seems to come out of the woodwork. His shiny, red face peers over his favorite jet-black clipboard. I've wondered more than once if the damned thing has a permanent spot next to his pillow.

"Ready as always," I respond with a smile that doesn't come close to matching Robert's enthusiasm. I know because he's told me.

"Let's try and get the first med-pass out by nine today, okay?" He varies the pitch of his voice, as one would to convince a child to do something unpleasant. *The dentist will have new toothbrushes after your cavity. You'll get a lollipop after your shots today.*

"Isn't that a bit risky?" I ask with a cock of my head to soften my opinion. It's nothing new that Robert's energy and ideas clash with mine. "I rush it as it is and can barely make it by ten."

"Chuck can do it," he says over his shoulder as he walks away.

"Chuck works the night shift," I grumble, knowing less than half the meds are passed out at night. I don't dare press the issue. If Robert had it his way, I'd work ten-hour shifts like everyone else. I just can't do that with Nick having a forty-five-minute commute each way and the boys starting school just before eight.

I grab the little paper cups for medications with shaky fingers. I'm not one for spontaneity. My brain was scrambled last week when the store was out of my usual brand of dish soap.

Robert is constantly adding tasks to my list, changing my hours, and wreaking havoc with my morning routine of getting the boys ready and out the door on time. He is a household name for us, but not in the same way as Kelly Clarkson or The Rock.

Denise and Rebecca mosey into the med room. The three of us have a 'surface chat' as I drop pills in one hundred little cups. They discuss light subjects such as the weather and what's new on TV, as if I have time to watch a show at night.

I listen to Rebecca recount her night school stories, and Denise excitedly talk about the possibility of moving. "I'll sure miss giving baths if I move," she says with seriousness before we giggle at her joke. "If I go, we should get together outside of work, maybe have drinks to say goodbye."

"Sounds good," I nod, knowing I'll never follow through with this engagement. I don't have time to fit a social life, well, into my life. These women are nice, but these friendships are as empty as the cookie jar I emptied last night. Nothing we talk about is profound.

My watch buzzes with the daily reminder of my dinner menu. "Darn, it's lasagna night," I say aloud, moving my hands as quickly as possible with the medicines.

"Why is that bad?" Rebecca asks as she leisurely files papers in charts. "I love lasagna."

"It takes forever to make, and I'm working until five-thirty today."

"Just make something else," Denise says with a swipe of a hand.

"You know I have my dinner schedule. It's lasagna night." The greens of my eyes flicker at the shock of her statement, comically showing dedication to my meal rotation. Without my schedule, I waffle back and forth, not knowing what to make, wasting precious evening time when I'm not working. "It's great that my kids aren't picky, but their taste buds refuse leftovers… which I left on the counter at home today."

"I don't know how you keep so strict with your schedules, Joanie. I say, just wing it!"

"I know, I'm weird," I say, brushing off her comment. People don't mean harm when putting their stamp of opinion on others' lives.

Denise has no idea what I'm going through. Life is easier when you work part-time, have one little kid who is an angel, and a husband who gets to work from home and does all the shopping, cooking, and cleaning. What Denise doesn't have a clue about is how much I've altered my life in ways to deal with these hang-ups. If that means I have a laminated meal schedule on the bulletin board at home with associated ingredient cards to take to the store, so be it. A mom needs to save time when she can!

A clanging noise approaches, and before I see him, I know it's Mr. Alders, one of our residents. He approaches with an angry look, complete with a night robe and slippers.

"I locked myself out of my room!"

"Again? Okay, let me get your key," Rebecca says from her reception area next door. She hands him a key, and he stares at it with apparent confusion.

"What am I supposed to do with this?" Mr. Alders asks, his face scrunching as if the key were foreign. He locks himself out of his room at least three times a week for extra attention.

"I'm not going to open it for you." It's a snarky response from Rebecca, as usual. She laughs it off as if it's meant to be a joke.

I glance at Denise, who excuses herself to avoid the situation. "I'll help you, Mr. Alders," I say, making a tick mark on my check-off list before abandoning the stressful task. These little interruptions are what make the arduous med-pass take longer. "Did you get new slippers?"

"My daughter brought them by. Do you like them?" he asks, sticking his right foot out of his long blue robe.

"They look cozy. Good morning, Mrs. Cline," I say to another resident, who pats me on the shoulder. I've grown to know each and every one of them. I know their favorite foods, medical histories, and daily routines. The patients make dealing with Robert's high-maintenance ways worth it.

Mrs. Cline makes eye contact with me. "Joanie, my toilet is making that hissing sound again. Do you think you can…"

"I'll stop by right after my med pass, no problem," I answer without skipping a beat. I help Mr. Alders into his apartment and return to my station, only to find Robert waiting for me with a scowl.

"And where have you been? This door is to remain locked when you leave, Joanie," he reprimands, his breath thick with the scent of coffee.

"I needed to help Mr. Alders into his apartment again. Denise was here when I left," I say in defense.

"It's *your responsibility*. I'm going to have to write you up for this," he says with a scribble on his clipboard.

"Write me up? Robert, I was gone for one minute."

"You know the rules," he says without heart. "And Joanie, remember that number fifteen has a different dose for his Vasotec. You have the old dosage on the sheet, I noticed."

"What?" I ask. With every medication pass, I diligently review the check-off sheet, matching each patient with every medicine and dosage he or she takes. "It doesn't show that for Mr. Miller," I say, looking at the master sheet.

"His doctor called last night and changed it," Robert says

irritably.

"Who took the call? They are supposed to update the list. Otherwise, how am I supposed to know?"

"You should be checking the charts."

I shake my head, ready to defend my stance, knowing my muted tones won't make a difference. "It would take hours to check every patient's chart every day, Robert. Any and all changes should go directly on the master sheet."

"I know the rules, but you're wrong here. Make sure you update the pill," he commands before leaving me in a cloud of anger.

I figure Robert will also write me up on talking back, even though I suspect he's the one who took the call. I swear my employee file is thicker than some of our patient's files. It's full of these little errors that are other employees' mess-ups, not mine. Robert doesn't see it like that, spending his days making these mundane reprimands to give himself a heightened sense of authority.

I continue sorting the meds, swiping at the tears of frustration before they leave streaks down my face.

After Robert's lecture, I diligently check the patient's medicine list against every pill as quickly as possible, my brain on high alert. I'm drained after nearly one hundred cups are labeled and filled accurately.

"There she is with our goodies!" Mrs. Grogan says, rubbing her hands together when she sees me enter the cafeteria.

Other residents joke about getting their 'happy pills,' thank me, and offer small hugs. Earning this affection does good for my soul. Lord knows I don't get enough of it at home.

After passing out the tiny cups of pills, I start my rounds

with my twenty assigned patients. There are five of us CNAs on duty during the day. We help with showers and baths, change sheets, stock apartments with necessities, and serve as a general friend and counselors. It's tiring, but the rewards of bringing happiness to my patients' lives are worth it.

I first stop by Mrs. Cline's apartment to make good on my promise to fix her toilet. "You know, my son-in-law tried to fix it over the weekend, but he's not very good at this sort of thing," she lilts in a gossipy tone. "Not like you. *You* can fix anything. They should fire that so-called maintenance guy and have you to it."

"I just have the touch," I say, not leading on to my past. It's true. I can fix just about everything, yet these little tasks at work are the only tinkering I practice. "My two brothers and I made birdhouses one time. They were so envious of mine. It was what my dad labeled 'the mansion of bird homes.'"

In college, my carpentry instructor said I was the most skilled and creative student in the program—possibly the best he had taught. Enrolling in carpentry school was a natural progression for me, having learned so much from my dad as a kid.

It's what I wanted to do for a living: make furniture or doing repairs for others. The associate's degree behind my name would have been a good selling point had I followed through with my nearly-forgotten plans to own a business.

Mrs. Cline squeezes my hand, a gesture that shows she is listening. "You're a magician, Joanie, thank you. That noise has been keeping me up the last two nights."

"I'm sorry about that. You should be good to go now," I say, accepting her hug. It feels good to be given recognition. I try hard in every area of my life, sometimes to a fault, and it's nice when others notice.

My phone dings in the hallway, reminding me to check on Dillon's behavior at school, as requested by his teacher. Nick and I have been called away from work several times to pick him up after he's repeatedly yanked on some poor little girls' hair or drawn all over the bathroom mirror with a permanent marker.

Today doesn't seem much different from the rest, with the report of Dillon having to sit on the sidelines during PE.

"What's wrong?" Brett, another CNA, asks.

"Oh, my son apparently played too hard during dodgeball."

"Is that even a thing for that game?"

"Apparently."

"Sounds like the teacher is hyper-focused on him."

"Exactly!" It's a perfect way to explain the feeling when I go to the school.

What can I do? We can't afford to send the boys to private school, and I'm definitely not cut out for homeschooling my kids.

"Hey, do you know where the extra wheelchair is?" Brett asks. "The one in my wing is missing."

I roll my eyes with a smile. "The night shift probably played that racing game with them again. Try the closet across from the breakroom."

"Great, thanks, Joanie."

"Joanie, do you know where the key to the supply closet is?" another CNA asks. "Mr. Alders wants the special soap for his bath."

"Yes, it's hanging on the lanyard behind the door in the med room." Robert made us turn in all our keys to the supply room, making it exponentially harder to access. He says we need to cut down on expenditures and thinks this will help, even though the last time I checked, we were under budget for this time of year.

My feet have wings as I fly through a million daily tasks. Dillon's negative progress report is like a dark cloud hanging above it all. I haven't had a sunny day since he started daycare four years ago at age two.

My bi-weekly conference with his teacher has wrung me dry with reports of Dillon being unaffected by any type of authority. When Nick and I discuss what to do, it usually ends with us staring at each other, awaiting the other to devise a brilliant idea of how to tame our sons.

I'm in a familiar daze as the minutes tick by, wracking my brain for ideas for being a better parent. The carpet I've been staring at fades into a watery blur until tears slide down my face. The dampness returns me to my current setting, and I nearly leap out of my skin when I see Robert standing right behind me.

"Robert! You scared me."

His chin is set as firmly as his grip on his clipboard. "You abandoned your post, Joanie."

What is this, the military?

"I had to fix a toilet, and…"

Robert laughs as if this has been a big prank on my behalf. "I'm joking. Gosh, you know I don't crack the whip."

Hardly.

"Go ahead and start your regular duties," he demands, wandering off.

"No, really?" I mumble, keeping my opinions to myself. I've secretly been vying for Robert's job. Lord knows we could use the extra money with the promotion. I've been looked over, however. Like everything else in my life, despite how hard I try, my flaws shine like as a spotlight.

Chapter 2 The Ultimate Shock

The report of my boys misbehaving during the after-school program is typical. They are in trouble for entirely different reasons, however. Morgan stands in front of the room in all his nine-year-old glory, putting kids in timeout when they don't follow his rules. Dillion is the opposite of a rule follower. With it being the third quarter of school, his antics are wearing thin on the staff. Messing with the teacher's things, jumping from desk to desk, and messing with other kids' cubbies are all part of his repertoire of mischief.

Perpetual embarrassment leaves me tucking my invisible tail between my legs on a daily basis. Their behavior reflects my lack of parenting skills. Nick and I haven't made parenting enough of a priority, chasing after our kids who are running the show. We've formulated plans but have yet to pull the trigger.

When Nick's mom, Marge, lived in town, she told me I needed a firmer hand when they were younger so they wouldn't get out of control when they were the age they are now. She watched the boys often when she lived here and was the only person who could control them. After she moved to Oregon, Morgan took it upon himself to try to be in charge. With my lenient tendencies, he has pretty much succeeded.

"Tough day at school?" I ask my oldest, lightly resting my hand on his shoulder. I should be used to the disappointment of his snub, but my feelings still fall as hard as my arm after he shrugs it off.

"The kids in the after-school program are so stupid," he says with attitude. "One kid went to the bathroom and left the door open. Then he didn't wash his hands!" I'm inwardly amused at his description of what being 'bad' is.

We rush to the car with the freezing rain fueling our feet. Dillon runs around the parking lot like a dog freshly freed from his leash. "Dillon, come over here!" I scold. No matter how fierce I try to sound, my quiet voice never rings as loud as I intend. Luckily, I'm the last parent of the day to pick up my kids, so there aren't any witnesses.

"There aren't any cars," Dillon returns, ignoring my command.

"Dillon, now!" Morgan says seriously, starting toward him. Dillon comes back to us, though he plays it cool like this was his decision.

Boys.

Morgan immediately gives his brother a noogie when we get in the car. "Morgan, be nice." My words land on deaf ears. Dillon whines before hitting his brother. "Guys, please don't." The interaction drains my nearly empty bucket. They know nothing of my hard day, nor would they care if I told them. Whether I like it or not, my night shift at home has just begun. At least at work, I get paid, *and* I occasionally get a break.

"What's for dinner?" Morgan inquires forcefully.

"It's lasagna night, so salad and sourdough…"

"We had that last week!" he complains.

"No, we didn't. We last had it four weeks ago," I say,

stopping at a red light and answering a text from Robert about the whereabouts of a key. "You know I have the meal rotation," I respond in defense of my schedule.

"I don't like your lasagna. The one at school is better." I ignore Morgan, wondering which one of my children is the more challenging– the nine-year-old treating me like a fifty's housewife or my six-year-old who runs around like a feral cat with catnip.

"Mom, Morgan hit me in the face," Dillon whines.

"Maybe you shouldn't play that handsy game," I suggest as they continue to bat each other's hands as quickly as possible.

I turn on a song by Bruno Mars, hoping to shift the focus away from their incessant need to annoy each other. I playfully belt out the chorus in off-key notes, turning my face to the backseat when we have another red light. The boys give me a surprised look and glance at each other before Dillon joins in. Phew, another backseat argument averted.

I glance at the clock every few seconds, longing to be home. Why I'm looking forward to preparing dinner and an evening of nightly chores is a mystery to me. Checking things off a self-made list makes me feel productive, fooling myself into thinking I've accomplished something.

"I do, too, know my alphabet!" Dillon screams, breaking my trance. Freezing air whooshes around the van after Dillon rolls down the back window.

"Hey, roll up the window!" I shriek, whipping around to see what's going on. Hairs that have escaped my ponytail throughout the day cover my face, blocking the view of my two-second peek of the backseat.

"I'm not stupid!" Dillon continues to yell. I look in the rearview mirror just in time to see Dillon's shoe flying from the car.

"Dillon! What are you doing?" I yell, nearly swerving off the road. I look back again to see shoe number two thrown out the window. I'd roll it up myself, but my controls have been broken for years, the aftermath of rowdy boys.

"I can't believe you threw your shoes out the window! What were you thinking?" I yell, unable to keep the mixture of shock and anger from my voice.

"Morgan called me stupid, and…."

"I don't care what he called you! Now I have to search for your shoes in the dark. And it's raining!" I find a place to pull over on the highway and back up slowly on the shoulder.

I slam the car door before tromping into the ravine with my useless phone flashlight. Heightened adrenaline helps me forget my fear of the darkness and what's beyond. "There's one!" I yell as if I've found an Easter egg.

I continue searching, glancing back at the van to spy my boys' faces pressed against the window. I lose my footing, and down I go, sliding a few inches in the mud on my side. I stand to assess the damage, thankful I didn't get hurt. Ten minutes later, when I'm soaked through, I call it quits.

With only one shoe, I return to the van in defeat, ashamed that I lost my temper and yelled before leaving the car. I grab a small rag to drape over the seat before sitting my muddy butt down.

"You'll have to wear your backup shoes until I can get you another pair after work tomorrow," I say apologetically. I'm more cold than angry at this point. I flip my turn signal on with my left hand as my right blasts the heater.

The boys continue to argue on our drive home, not giving one care that I'm shivering and starving. I allow my tears to mix with the rain on my face. The worst part is that this isn't an unusual day for me.

***

Our dark-red, one-story house awaits us under a dark sky, the same as it was when I left this morning. I park in the narrow driveway and push the button for the boys to exit on the left so they don't run through the muddy yard to the right of the van.

Ignoring the open sliding door, Morgan wrenches the right door open. Before I can tell them to avoid the mud that is a direct result of Nick and I having neglected our yard, the boys have darted into the house, no doubt tracking footprints everywhere. In Dillon's case, it's sock prints.

"No, not that way!" I yell to a now empty van.

Deflation keeps me rooted in my seat for a moment as I hear the rain and sleet pounding against the van. The song 'Fix You' from Coldplay comes on, stopping my hand on its way to pulling the keys out of the ignition.

"I *have been* trying my best, darn it!" I say back to the song. And no, I haven't succeeded at any of it. I breathe in sharply before allowing my shoulders to sag forward. These lyrics say it all for me. I stop the song before the words about tears streaming down your face have the same effect on me. I don't need to cry for a third time today. Although, it wouldn't be the first time I've cried while making dinner.

"Don't worry, I'll bring all this stuff in!" I say in frustration. The boys have tossed everything out of their bags before heading inside, something they do every day.

Rain and sleet pelt my face with the force of the fifteen-mile-per-hour wind that I swear hasn't stopped since

October. I tell myself I like living here, even if my body craves sunshine most of the time.

With both arms full, I make it through the front door with my wet ponytail dripping down my back. The scent of lilac candles meets my nose, signaling I'm home. It does the trick of covering up the damp smell we can never find the source of in this rental house.

I trip on Morgan's shoes in what we call a foyer, which is a four-by-four stretch of linoleum. I toss Dillon's one shoe on the pile, which is literally inches away from the empty shoe cozy I've built.

"That's better," I say after my elbow finds the light switch, though it does little to help the space it falls on. "Better-ish," I mumble. The living room beyond the foyer barely has enough space for a loveseat, a small couch facing the TV, and an ottoman. The plain brown furniture and white walls do nothing to inspire decor in the room.

In my twenties, I learned firsthand that ivory, cream, and eggshell are pretty much just white. It's all boring if you ask me. I've always wanted to change this room up with splashes of color but could never decide which one to go with. Tiny homes can be cute, but I'm better with tools and wood than adding feminine touches of color and flare that make a place feel homey.

I pass the same garage sale pictures of a waterfall or meadow that someone, at some point, enjoyed firsthand. This small square of a living room would look amazing with the shelves I made for this space. Like all my other half-done projects, the shelves are tucked away under a thick layer of dust in the garage.

After shedding myself of the wet, muddy scrubs, I make it to my nightly post in the kitchen. First, I feed the leftover meatloaf I left on the counter this morning to the garbage disposal. "Such a waste."

I text Nick before getting started on dinner to see what time he'll be home. I drag out the lasagna ingredients from multiple cabinets, quickly filling the little counter space I have to prepare our meals. I like to save time by boiling the lasagna noodles first, even though it takes almost fifteen minutes before the first hints of baby bubbles appear due to our ancient electric stove.

My phone tings a wolf whistle, reminding me of when Nick makes this noise for me in person.

Miss me? Nick

Always. I reply, with my shoulders sinking at the trueness of the one-word answer. Our marriage is held together by strings of text messaging and maybe an hour or two of in person time at night. It's not enough, and my skin always misses the touch of his fingertips.

I need to make sure I have dinner ready for you when you get home. Joanie

He always tells me I don't have to rush home and make his meals. Call me old-fashioned, but I like to serve a hot meal to my family. Nick always appreciates this, especially after working ten to twelve-hour days at the manufacturing plant.

I'm finishing up for the day. Did 'Mr. Uptight' give you any guff today? Nick

Don't you know it? I reply, recalling the bouts of tears Robert caused.

A banging noise in the boys' room sends me running to check on them. Dillon pops up from the floor, obviously after jumping from his dresser. It's 'fun' for them to try and launch onto the top bunk from the other pieces of furniture in their room.

"Dillon, stop jumping like that," Morgan chides for me. "You'll break your arm one day."

Dillon turns his gaze on me, his face breaking into a devious smile. He hunches over and tiptoes towards the dresser in Grinch-like fashion. "Don't do it…" I say with a wag of my finger. He stops, but probably only for show while I'm here.

I leave their door open and rush back into the kitchen to start dinner. I switch on an upbeat playlist to jump-start my body, begging me to slow down for the day. The music works, but in my haste, I bang my hip on an open drawer.

"These darned hips. Ugh, it's broken again," I grumble, unable to shut the drawer. This narrow house with its tiny passageways was not built for hips like mine; I have the bruises to prove it.

I pop the dinner in the oven at record speed and return to the broken drawer. Is it weird that this fix-it project has me excited? I wiggle it in and out to diagnose the problem, knowing what to do in only a few seconds.

"We're hungry!" Dillon's shouting causes me to flinch. It's not like I don't know they are home with me. "Are you sticking your tongue out again, Mom?"

I close my eyes for a second, the memory of being teased for such a thing lovingly coming back to me. "You can get a snack, but it needs to be applesauce or a granola bar. Dillon!" My calm words escalate into a holler when he snags a bag of chips from the stand-alone cupboard I made to give us more space for food.

"I got chips, Morgan!" he screams, running away proudly with the red bag in the air.

"Dinner will be ready soon… Dillon!" But he's gone,

surely littering their floor with crumbs that our geriatric vacuum cleaner will never see. As if there's even an inch of visible carpet in their room.

Some moms threaten that the dad will put his foot down when he gets home. In truth, Nick plays with the boys like he's one of them, throwing all my so-called rules out the window.

I ignore the trickle of toys and clothes on my path to my room. Thirty seconds later, I head to the garage with the laundry mission at the forefront of my mind. I move the stack of clean clothes aside to access the buttons, wondering if I will ever catch up.

I turn my back on the unfinished woodworking projects that fill this space. The garage serves as a graveyard for my creations. Instead of giving myself permission to feel pride in having completed these pieces with my own two hands, I use another descriptive word: disappointment.

Once I had the boys, I no longer had time to flex my carpentry skills. My dream was to start my own furniture shop and take custom orders. Starting a business is risky, though, even in the best economy. With Nick and I already up to our eyeballs in debt, we have nothing extra to give to this once-upon-a-time passion.

Twenty minutes later, after I've finished folding clothes and setting the table, the boys run from their room as the sound of a truck alerts us to their father's arrival.

"Dad!" they scream, flinging themselves at his torso. As always, I look on with sorrow, wondering what I've done to be deprived of this affection from them.

"There are my boys! And my beautiful wife," Nick says with a kiss, complete with eye contact. His love trickles into the empty bucket that my boys drain. They have more fun with a burly dad instead of boring ol' mom. I've always been confused by this. It's not like I'm a girly girl. I can prove it with this face void of makeup and my hair residing in a daily braid or ponytail.

"Dinner isn't quite ready." I scrunch my nose to show I'm sorry.

"No worries. You work more than I do since you have the boys, hon. I don't mind if you wait for me to get home so I can help with dinner. But first…" he hands me a small wrapped box.

"What is this?" I ask with a crack to my voice. The boys look on with curiosity.

"Why don't we get a present?" Dillon whines.

"Because you haven't been married to me for fourteen years," Nick responds proudly.

"I thought we were going to save our money this year." My smile indicates I'm obviously not too upset. My teeth grind together, knowing I'll have to go over our budget yet again with my husband, who keeps his blinders on during this topic. Nick is Nick, and sometimes he does what he wants without consulting me.

"I know our anniversary was over the weekend, but we missed it… just like we missed Valentine's Day," Nick says quietly, his eyes focused on me. At least I'm not the only one who misses our time together.

My expression shifts into one of shock upon seeing the ruby earrings. "My birthstone. Nick, these are gorgeous. What do you think?" I say, snapping out of my penny-pinching mode and holding the studded earrings up to my ears.

"Eww, earrings are for girls," Dillon yells before both boys rush to their room again.

"Alone time." Nick engages me in a soft kiss before

pulling back. He gives me my special look. It sounds silly, but it's a knowing expression that we'll be together forever. We got married when we were just eighteen, with all the expected warnings from our family to not go through with it. "Look at us now," Nick says with a kiss on my hand, showing he recalls the same memory.

It's more than determination to prove to everyone who didn't believe we'd last. Nick and I have been best friends since our early high school days. The tight rope we wound those first several years has since splintered in several spots. It still holds, even though we've ignored the frayed ends and splinters along the way.

I hold the jewelry box to my chest, pushing the financial argument aside. I lean into Nick, surrounding myself with his familiar hardness. I need this human contact even on the easiest of days. It's one reason I've adopted my silent treatment when difficult topics such as money or parenting come along. Rocking the boat isn't part of my persona.

Though Nick isn't much taller than my short stature, he makes up for it in broadness. He's packed with muscle and a couple of his own squishy parts that make me feel more comfortable with my own. I scratch his broad back as he walks away to change, bringing another touch of love through my fingertips.

He jogs the few steps down the hall, dodging the toys on the floor like an obstacle course. While my mind is full of complaints about this tiny, messy rental, he hardly utters a negative word.

Minutes later, my mouth waters from the smells and sights of the bubbly, cheesy lasagna when I pull it from the oven. I give it a few minutes to cool off while I prep our sourdough bread and salads. Nick does his best to help, but the boys demand his attention, telling him about their day.

"Dinner time," I announce. The three scramble to the table and the boys almost instantly kick at each other underneath. "Guys, please don't," I say, though my soft-spoken voice can barely be heard above their noise.

"Your mom said to stop," Nick demands with a booming voice.

"I got an 'A' on my Oregon Trail project!" Morgan says to Nick.

"That's great, Morg!" Nick replies. I've been with the boys for two hours now. Why didn't Morgan tell me about this?

I ignore the ding of a text from Robert and fill Nick in with the day's highlights while the boys shovel food into their mouths. Four of my bites are one of theirs. Nick tells us about his day, which he says is a repeat of all the others.

"Dingus here threw his shoes out the car window," Morgan interjects with a tattling tone.

"You did what?" Nick asks, pointing his vehemence at Dillon.

"Morgan was calling me stupid and…."

"I don't care what he was doing; you don't throw your shoes out of the window!" Nick scolds.

"Mom got soaked and muddy," Morgan says, continuing his tattling session.

"I could only find one," I say in defeat. Nick sends an angry look at the boys before chewing both of them out.

"This family is stupid!" Dillon yells, bumping the table as he stands. I spring into action, grabbing two half-empty glasses of milk with each hand before they topple over. Dillon then does the unthinkable, or, at least, I would have thought so before I had kids.

"Don't even think about it!" Nick growls. It's too late. In anger, Dillon throws his glass of milk in the living room. The carpet has already seen nearly every type of liquid on the planet. Why not add milk?

And to think I was worried about spilled milk on the table.

"Well, I guess that's what happens when you can't control him," Morgan says, popping the last bite of bread into his mouth. He saunters away from the table as if nothing has happened.

Chapter 3 Inflexible News

The boys play in their room, leaving Nick and me to clean up the dinner mess. These thirty minutes are usually my favorite of the day when we are uninterrupted and can catch up with each other. Only tonight, I scrub the dishes while Nick uses cleaner to deal with the milky carpet.

"Thank you. Our house is starting to smell like sour milk even without this new addition to all those stains," I mutter, ignoring the real reason for the spot-bot to be dragged out of the garage.

"It's what I always want to do at the end of a long day," Nick says with a smile that brings out his dimples.

He joins me in the kitchen after throwing something in the drawer. "Of course you fixed it," he says with a twinkle in his eye, pulling the previously broken drawer out before pushing it back in. "So, um, I have something to tell you." He pushes his palms down his legs, igniting a flourish of butterflies in my stomach. This is his tell-tale sign that he's about to drop a bomb.

"Must be something big for you to bring out the palms," I nervously laugh.

"Yeah, well," he breathes, looking down at his feet. Yikes! What's this about? He turns his blue eyes to me with a nod as if he's just finished an internal pep-talk. His round, scruffy face does little to soften my nerves. The last time he had news, he had gotten in a car accident that totaled his truck that insurance barely paid for. "You know how you always say how much you hate living here?"

"'Hate' is a bit harsh for me. I just don't like how cold it is, as evidenced by…" I hold my hand out towards the back porch and remain quiet for us to listen as sleet pounds against the porch cover. "Should I leave this on the counter now or wait until tomorrow?" I tease as I package the leftovers.

"Forgot it again, huh?" he asks with a tilt of his head.

"I grabbed a salad from the kitchen at work. Skipping a meal wouldn't have killed me." It hasn't escaped me that I'm changing the subject, nor are we addressing Dillon's umpteenth fit of the month. Yes, it's easier to not buckle down with discipline, but that doesn't mean the issues are solved.

He pulls me into his relaxed stance against the chipped corners of the countertops. "You look great, and should eat every meal," he says, wrapping his arms around my thick-ish waist for a full-on hug. He rests his head on my shoulder, sighing deeply in my ear. "We'll have this wherever we go."

"What does that mean?" I ask lightly, my gut tightening as if by a wrench.

His eyes avert yet again, unable to match mine before answering. "I've been offered a job. A promotion," he says softly with a side smile.

"Really? That's great!" I eye his face in confusion from how his drab tone clashes against the exciting news. I grasp his upper arms and give him a little shake. "What's wrong? It can't possibly be more hours, could it?"

"No, that's not it…" His words rush out in a breath he's been holding. I scrunch my shoulders in question, waiting for the bad news part of this. "It means we would have to move."

"Move?"

"To Oregon."

My stomach sinks. I'm usually an expert at hiding my emotions, but this news puts me to the test.

A test I fail.

All I know about Oregon is that Morgan has been doing his covered wagon project about the Oregon Trail, and that it has miles of open land. Open land similar to the acreage that I grew up on. Acreage that I was left alone in when my brothers thought it was funny to leave me stranded in the middle of a field. I don't have to dig far to conjure up the frightful feelings from when they would play tag with me and dart out of sight. They are great men now, but they were much like my sons back then, ornery to the bone.

It doesn't take long to get sucked into the trenches I've dug for myself. We can't possibly move! The house isn't perfect, but we've grown comfortable here. Ish. We are rooted in work and school. I have my schedule down to the minute most days. It's what I know, this consistency. Some call it a flaw to stick so stringently to a routine. It's my way of dealing with my realm of existence.

Nick's eyes roam over my face, analyzing my non-verbal responses as he reaches out to me. "That could have been the widest array of emotions I've ever seen," he observes.

"Nick, I can't imagine moving with the boys. We can't trade our lives for new ones. I'm already pushed to the limit and can barely juggle work, the boys, cooking, and cleaning."

Nick knows how much I despise change. We're comfortable here. Ish. Moving would be a lot of work, not to mention saying goodbye to my patients. This last thought brings tears to my eyes.

I step back, adding distance between us, needing to digest this possibility.

"I know it's big news to spring on you. It's a big promotion." He continues to lean against the counter with his palms pressing against the counter. It would help if he could stop looking so good at this moment. What can I say? I still find my husband attractive.

And I miss him terribly.

"I'm sorry. You know how I get stuck in my own cement. It's hard to imagine. I have parent-teacher conferences next week for the boys, and I'm covering for Denise at work at the end of the month." I turn my back on him for a moment to gather my thoughts. "What's the job?" I say, attempting to let go of the grip of anxiety that accompanies change.

His face morphs into a smile of knowing. "Assistant Plant Manager at the biggest mill in the region."

"Whoa, what a title! How'd you land that?" The questions are real, even though I'm so in my head that I can barely comprehend Nick's answers.

"My dad heard about the opening in Garden Valley, and I tried for it." He spreads his hands out wide with an expression that shows his disbelief.

I hesitate before answering, now feeling like a minor betrayal is at play. This type of job isn't taken lightly, nor is it given overnight. I'm sure he's been trying for it for a while.

"It pays a lot more than I'm making here, and I'll be on the fast track to being the Plant Manager one day," he says, eagerness rising in his voice. "There are pay raises, bonuses, and great benefits. Joanie, you won't have to work anymore! Well, unless you want to," he says in an enticing voice.

"You're kidding about this, right?" My words have him

nodding in excitement, even though he misreads my meaning. "Are you really thinking of doing this?" The shock and fear ring clear through my voice, something I'm hoping Nick will hear.

He tilts his head with a sorrowful sigh. "How can we not, Joanie? We've been strapped for cash for years, and we both know it won't get any better for us here. Houses are cheap in that town, and we'll be close to my parents and sister. We can finally be back with family again."

I have to admit, this is a good selling point.

"Nick, we'd have to uproot everything. It'll all change with this, from me quitting my job to where we put the silverware. I can't up and leave my patients. And it's all the way across the country!"

"It isn't," he says with a smile at my exaggeration. "Sure, it's a few states over, but…."

"But what?"

"Butt what, butt what!" the boys chant, tromping into the kitchen with a force that shakes the floor.

"Hey, boys," Nick says with a hopeful voice. I furiously shake my head. We need more discussion before we bring the boys into the mix. "What would you say if I told you we have a chance to move to Oregon?"

"Are there still covered wagons there?" Morgan asks with interest. "I've been wanting to ride in one."

"Isn't an organ something in our body?" Dillon asks with disgust.

"Gross!" Morgan yells. "We're going to live in someone's body." The boys laugh at this childish joke. I look at my family with the most disconnected feeling I've ever had. I feel miles away from their happiness, shoving down a scream that is clawing to come out to stop this celebration.

"No, guys, I'm serious. I've been offered a job out there."

Wait a minute; he was already offered the job?

"The town has a lot of open land. We've seen pictures from my parents. It's a different vibe than here and has that hometown feel. We can have a farm! Maybe Mom will build you guys a treehouse."

The boys look at each other with excited eyes. "Come on, Dill Pickle, let's pack!" Morgan runs to their room with Dillon following his big brother's lead.

"Now, wait a minute!" I say as everyone runs past my protests. "I can't believe you told them. That's just not fair, Nick!" Even my pursed lips can't keep my words caged right now.

"Joanie," Nick says, missing my hand by an inch as I stomp by. I throw my arms up in disgust. Not only has he accepted the position without discussing it with me, but he just got the boys on his side. He doesn't follow, allowing me the time to mull over the news.

My phone dings with another text from Robert, telling me I rounded my time for the med pass to ten o'clock instead of writing the exact time. His dull excuses for writing me up are sharpened by his persistence to find my errors.

Robert, I know how to tell time. I know about your rounding rule; it was exactly ten o'clock when I finished. Joanie

I can't help but take my anger out on him. I close myself in our room, roughly picking up clothes and throwing them in the hamper. The disaster in my room is of my own making. One thing's for sure; the boys get their messiness from me.

My eyes shift to the stuffed bunny on our bed, Annabelle. Throwing myself onto the pillows, I clutch the childhood toy to my chest, allowing myself to feel a sliver of comfort.

How could Nick have accepted this job without asking me first? Couldn't he have let me in on the application and interview process? Darn it! We're supposed to be in this rat race together, not have one of us jump over the fence to snack on the greener grass alone. I've been entirely left out of the equation of this decision.

I sit on the bed and listen to Nick make his lunch across our microscopic house. I used to make his lunches, but he insists on preparing his own. *"I don't see why you need to make another meal that you're not going to enjoy,"* he said.

Would life slow down after this move? Nick said I wouldn't have to work. I love my job. Well, 'love' might be a little strong, but I've made connections at work. What in the heck would I do without a job? I have always worked and have taken pride in contributing to the bills.

The negatives stack up like dominos. Nick might be crushed by my 'no' answer, but that's where I'm leaning.

Nick gets the boys ready for bed tonight. There's no wrangling involved when he does it. The boys simply follow his directions.

I take my time in the shower, using the exfoliating scrubs to wash the added anxiety down the drain. Do I have to be so stubborn every time my routine is challenged?

"It's a big deal!" I say to the washcloth, throwing it against the shower wall. It gives zero satisfaction, only traveling the distance of a foot in our tiny shower tube.

I like being here. I have a couple of friends and… "acquaintances," I glumly correct. I have a job that… isn't exactly perfect, I think, picturing Robert clutching his clipboard as he writes me up for something mundane. I've tried for his job for years without serious consideration from management.

My mouth grows tense, hating that I can't grab hold of a concrete reason to stay in the life we've made. I think back to the conversation today with Denise, anticipating her own move. Was that a coincidence, or what? She seems to be able to pick up and leave. For a moment, I felt envious of her upcoming adventures.

Nick has climbed his way up the rungs in the lumber industry, only to be met with a dead end to the progression of his career.

Okay, so what if I join Nick's excitement for this change? My eyebrows perk at the thought of being closer to my family, who all live in Washington State. That would be a long car ride away instead of a hefty plane ticket expense and a car rental.

Did Nick say we'd live in the same town as his family? I have missed them since they moved. We used to get together all the time. His sister, Brooke, and I were close and would get our kids together to play on the weekends. Empty promises of visiting were given when they left, though we didn't intend for them to be.

Having family nearby means I'll get help with the boys. I think back to the days when Morgan and Dillon behaved better. It was because Nick's parents offered them the right type of discipline. They've always been a handful, but their fits have been nearly every night. And now they are getting written up at school all the time.

Kind of like how I got written up *again* at work today.

After my shower, I do a quick search and see that Oregon gets more rain than snow, four distinct seasons, and 200-plus days of sunshine. It's a no-brainer that the weather wins high marks compared to the perpetual cold we shield ourselves from here. Still, no one in the pictures shares my darker Indian features, making me wonder if the boys and I will be outsiders in this area. We haven't had trouble with this so far, but it could be a big bullet on my con list.

I hardly glance Nick's way when I step out of the bathroom. The scent of my coconut moisturizer trails behind me as I leave our room to say a quick goodnight to the boys. I lean in for hugs, hoping they'll return a small amount of affection.

"Night, night, guys," I say.

"Eww, Mom kisses," Dillon responds, making his brother laugh.

Silent footsteps take me back to our bedroom. I hope I can finish tonight's discussion without bursting into tears. Nick has always been as sweet as they come, never raising his voice or straying in any sense of the term from our marriage. His only fundamental flaw is occasionally overspending our budget. Discovering that he's kept this job news from me has added to this single-item list. A jolt of pain jabs at my heart. He obviously didn't include me because he didn't want my party pooper opinion.

Nick presses his ear to his shoulder as he lifts the comforter and gestures for me to lie down. I curl up in the space of his oversized arms, a familiar position we repeat every night so he can cuddle me from behind. I think I would have agreed to this move if he'd asked while we were in this position.

"I'm sorry I dumped the news on you." His voice vibrates through me, his warm body flush against my back. "Honestly, I thought it was a long shot. I'm still stunned that they picked me! They only offered me the job today. The more I think about it, the more I'm convinced this will be great for our family. For you," he says, tilting my chin back to lock eyes in the dim light. "I love how your eyes glow green after your showers," he says, kissing my cheek. "I didn't think you would approve of me applying for the job."

"You've got me there," I say boldly before I can second-guess myself. It's not my style to speak up for myself, but he needs to know I'm not on his side.

"They offered, but I haven't accepted the position yet. Your opinion means everything, and we can come up with a decision together. We can talk this weekend."

"I work Saturday, and your week starts on Sunday," I say quietly. Another weekend of not seeing each other adds to the deep well of longing I have for him.

"With my raise, you wouldn't have to work," Nick repeats.

I'd miss my patients, but not having to deal with Robert watching my every move is enticing. I used to work part-time Monday through Friday with the occasional Saturday thrown in. Lately, it's more than full-time, and every Saturday, which has tipped my weekly total to fifty hours.

"Maybe it's an idea to explore," I cave.

"What was that mumbling?" he asks. My giggles ring through the darkness when he tickles my side. "Go about your next couple days and ask yourself if it's time to see what else is out there for us."

I take a deep breath, feeding my inner self with his optimism. "It does sound like a good opportunity for you. Do you think the airlines would take the boys across state lines if we move?" We share a good laugh, with me flashing on the myriad of struggles we've had with the boys.

Laughter.

It's something that doesn't happen often enough in my

day. It provides comfort at this moment, easing the weight of the news that weighs ten tons.

"They get four seasons in Oregon," Nick says, rubbing my arm with his calloused hand.

One of my favorite things is to watch the weather change and not have it stuck on cold like it is here. "I'm not about to stake this decision solely on the weather. This is a lot to handle. Taking us away from everything we know feels overwhelming. You've had time to think about this; I haven't." I allow the floodgates to open with this topic, having kept my thoughts to myself for too long.

"I'm sorry I didn't tell you. It's a big step up for me. I wanted to focus and go for it, not worry that you'd say no," he says with longing. "I know how much stress you're under every day and how it bothers you that the house isn't clean."

"It's not like I don't add to the mess." Not contributing financially would bother me greatly. I'm sure I would get a job if we moved. Besides, what the heck would I do by myself all day?

****

I get up shortly after Nick leaves at his usual five o'clock time. His forty-five-minute commute to and from work has played a big part in keeping us apart.

"Make sure you give yourself enough time to get to work," Nick whispers before he leaves. "I shoveled the driveway behind your van, but it's really coming down out there."

The weather app shows dark blue shades covering our town on the radar, indicating snow is on top of us.

"I wonder…" I bite my tongue while I type out a text to Nick. I picture him driving, listening to my words spoken with a computer voice.

Did you say it's in the same town your parents live in? Joanie

Yup, Garden Valley. Nick

A smiley face emoji with hearts surrounding it flies over the screen, yet another indication that Nick is glossing over my whole package of emotions. This has happened before, with Nick saying he'll consider my opinion but then ultimately making the decision. My wants and needs fade away when he's got an idea, yet I go along and adapt.

I research the zip code for Garden Valley and type it into the weather app. It's even earlier there, but a large sun and passing clouds fill my screen with the promise of a fifty-degree day. The seven-day forecast has rain on a few days, with the low temperatures being above our highs.

I slink out of bed and into an extra layer of clothing before examining our dimly lit bedroom.

Less than impressive.

I stroll around the house, noting cabinets, baskets, and chests taking up every nook and corner to discreetly hold our stuff. Even the top of the ottoman has blankets stacked on it since the linen closet in the hall is where I keep the slow cooker, bread machine, and canned foods.

As much as my anxiety has flourished with the news of moving, the sights of the house that barely contain us confirms that a change might just be what our family needs.

Chapter 4 The Pro-Con Debate

Snow dumps on Fargo one flake at a time over the next few days. I love watching the weather from the comfort of my home, but driving in it adds to the cons list for this town.

The unknowns surrounding this decision to move gnaw at my gut. Where will we live? What is the town like? Will we have to scrunch ourselves in a hotel room until we find a house? How are the schools? Will they accept Morgan's and Dillon's challenging behaviors? Will we be the only Indians in town?

This last one hasn't been a huge deal in our lives, especially since I swear my brothers got most of the Indian DNA. I'm grasping at short straws to add to my con list.

I shuffle the boys into the van ten minutes later than I want this morning, fighting the urge to literally push them to go faster. I don't need Robert to write me up because I'm late again.

"Yikes, it's slippery out here. Be careful," I tell the boys after slipping on the icy driveway.

"That looks like fun!" Dillon says, running and purposely sliding.

"Dillon, stop! You're going to break your arm," Morgan scolds.

Driving isn't any calmer. My studded tires do little to grip the road. After three slips and a skid halfway into an intersection, I finally make it to work.

I receive a notification when I'm walking in. A picture on Instagram shows my sister-in-law, Brooke, by a beautiful lake. Familiar faces of Nick's side of the family smile at me with the caption 'Enjoying unseasonably warm weather in Garden Valley.' The beautiful background of a green field and full-grown willow trees in bloom brings up memories of growing up in an area like this, even though my memories of being abandoned in large meadows by my brothers aren't as shiny.

I pelt Nick with a multitude of texts throughout the day, sneaking my phone so Robert doesn't catch me. Unfortunately, Nick has had to work late the last few nights, taking away the precious time we need to sort through this decision.

How is the housing market in Garden Valley? Do you remember how much notice we need to give our landlord? How would we get all our stuff and cars to Oregon? Joanie

It sounds like you're leaning toward yes! Nick

"Joanie!" Robert shouts as he stomps my way. Geesh, it's just a text. It's not like I'm stealing something or being rude like Rebecca. This is one of his big pet peeves, though, and I know it. "You know…"

"Yes, I know I'm not supposed to text." Robert is taken aback by the snarky tone, as evidenced by his frown.

"I think someone needs to be moved to the front desk today," he sings with a scribble. I cross my arms and curl my lips together. "I found another error with your med-pass this morning, so I think a time-out is due."

A time-out?

"What 'mundane mistake' did you find?" Unfortunately, I blurt the first thought that comes to mind, my shield having chaffed away due to the upheaval in my life.

"Joanie," he says, shifting his clipboard to rest against his belly, "you know you're supposed to pass the cup out and check the number off the list. You were doing three or four cups at a time before crossing them off."

"You've got to be kidding me," I mutter.

"What was that?"

"You know how diligent I am. I wouldn't do anything to hurt our patients," I say, biting my lip. The threat of tears clogs my throat. I turn away from him and start towards the front desk, ready to face my sentence of torture for the day.

"Which is why I'm shocked that you keep doing these things," he says, following me.

A man comes in, requesting to visit Mrs. Cline. "Okay, what's your name?" I ask.

The man pauses with insult. "I'm her friend, Daniel."

I look through the guest list but don't see his name. "Sir, I'm sorry, but I don't have you on her list of expected guests. If you're not a family member, we have a process to see our residents and…"

"Joanie! What's going on?" Robert interrupts.

My whole body tenses at the sound of Robert's voice behind me. There is usually slight tension between us, but never like this.

"This man claims to be Mrs. Cline's friend, but I don't see him on the list."

"Oh yes, I updated the list today. I remember seeing that Mrs. Cline has additional guests," Robert says as if his snafu isn't a big deal when I get to feel the embarrassment of his mistake.

"Did you put the updated list in the book?" Robert's lips squish together in a sneer as I continue. "I remember how you wrote Rebecca up a few days ago for doing the same thing."

The guest's eyes ping-pong between Robert and me, shifting his weight and growing impatient with our scuffle. "If this is how management is around here, I should help my friend look for another place to live." The automatic doors cling shut behind the man after he storms off.

Robert's face glows red as he frantically jots a note on his clipboard. "Joanie, you might have just cost us a client."

I cross my arms, willing myself to keep quiet. My job would be nearly perfect if it weren't for Robert. My mom always says it only takes one apple to spoil the bunch.

Robert's petty complaints move to the backseat as my mind shifts to the golden opportunity I've been presented with to change my life. Everything I've been holding in all these years boils to the surface.

My voice is calm but shaky as I continue to test my limits. "I do everything you ask, including being reduced to sitting in this horrible front desk position today. It's a bad move when you know I'm one of the few staff here qualified to care for our residents."

"See, that's what I'm talking about, Joanie. This attitude crosses the line," he says with a sigh. "I'm going to have to let you go."

"What?" I say, standing so quickly that my chair flips over. If I thought my stomach was in knots when Nick told me about his new job, that was nothing compared to the tumble cycle it's on now. "Robert, I've been here for eight years and am one of the best employees. I barely take any time off. I've never called in sick."

"Your kids are sick all the time."

"They are not, and you know it!" I yell. I angrily swipe at

a tear, hating that Robert has a visual of how he's gotten to me. I'm rarely this outspoken, but Nick's news has opened a trapped door of emotions.

"I've only seen a decline in the quality of work from you, Joanie, and this outburst is unheard of. I'm surprised I've put up with it this long. This will be your last day. Make sure to turn in your badge and jacket by the end of your shift," he says with a disconnected tone, writing on his clipboard.

I promptly take my white jacket off and lay it on the counter. "I'm not going to stay that long. Good luck running this place without me," I grumble, heading for the breakroom to gather my things.

Not two minutes after Robert has fired me, I'm out of here. Tears flow down my face as I make the embarrassing walk through the glass doors, wondering if I'll be able to come back and say goodbye to all of my friends I've cared for all these years.

My brain has been scrutinizing the decision about moving when fate has made it for me. It looks like we're moving to Oregon.

***

Since Nick and I told the boys of our final decision to move, they have been on the phone with their grandparents every night, hooting and hollering their joy.

Everyone is excited… except me.

I merely float through the packing process with a disconnected feeling, finding myself knee-deep in boxes. Now that I no longer have ties here and Nick has accepted the job, there's no going back.

Our plans to pack together and tie up all the loose ends are frayed when Nick is asked to start his job as soon as possible. The previous assistant plant manager decided to retire early, leaving the mill desperate for my husband.

"You can all come with me," Nick says sheepishly upon giving me the news. "We can pack and leave here in a day or two."

"I can't just up and leave! The boys have school, and I don't think it's fair to take them out this close to spring break." I frantically clean the bathroom, my movements matching my current state. "Plus, our landlord wants this place scrubbed clean before we go, and I'm nowhere near that point. I don't want to pay a thousand-dollar cleaning fine."

"We'll pack as much as we can together before I go. Don't worry, I won't leave it all on your lap," Nick says smoothly, patting the bed. "Come here. It's late. Sit down and relax a little." I oblige, knowing how badly my mind needs grounding. "Listen, I'll schedule a moving truck, fill it to the brim, and leave you with whatever you can't live without for a couple of weeks." I open my mouth to disagree, but he continues. "The mill is giving me a moving allowance. We'll hire a team. They can move all our things to Garden Valley. The time will go by so fast before we're all together again."

He threads his hand behind my head, kneading the knot on my neck. "I'll miss those plump lips of yours."

"We won't see each other for almost three weeks," I say with real tears. While we don't see each other much on a typical week, at least I get a daily dose of him. My chest is already filled with the loneliness I know is coming my way. Nick is the only person who has been there for me in my small world. Lord knows the boys won't be keeping me company.

"I'm sorry. It wasn't in the plan to move this soon. Management said late May, but they've been inundated with orders. Without an assistant plant manager, you do the math." There's no point hiding my tears when he firmly grips my hand to keep me from escaping to cry. "I know, being apart is the hardest part of this whole thing," he says, running his hand down my arm. It's enough to increase my need for him, my unquenchable requirement for his touch. "What do you say we make up for some of that lost time?"

Chapter 5 Parenting Tests

We've finally made it to the boys' last day of school. Even though dealing with their behavior issues has been like a part-time job, especially since I lost mine. There's something to be said that they haven't been kicked out of school.

Only an hour after I dropped the boys off at school on their last day, I get a call saying that Dillon had hurt his arm by falling off the play structure.

Apparently, we aren't over the hurdle yet.

"He's already had recess?" I ask with a glance at my watch. I peek outside the kitchen window at the snow, wondering why they'd let the kids out in this weather.

"No. Dillon claimed he had to go to the bathroom and snuck outside to play." The nurse says with the same irritation that everyone else at the school has had with me, the one that says, 'We've had to deal with your kids' behavior because you're a bad parent.' And no, this isn't in my head; the principal has said those exact words to me.

What I thought would be days full of packing have been filled with dealing with our disgruntled landlord. He has toured our house three times, writing on his own clipboard a list of repairs.

Now, my day of last-minute packing has been completely derailed by taking Dillon to urgent care. He stayed still for his x-ray but is now bored and getting into everything in the bland waiting room.

"That lady has a mustache!" He laughs and points at an older woman. I apologize when she huffs in response. The assistant opens the door to call another patient. Dillon accepts this as an invitation and tries to go through the door.

"Oops, sorry, buddy. It's not your turn yet," the assistant says, sticking her foot out to block him from crossing the threshold. To her surprise, Dillon persists. "Um, you can't come back here. It's not your turn!"

I jump up to help, but he won't come with me back to our seat. I wrap my arms around his middle, and he instantly turns into a wet noddle, trying to wriggle free.

"Ouch, you're hurting my arm," he dramatically whines.

"I'm not touching your arm, Dillon. Come sit down," I say with frustration.

The other waiting room occupants stare at the entertainment we are providing. They are no doubt offering their own judgment and parenting solutions to my problem— as if I haven't already tried everything out there!

I finally settle him down with bribes of butterscotch candies and a kid magazine.

Wish you were here to help me with our terror child. Joanie

Me too! Sorry, you have to go through that alone. Nick

Forty long minutes later, we get to wait in a leaf-green exam room. Dillon explores each bottle and container full of Q-tips and cotton balls. He opens every jar, drawer, and cabinet as if on a desperate mission to find a secret cure to a devastating crisis.

"Those are for patients," the assistant says, trying to get Dillon to stop while looking at me to help.

"Dillon, stop!" I scold, trying to pull him back.

"Stop touching me!" he yells, wiggling around uncontrollably. The door squeaks open, and in walks a frowning doctor, his eyebrows furrowed.

"So, this is the little guy who is disrupting my office. I'm Doctor Williams. Why don't you settle down so I can show you your x-ray."

Dillon peels back his energy at the sound of the doctor's deep voice, but only long enough to sit down and bounce right back up. Every muscle in my body is clenched, prepared to leap into action if he starts throwing things.

The doctor plays the waiting game, staying still until Dillon does the same. To my surprise, it works.

"Well, Mom, it's broken. You can see here," the doctor says, pointing at the gap between bones in the X-ray. Dillon sits on the doctor's rolling stool and begins to spin in place until Dr. Williams pulls him closer to the X-ray, naming off bones and explaining the plan to mend them. Dillon finally stays still with interest.

"What do you say you bring him back in a few weeks, and we'll check his progress?"

"We're moving, so we'll have to find somewhere in Garden Valley. It's in Oregon."

"We'll send over the records once you're settled," the doctor says quickly before excusing himself from our problems. The technician stays to wrap Dillon's cast, giving me glances of annoyance every time he acts up.

After three hours at the doctor's office, Dillon and I emerge with his broken left arm in a lime-green cast that extends past his elbow down to the tips of his fingers.

"Dad sends his apologies and can't wait to give you a big hug in a few days." I show Dillon the selfie of Nick's sad face. I miss him so much that I can barely tear my eyes away from the screen. "C'mon, we have to run to the store and pick up this prescription before we grab your brother from school."

"The store is boring," Dillon whines, dragging his feet on the pavement.

"Then maybe you shouldn't have snuck out on the playground today." Sympathy has left my voice now that I have to run the last of my errands with Dillon in tow and scramble to get done in time to pick Morgan up. As if I don't already have a hard time driving Nick's monster of a truck around town.

The store certainly isn't dull, at least not for me. You know that mom who runs around to catch her kids? That's me. You'd think a kid who just broke his arm wouldn't have enough energy to run amuck in the grocery store, yet here I am, chasing him as if we're playing 'duck-duck-goose.' This is why I used to go grocery shopping alone after my shift on Saturday nights.

A few swats to the rear end would do my boys some good, but I've always told myself it's not my style. I'm sure I'll figure out what my parenting style is one of these years…

"Aww, you broke your arm," a woman at the grocery store says, her voice thick with compassion. Dillon hangs his head. Great, now he'll get more attention and praise for his naughty behavior.

Morgan throws his bag over his shoulder when we pick him up ten minutes late. It's his tell-tale angry gesture, and I know I'm in for a rough evening.

"What happened to you, Dingus?" Morgan asks his brother with evident irritation.

"Broke it," Dillon replies, copying Morgan's annoyance. "And it's all your fault," Dillon says to his brother.

"How so? It's not my fault you're stupid," Morgan spits back.

"You're always telling me I'm going to break it. And now none of my friends will be able to sign my cast," Dillon says, aiming his anger at me. Morgan glares at me as well, grumbling something about how stupid this move is.

I'm at a loss for words. So far, they've been way more excited about this move than I have. What's with this switch?

"We'll all make new friends," I say on our last walk through this parking lot. My voice is drab, knowing out of all of us, I have the hardest time making friends.

Morgan breaks away from Dillon and me and stomps off towards the truck, yelling over his shoulder. "This is stupid! I don't want to leave my friends," he yells. Dillon follows suit, sticking his tongue out at me.

It's a childish gesture that still hurts. Every time they treat me this way, they drill deeper into my heart, leaving a hole that feels like it'll never heal.

***

"You'll be here in just a couple of days!" Nick's sister, Brooke, yells through the speakerphone as I clean up after dinner. We've spoken a few times since the news. Her naturally optimistic persona has been infectious, nearly swaying me to agree with this move.

"The boys were sad about it today," I say gloomily. "They went straight to their room after school and refused to eat dinner with me. I left meatloaf on the floor in front of their doors like they're in prison." I don't blame them for being angry, but why does it have to be aimed at me?

"Oh, they'll be okay after a few days. Kids are resilient." She flips into speed-talk mode, filling me in on the town. She has one setting: hyper. It must be where Dillon gets it from. Where I'm a stickler for schedules and lists, Brooke is a free spirit floating in the wind.

My phone chimes with a text that causes me to roll my eyes. "Can you believe that Robert has the nerve to keep texting me?"

"The jerk who fired you?" Brooke asks in disbelief.

"That'd be him."

"You're not answering him, are you?"

"Gosh, no. I'm sure he can figure out where the stupid keys are and how Mrs. Cline likes her bubble baths," I say, rolling my eyes. I've sent one text to Robert since he fired me, asking if I could come back and say goodbye to my patients. He denied my request, saying it would be too disruptive for them. While this hurt, it's one thing that has had a clean break in this move.

"You're going to love it here. You'll fit right in. They have a bunch of tribal gatherings that you could join."

"I haven't done that in years," I say with unintentional longing. My family is big into our Indian tribe in Washington, but it's something I've let slip from my life through the years.

"I've been house-hunting for you," Brooke sings. "There's not much to choose from, but a gem just came on the market."

"Oh? I'll have to take a look when I get there."

"I sent the specs to Nick yesterday, and we walked through it today. I think it'd be perfect for you guys, Joanie. Nick said he might put an offer on it."

The unwelcome surprise hits me as squarely in the nose as the dodgeballs used to in elementary school. I've met my spontaneity quota for the next decade.

"What? He wouldn't do that without me," I say with initial confidence. Or, at least, I never thought he'd do that. He did just take a job halfway across the country without talking to me first.

"Come on, go with the flow!" Brooke encourages as if reading my mind.

"I'm doing my best, but you know I'm more like a rock than water."

"I'd love to help you guys move in when you get here, but it's our spring break. We've had a vacation planned for Disneyland forever."

"The Disney trip, huh? Your kids will love that. Mine would probably spend the whole time running away from me." My phone buzzes with a call from Nick. "Brooke, I've got to go. Nick's calling."

"Remember, I get the credit for finding the house! Good luck with the move!"

"Thank you. Hi, honey!" I say with a little too much chipperness in my voice. I'm curious if he'll even tell me about the news of the house he and Brooke looked at or if he'll buy it all on his own.

"Hey, hey! I sure miss you! Guess where I'm going?" The noise of driving is added to his voice, a big clue to the answer to this riddle.

"To the hot new house on the market?" I answer with a knowing tone.

"My sister is such a blabbermouth. I wanted it to be a surprise," he says.

"Because I do so well with surprises?" If it weren't for Brooke giving me a half-minute's notice about the house, this would have been more of a bite.

"Sorry, I wanted to call you earlier but just got off work. How's Dillon's arm? How are the boys?"

"Mad at me, as usual. Dillon is fine and milking his injury. It sounds like you've had a long day," I say, looking at my watch and doing the math for the time difference. I've been harboring the worry that Nick will work even more at this new job. With him easily knocking out sixty-hour work weeks here in Fargo, we could slip into the same routine of hardly seeing each other. With or without a job, that would bring me the same misery I have here.

"Don't worry, it's just the newbie schedule with all the training. I might as well learn all I can since you guys aren't here yet." My voice stays buried in my throat, forever to be locked away in the vault that's suffering from overcrowding. "How's the packing going?"

"Surprisingly well. I've been finishing with all those little things left in drawers and cabinets that no one knows what to do with. I'll be done in the morning." I pause to indulge in a long yawn.

"Still not sleeping well, huh?"

"You know I can't sleep when you're gone. I'm positive these noises don't happen when you're home." Even as I say this, I take a peek over my shoulder. There's something about voicing fears that makes them more real, and with the person who makes me feel safe being in Oregon, I've been checking the locks more than I'd like to admit.

"There's nothing in the dark that's not there when it's light. Hold tight, sweetheart; you'll be here soon."

And then what?

Nick has reminded me with almost every call that I won't have to work. It's a badge of honor for him to be able to support the four of us. Me and being alone isn't a combination I want to try out long-term. I understand his pride, but I have a feeling this move will leave me by myself all day.

In a new town.

Possibly at a hotel.

While the boys are at school and Nick is at work.

"I'm sure I'll be finding a job when I'm there," I say once again, sorting through my toiletries. "Tell me about this house." I don't know if this is better territory, but at least we won't have the job conversation again.

"That's the great news of the day!"

Like the good news that has me packing this house? Or the news that is making it so the boys hate me even more? Or how about the news that has taken Nick away from us for almost a month? This is the news that has put me on a whole new trajectory, where my future is an endless black abyss and is about as entertaining as white noise.

"Can we switch to video so I can see?"

"Sure!" Nick says through the sound of the van door closing. "It's a pretty nice house," he says in the same excitement he had when he told me about the job. "It's on acreage and is the previous assistant manager's if you can believe it. It'll be just like when you were growing up, Joanie."

My stomach does somersaults at this shout-out. I can't pinpoint if this is due to the uncertainty of the move or the mention of my childhood woes.

"You can't just buy the first house for sale," I say with a light chuckle as I put my earbuds in to free up my hands. "And, Nick, I'd like to be there before you do something this big."

"Don't worry." Nick gives commentary on the outside of the house as he pans the phone around for me to see.

Even through the colors of dusk I can make out the glow of a town beyond empty land.

Memories drown out his voice as visions of me running in green fields fill my thoughts. My brother's 'game' of hiding from me finally stopped, but not until it was nearly too late. The mountain lion was within feet of pouncing on its prey, which, unfortunately, was a ten-year-old version of me. They were able to scare it off easily enough with the help of my dad, but the memory still brings goosebumps to my skin.

"This is a rare find around here," Nick continues. "Hello? What do you think?"

"I'll take a look at the house when I get there," I say quickly, coming back to the call. Silence hangs in the air, and I sense there's more Nick is keeping from me. "What else aren't you telling me?" I squeeze my eyes with a hand on my forehead.

"Okay, so don't be mad, but I put an offer on it."

"You what?" I shriek. "Nick, you can't just do that without me!"

"This house is perfect for us! People snatch houses up around here, and this one is new on the market. We need to jump on it right away. And the deal has a bonus that I can't wait to show you!" Who is this spontaneous man, and where is my predictable husband? Some people may like this in a relationship, but not me. "Just look at it!" he says, panning the screen around in the dark.

"Nick, it's too dark, and I can't see a thing," I huff with irritation.

"Hmm, I can't make it any lighter. They were in the middle of a remodel, and from the looks of it, they haven't gotten to the light fixtures," he says with a funny expression as he's looking up with the phone right in his face. "Can you see *anything?*"

"Not really."

"I know I didn't wait for you, but I have an 'in' since I took over Glen's job. He said he doesn't mind if we move in immediately. Now you don't have to worry about we'll be staying when you and the boys get here! You're going to love it here, hon. With this new house, you will have *plenty* to do."

What's that supposed to mean?

"After you get here and see it, we can back out if you don't like it."

But then we won't have a place to live. No pressure or anything.

"Honey, you're losing reception or something. The screen just went dark." The blackness is a visual representation of the dread that's currently piling onto my chest.

"Oh… happened earlier... sorry... tomorrow."

"Nick? Nick!" I shout. I stand in my lonesomeness as the seconds tick by. I stare at the screen, hoping he'll call back. "Darn it!" I say, tossing my phone on the bed.

It's not uncommon for Nick to take the lead in making these decisions, but it's never been like this. I've been left out of the puzzle, a forgotten piece, even though I know Nick wants me to be as strong as the corner piece.

I give up after a half hour of trying to settle the boys down, needing to lay down and rest my tired body. It's a win that they are in their beds, even if they still throw around stuffed animals that I've already packed twice.

A unique jingle comes from my phone. "Great, now I have to deal with you on my three days of torturous driving," I utter to the period app that has reminded me of my womanly status. "Whoops!" I jump out of bed to pop my birth control pill that I have forgotten again. Even if it is a placebo, I've never missed one over the years, except for I've missed three now ever since someone grabbed my life like a snow globe and gave it a good shake.

I fall with my face in my pillow and release a scream until my throat is coarse. A creak in the hallway pops me up on my knees. I freeze like the coward I am and switch on a light for a false sense of security. After a full minute, I check the locks in the house yet again to see if this will settle my angst. No such luck.

After deleting and re-writing several different text messages to Nick, I finally hit the send button.

Please wait a few days until I get into town before making any more drastic decisions without me. Joanie

I stare at my screen, awaiting his answer, but nothing comes. It looks like the new town has poor cell reception.

Great.

I kick my feet against the bed as if I'm a toddler who just had a toy taken away. I hate everything about this move, how it has pulled Nick and me apart, how the boys have another reason to be mad at me, and how I have no idea what I'm stepping into.

I lay awake with dread, but this time, it's not about the unknown town. Tomorrow morning, I'll be stuck in a truck for three days with two Tasmanian Devils.

Chapter 6 Road Trip

After two hours of scrounging up our final items, I stuff the last bag in Nick's truck. It sounded like such a luxury to hire movers and make life easier, but add two kids who think it's fun to dart between the men carrying boxes and furniture, and there's chaos.

I've grown somewhat accustomed to Nick's beast of a vehicle, but it's not nearly as easy to drive as my trusty white van. "This thing has so many buttons and gadgets that I swear this truck is smarter than I am," I mutter as the boys settle in the back seat.

I tap the touch-screen of the truck's navigation system to enter our first destination, which is seven hours away. My stomach erupts in flurries. I don't think I've ever driven this distance, and certainly not without Nick. I've never been in charge of the boys this long by myself either, and look how that's turning out.

Bad comparison.

With the three of us strapped in, I take one last look at our tiny house and pull away, praying everything will go as planned.

"Say goodbye to the house, boys." We each give a wave, mine filled with tears.

It's this last moment that I've been dreading the most. This is where I brought the boys home, bundled in the baby blankets and little beanies. They had all their special first moments here. Their first snub towards me was here, but I don't allow that to dampen my reminiscing.

Hide-and-seek and tickle games leave imprints of laughter in my ears. Those were when times were better. Nick's family lived close by, and the boys allowed me into their lives. Things have changed since then, but the memories will remain forever in this tiny home.

Just as easily as I back the truck out of the driveway, our stamp on this place will be gone. We are moving out today, and our landlord has already rented our home to new tenants starting tomorrow. I sigh, knowing this chapter of my life is over, and though it wasn't perfect, there's nothing I can do but turn the page.

***

"Is there anything but the road and wilderness out here?" My angst goes unnoticed by the boys glued to their movie playing in the backseat. I stretch up to the windshield to see through the rain threatening to turn into snow this last hour. Relief fills my chest when the hotel comes into view.

Our first night at a hotel brings a fear worse than snow to life: having the boys out in the world and being unable to control them. Morgan and Dillon jump from bed to bed, causing the neighbors to pound on the walls and yell unflattering variations of "Shut up!"

"Boys, I'm tired from driving all day, and we all need to go to bed." I yawn on my way to the bathroom to change into pajamas. Through the crack in the door, I see Morgan whispering something in Dillon's ear. Before I can slip into my comfy pants, the two of them tear out of the room. I barely pull up my pants and run after them as they sprint down the hall, knocking on doors.

Through the grace of God, we settle into our beds around midnight, and the boys fall right to sleep. I'm shocked that we haven't gotten kicked out of the hotel by the time we finished our complimentary breakfast the next morning. I practically run through the slushy snow to the truck with our belongings, ready to put this hotel experience behind us.

It's a heroic effort when a mom embarks on the challenge of taking her kids out of town by herself.

"Boys, stop doing that hand thing!" I say, breaking up yet another fight in the back seat on our fifth hour. "Dillon, you'll hurt your brother with your cast if you keep doing that."

"More like he'll infect me with his stink. You shouldn't have gone swimming last night. It reeks!" Morgan says, plugging his nose. "Mom, Dillon stuck his finger in my eye!"

"I'd like to pull over and let you guys run around, but this rainy-snow stuff isn't letting up. Why don't you put another movie in?" I ask with a yawn.

"We're bored of movies," Dillon moans. "Mom! Morgan just said the 'assistant F-word.'"

"The assistant F-word?" I ask.

"He just said he's frickin' bored."

My laughter eases the tension in my shoulders that have been shrugged up to my ears since we pulled out of the driveway. No matter how frustrating my boys can be, their phrasing is sometimes hilarious.

"Maybe you can play a game. I put those dinosaur cards in your bag." Morgan pulls the cards out of the bag and flips them over, contemplating if he should go along with my suggestion.

Minutes later, they happily play 'Go Fish.' It's one of the rare moments they have been good, except when zoned out watching a movie. I sear it into memory, asking it to replace the many not-so-great moments that have filled my mind.

"Do you know the strategy with this game?" I ask, eyeing them through the rearview mirror. "Pay attention to the cards the other person is asking for. Then, if you draw that card, you ask for that card since you know they have it."

"Seems logical," Morgan says, sticking his lip out and nodding.

Thank goodness the day is uneventful. We stop at a rest area for snacks, and I stretch my legs while the boys run around the grassy area.

Our road is lined with a thick forest surrounded by the darkness of the mountains. The boys play more games but grow tired in the late afternoon. The rocking of the truck and the white noise from the road do the trick of lulling them to sleep.

"Must be nice," I utter with a yawn.

The signs fly by, with me contemplating driving into the night instead of stopping at the scheduled stop that's only twenty minutes away. Do I dare risk passing this town and hope another will come before the night's end? I could get dozens of miles under our wheels with the boys still asleep.

Dozens of *quiet* miles.

"I'm doing it," I whisper, gripping the wheel in defiance as I drive right by our turnoff. A glance back at the boys shows they are fast asleep. I do my best to relax into this decision, hoping this is a good idea.

Two hours of silence tick by like the lines on the road. I might as well be driving to a foreign country, for I know little about the town I'm inching toward. Through all my anxiety of being fired, packing and fretting this drive, I've barely allowed myself to visualize what's in store for me in Garden Valley.

Have I been unable to, or have I purposely ignored this deep contemplation?

Every mile brings me closer to my dreaded future, the one I can't plan for. The one where I see myself in empty rooms, waiting out the daylight hours until I get to see my husband again. The unknowns are what have been repelling me from this change.

What else besides a midlife crisis could explain Nick's rash decisions? We are typically in sync with everything from what to eat, decorations for holidays, movies, songs, and nearly everything else during the years. Despite not seeing each other much, our marriage might be smooth despite the task of parenting. That road is filled with rocks and potholes.

I'm apprehensive about being a stay-at-home mom and wife. At first, I'll unpack in the house, which I hardly had a visual of. He mentioned it's in the middle of a remodel, so maybe I'll work on that.

No matter how I try to fill my days, one thing is certain: my planner is entirely empty.

The boys wake up at nine at night, complaining of grumbling tummies and thirsty tongues. I packed tons of snacks, juices, and water, but they have eaten all the good stuff and had grown bored with their remaining selection.

"I don't want any more apples," Dillon groans before taking a huge bite.

"Don't eat it like that!" Morgan snaps, "You'll choke."

"We have more food in the back, but you'll have to wait until I pull over," I interrupt.

"It's snowing!" Dillon says, pressing himself against the window.

"Yeah, it has been for about an hour," I say quietly, the pit in my stomach growing with each flake. I angle my face to inconspicuously wipe an anxious tear on my shoulder. I hate driving at night. I hate driving in the snow. These elements are combined to conjure another monstrous fear that has come to life. "I don't see a restaurant or hotel around anywhere."

I stretch toward the windshield and then to my driver's side window as if this will help me see past my headlights. The snow builds on the side of the road like it's stacking up against me. I wonder if the boys have the weather on their side, making this trek harder for me.

I yawn again, trying to ignore my body's call for sleep. I zoom out of my map a few times only to find more open land. I guess I chose to stop at that last location for a reason. My worried eyes flicker down to the gas gauge that's luckily still half full. At least I haven't messed that up. We've got to come upon a town at some point, right?

"Mom, make Dillon stop that annoying noise!" Morgan whines.

I do my best to ignore them, but Dillon's screech is like grating something on the back of my neck. The snow picks up, blocking my view further.

"Dillon, honey, that's a little annoying." He continues the high-pitched screech as I hit the zoom-out button again on the map. "Dillon, please don't do that anymore."

Screech, screech, screech.

"Dillon! Mommy is trying to find a place for us to sleep tonight!" My hands fasten to the wheel as I crane my neck to face the boys for a few seconds, hoping they can see my angry face in the dark. It's not like me to be mean, but a person can only take so much.

It works for a minute or two before Morgan complains yet again. "When are we going to stop? I have to pee."

"I don't know," I say in a worried voice that I hope they can't hear. Or, maybe it'd be good if they understood our situation so they would start behaving better.

I have no idea what's in store for us tonight. My slow speed in this weather has stretched the miles longer than I would have liked. We go miles before seeing the comfort of another car. Snow is beautiful when snuggling on a cozy couch inside, but not when in survival mode.

"Mom, you don't like driving in the snow," Morgan says, his voice having changed to one of concern.

"I sure don't." I slow my speed to thirty miles per hour for a while longer before my yawns make me decide to relinquish to the night. I pull into an empty truck turnout serving as our stopping spot.

"What are we doing?" Morgan asks, looking out his window. "I don't see a hotel."

"There isn't a hotel. I'm sorry, but Mommy kind of messed up. But guess what," I say with as much enthusiasm as I can muster, "we get to have a slumber party in the car! I have blankets and pillows in the back and everything."

And I do because I'm a mom with an over-active imagination and two little kids. You never know if this exact scenario is going to happen. For the last three weeks, I have entertained thoughts of us being stranded on the side of the road in the middle of a blizzard with no phone. Great job, prophetic mind.

With my eyes free from the road, I search the map for the closest town. "Ugh, it's two hours away. This would be fine during the day, but I hardly slept last night, and I'm exhausted."

"I'm not tired at all," Dillon says, bouncing in his seat.

"Yeah, well, I didn't get a two-hour nap. One bar!" I scream with a glance at my phone. I tap a 'we're okay' message to Nick and push send to quickly get it to him. I type out yet another message explaining where we are and the plan tonight, assuring him we are okay. At least, I hope we are. With one shift in my seat, the phone switches back to not having service. "Stay here. I'm going to run to the back for a minute."

I dash through the flurries of snow to the back of the truck to grab snacks, blankets, pillows, and the battery-operated heater I hope will work. A bitter cold makes its way to my skin almost instantly, and I mumble curses about Nick not being here with us.

I head back to the driver's door just in time to see Dillon's feet disappear at the front of the truck. My heart leaps into my throat at the thought of one or both of the boys getting lost in the darkness of this storm.

"Dillon, no! We can't play in the snow right now!" I rush to the front of the truck and thankfully see him standing by the passenger side headlight. He turns to give me a look of disgust upon seeing me.

"I'm peeing!" he yells, returning to his task.

"Oh, of course," I say, giving him some privacy but keeping him in my peripheral vision.

"I am, too," Morgan says behind me.

"NO running off!" I yell loud enough for the whole forest to hear. "It's freezing out here, and…" The boys rush past me to jump back into the truck. I follow and try not to laugh as they bundle under the blankets I hand them.

"It's cold out there!" Morgan says with a shiver.

"And scary!" Dillon adds. He looks at his brother, who rolls his eyes and shakes his head. "It is! It's dark and snowing, and I couldn't see."

I laugh, and to my surprise, the boys go along with our car sleepover. They wait in the front seat while I lay the back seat down for the three of us to sleep on. They can't keep their hands off each other, which grows old about ten seconds after it starts.

We scrunch together under blankets, with me in the middle to keep them apart. Luckily the battery heater works like a charm, even though I worry about it lasting the night.

We dig into dried apples, nuts, and chips and watch the rest of the movie they started earlier. The boys play their smack-the-head game around me, thoroughly driving me nuts.

"Mommy's *tired*. Can't you guys just be good for tonight?" The harshness in my voice startles me, but it does the trick for the boys. "I know you've been stuck in the truck all day."

"Stuck in the truck," the boys rhyme. It's enough to make me smile.

"Maybe we can find a place for breakfast in the morning."

"It's cold in here," whines Dillon. "And my arm hurts."

"I'm sorry, honey. I haven't even asked about your arm." I grab my bag from the front seat and pour him a dose of liquid medicine before settling back in. "I'm chilled, too. But wait!" I say, wiggling out of the covers again and getting into the glove box. "I've always wondered if this trick works." I pull out a large candle and lighter as the boys' eyes stay on me.

"What the heck are you going to do with that?" Morgan asks with interest.

"Believe it or not, I've heard that lighting a candle in the car will keep you warm through the night." I use one of the thick paper plates to light the bottom of the candle, dripping wax down to hold it in place.

"I want to light it!" Dillon says, throwing himself forward. The candle knocks out of my hand, falls on the passenger floor, and rolls under the seat.

"Great job, Dingus," Morgan scolds. "Now we're going to freeze to death tonight."

"We won't freeze to death," I say with irritation, stretching to reach the candle. "But this is a good example of what *not* to do. You guys wouldn't want to set Daddy's truck on fire, would you?" They shake their heads, with me wondering if this is one of the worst ideas I've ever had, to camp here by the side of the road with two unruly kids and a lit flame.

I yawn again, figuring I no longer have a choice. I light the candle and rest it on the console. "There," I say before getting between the boys and re-fixing our covers. "When I bought this, it said it has twelve hours of burning time. I'm sure we won't sleep that long. *No one touches the candle!*" I say forcefully.

To my surprise, they huddle at my sides, pushing their cold noses against me. Their affection nearly brings me to tears, even though I know it's because they are cold. I allow their weight against my body to warm my soul, clinging to the positive side of this situation.

I hug my bunny, Annabelle, to my stomach and see the boys doing the same with their stuffies.

"Hello, I'm Annabelle," I say sweetly. "What's your

name?"

"I'm Marley the Monkey," Dillon says in a quirky voice.

"Nice to meet you, Marley. And who are you?" I make Annabelle ask for Morgan's stuffed dinosaur.

"I'm Tony the T-rex," Morgan answers.

"Tony? That doesn't sound like a tough name."

"Oh yeah? I bet I could bite your head off, Annabelle," Morgan roars.

"I'll save you, Annabelle!" Dillon makes a farting noise with his mouth while bending his monkey over. "These farts are deadly, but watch it! Sometimes a little turd comes out." I cuddle my bunny to my chest and laugh.

The rest of the night is relatively uneventful. The candle does the trick and keeps us warm as light snow blows against the window. In the morning, however, I wake to catch Dillon poking at the flame.

"Dillon, no!" I yell when he has his stuffed monkey too close. The monkey's foot catches fire before it quickly spreads to its stomach. The fire is too big to put out with my hands, so I grab the monkey's head, open the door, and fling it out in the snow. I follow the monkey as quickly as possible, climbing over Morgan, who is getting a rude awakening to the day.

I throw snow on the monkey, barely noticing my socks soaking through. Ten seconds later, the crisis is averted, with the boys looking on in awe at my ability to quickly resolve this issue.

"You were fast, Mom," Morgan says, looking at Dillon for confirmation.

"Yeah, well, I had a lot of practice in my woodshop classes. Some of those guys were curious like you guys and would always start fires."

"My monkey butts," Dillon says, taking the wet, slightly charred monkey.

"You were playing with the fire, weren't you?" Morgan asks with a shove to his brother.

"I was just playing with the wax," Dillon says with a shove back.

"And the fire is still lit, so that's enough!" I scold, climbing into the front seat and blowing out the flame that probably saved us from freezing during the night.

At least we don't make headlines like *Mom and two kids found dead on the highway*. It wasn't the most restful night, which I am secretly blaming Nick for, but I did get a few hours of sleep.

Not a half hour away is a town I must have skipped over on the digital map in my frantic state. "Figures," I say, pulling into the first store. The boys run wild in the store, releasing pent-up energy and pulling out their usual grocery store behavior. I give them a pass, figuring we'll never see anyone in this store again.

We load up on muffins, bagels, yogurt parfaits, and whatever else tickles our taste buds. I call Nick when I have enough service to fill him in on our adventures, and I'm happy to report that we are back on the road.

"It's our last day in the truck," I say as an encouragement to the boys.

"Yay!" they holler in excitement.

While we're unusually on the same page, this means that I'm even closer to facing yet another fear: viewing the town and house that has barely formed an image in my mind.

Chapter 7 Look Who's Coming to Town

After three days cooped up in the truck, a fire, and several stink bombs wafting from the back seat, I finally take the exit towards Garden Valley.

"This is the town," I say, holding my breath as I formulate my first impression. One thing's for sure: the dominant color in Garden Valley is green; its beauty butting against my stubbornness.

Neighborhoods with sprawling grasses veer off of the main road. The valley part of the name is accurate, with the whole town is nestled at the center of a circular series of mountain ranges. Endless hills of green stretch beyond how far my eyes can see. The expertly taken pictures on the website didn't do this place justice.

"The lot sizes here are huge!" I say with a voice of surprise, thinking back to our tiny home on an even smaller lot.

I drive below the speed limit to take in the new sights. The sun rests behind a distant mountain, casting the town in shadows, but it's far from eerie. With light traffic and grazing animals, the town has a comfy feel, as if it is winding down for the day.

I can't put my finger on an odd feeling until I realize

what it is. The neighborhoods have house after house, as expected, but each home has a large area of land instead of being right next to each other. Most boast pastures with horses and farm animals. Every yard or field is manicured with flowery landscaping, showing the townsfolk's pride in their homes.

"There's cows in the front yard!" Dillon giggles.

"That yard has six horses!" Morgan says, plastering his face against the window.

"Our neighbors growing up had horses. I've always liked watching their tails swish." This easy back-and-forth conversation with the boys has happened a few times on this trip. Even with my anxiety at the top of the scale, I've been present enough to enjoy these little moments.

I wonder if the 'score of a house' that Nick found has any of these features we're enjoying. "Probably not," I puff, still in high irritation. Hills rest around the sprawling flat land, giving it depth and personality. I learned with my research that Garden Valley gets, on average, a foot of rain in the spring alone, obviously enough to feed the greenery dancing before my eyes.

"Can we get a horse?" Morgan asks. I can see the hope in his eyes through the rearview mirror.

"What about chickens?" Dillon asks.

"That person has a pool!" Morgan squeals.

A sign draped across two old-fashioned street lamps greets, "Welcome to Garden Valley," solidifying our arrival.

I call Nick with the news that we've arrived. "We're a little late, but we made it!" The excitement in my voice is for the fact that I'll soon be wrapping my arms around my husband, not for physically being here.

"Great! I'm at the house. You have the address, right?"

"It's in the GPS." The thrill of soon seeing his round, tanned face rips through my body, giving me a second wind after this long drive.

Nick texted me this morning that the movers had already dropped everything off, and he took the day off to unpack as much as possible before we arrived. On the outside, everything is falling into place. I agreed to move, but it will take more than a few well-aligned plans to win me over.

The houses spread further apart as we drive deeper into the countryside. I keep the truck on the narrow road leading to a dirt turnoff. It's hard to believe that this town has a population of five thousand, for I've seen more trees than houses.

"There's Daddy!" Morgan yells, pointing his finger at Nick, trotting his way down the dirt road.

Nick opens the door and hops in, putting my passenger, Annabelle, on his lap before filling the empty space.

"Joanie!" he booms with a serene smile, finally connecting his eyes with mine. No matter how upset I've been with him, the awkward car hug fills me with much-needed relief. My body relaxes for the first time in the almost three weeks since he left, my anger flying out the window.

"Hi, boys!" Nick says with high-fives. "It's a little ripe smelling in here."

"Oh yes, the boys have had multiple farting contests," I say with a fake smile.

"That must have been fun," Nick says sarcastically. "Dillon, I know green is your favorite color, man, but come on," Nick says with a touch to his new cast. "Aww, your monkey has seen better days," he says of the charred spots on Dillon's stuffed animal. "How was the drive?" After fifteen years together, I know my husband's bobbing knees and extra decibels in his voice points to heightened nerves.

"It wasn't terrible," I answer through gritted teeth. I'm not about to list all the boys' wrongdoings while they are in the back seat. After all, we did have a couple of heart-to-heart moments.

"It was looooooong!" Morgan drags the last word out to emphasize the fact.

"I bet. Ready to see the house? It's up there to the left," he says, pointing the way before lowering his voice. "Keep an open mind, okay?"

That doesn't sound good.

Judging by the row of mailboxes we passed at the end of the road, our house isn't the only one up this dirt road. We pass several horses grazing on the right side of the road beyond a sturdy white fence that travels beyond my sight. The animals would offer some solace if not for the knot pulsing in my stomach.

"Everything is so spread out here." My mind lacked imagination when visualizing where we would live, creating stories of peeing in an outhouse and driving an hour to the nearest grocery store.

The tires crunch past an empty field with grass as high as my knees. A willow tree up the hill sits outside a house that looks like it was pure white at one point. My eyes stay glued to it, formulating my first impression of the town. It's too rustic for my taste, even from this distance. It looks older than Nick and I combined, with siding that was probably in need of redoing a decade ago. The windows on the top floor are boarded, and the porch looks ready to crumble.

If this is my first impression of this town, I'd have to say, *Yikes*.

My eyes stay forward, awaiting our own house to come

into view. I haven't focused on the addresses, which I regret because the suspense is killing me.

"Take this driveway," Nick says with a nod to the left.

"Wait, are you sure?"

"Yup," he says with confidence.

"Here?" At this rundown house? This is the *yikes* house! This is the great find that Nick was excited about?

"Look at the tire swing, Dill!" Morgan hollers, unbuckling himself and pulling on my seat from behind.

I thread the truck between rows of angry-looking rose bushes that lead to what my mind labels as a mud pit. The truck drifts to a stop at the top of the hill in the gravel driveway beside a house way past its prime.

I'm in shock from head to toe, unable to form words. The truck jolts to a stop, rocking front and back in a way that does nothing to soothe my anxiety from seeing the dilapidated house in front of us.

"Go sniff it out, boys!" Nick says, getting out of the truck and keeping his eyes on me.

"Wait, Nick, I want to be able to see them. Boys, don't go too far!" I shout.

"I've walked the perimeter of the yard, and it's secure. Come on out and take a look, Joanie." I move slowly, partly because of my cramped muscles, but mainly from the shock of what lies before me. "So, I know it needs a little work."

"A little?" The screen door hangs sideways on the hinges, the windows are filthy, and I fear that it will crumble if I look at the front porch too hard. This is what I can see from the outside of the house for thirty seconds in the dusk!

"It needs a bit of curb appeal." It's a light way of saying I could work on the yard for the rest of my life and never be done.

To the right of the house is a stand-alone garage with matching chipped paint and siding that needs replacing. The garage door has a big pink bow, which I assume is Nick's way of giving us a present.

"I told the guys at work that my wife is 'Mrs. Fix-It' and would love a project."

"A project, yes, not four hundred of them." I take a few seconds after getting out of the truck to move this way and that. My cramped muscles appreciate being stretched into a standing position.

Nick comes to my side and circles me into a hug. He pulls back and embraces me in a kiss. Being with him again is nearly enough to snap me out of the unease about what's ahead with this tour.

"I've missed you. I have a good feeling about this place. It's getting dark, so let me give you a quick tour from the top of the hill here."

The cobblestone walkway is mostly buried under a thick layer of mud and weeds. I carefully hop from one stone to another to keep my shoes their original color. Nick takes my hand to steady my wobbly legs, helping me to the right side of the house where a side door sits.

My eyes strain to make anything out in the darkness that has settled around the property. Lights shine beyond our street, indicating invisible houses amongst the darkening sky. The spectacular view of the valley lying dormant under a frame of mountains is hard to miss, even in the dim light. An eagerness to see what lies in the nightfall will have to wait until the morning.

"Just wait 'til you see the view!" Nick says excitedly.

"Our last house had a view… of our four neighbors' houses," I say, grateful that my sense of humor is still intact.

"Isn't that the truth?" Nick says with a laugh. "So, way down there is the barn, and over here is the old chicken coop. There's a pond down there past the pasture, which can be used if we want a horse. A horse, Joanie!" He grabs my arms and gives them a little shake. "And this…" he says, with his hands spread wide, "is the house!" I fail to join him in his excitement. All I see is a dingy-looking building needing much more than paint. "What do you think?"

My insides are screaming to run away, to crawl back to the comfort of North Dakota. "I think we should get the place inspected before we set foot inside," I blurt. Nick's face falls, and I jump in to hold up his spirits before they crash. "How many acres is this?" I ask to skirt the truth. My stomach jolts with this question, dreading the answer. We had such a small lot where we lived that I didn't think to ask. Nick had said this house is on acreage… but this?

Nick pauses before giving a boastful answer. "Fifteen."

"What?" I say with a jolted shake of my head, finally understanding the land beyond my feet. "You bought a farm? That wasn't part of the photos you sent." He nods with a smile. Nick knows everything about my upbringing and how I haven't wanted to live in the open. Why would he do this?

"I know! It's not functional, but it has a barn, pastures, and everything." He stays silent, holding his breath in anticipation of my answer. I'm far from giving my verdict. Unspoken words float in the air. We both know I would never have agreed to be here had I known about the acreage.

"It's dark," I say with a tilt of my head to soften my non-answer. "Where are the boys?" I ask to take the spotlight off me.

"Right there. See?" He leans into me and stretches his thick arm to point.

"They're all the way over there? Morgan! Dillon! You're too far!" I yell. The boys register nothing of my calls to them.

"Boys, make sure you stay close!" Nick yells before turning his attention back to me. "I have a surprise," Nick says, leading me to the unattached garage. I follow in a daze, wondering how we got here in just a few short weeks.

Nick manually opens the garage door, which creaks in protest. His proud grin makes me wonder what his definition of "surprise" means. I fan my hand before my face to brush away the dust that greets my nose. He clicks on a light, illuminating a room full of steel woodworking machinery. It takes a moment to register this crafter's dream.

"For an extra five grand, I got all this… for you!" He spreads his arms wide to showcase a surface planer, a table saw, a jointer, a couple other machines, and multiple tool chests.

"You're kidding?"

As much as I've been repelling my woodworking skills, he's attaching the hook with this. I've been wanting to dive back into my craft. I can't help it; I've been a tinkerer my entire life. Being the only girl in a house with two older brothers will do that to someone. Until I was four, I thought my nickname, Jon, was my actual name.

I'm momentarily taken from the shambles behind me and delivered into my element in this garage full of dusty machines and tools. It doesn't take but a few seconds to form an opinion of the equipment that appears to be in good condition.

My chest is weighed down with a mixture of fear and excitement. I reach my hand out to touch the surface planer but pull it back, the fear, unfortunately, is dominating. I seriously doubt that I can pick up where I left off.

"What do you think?" Nick asks, curling his lips in anticipation. He's worried I won't like it. "You've talked over the years about wanting to get back to your woodworking, and now you can! You'll be sticking your tongue out in no time." Nick tickles my side with the tease.

"It's all a bit older, but it doesn't matter if everything has been taken care of, which it looks like it is," I say quietly. I'm far from tallying my final score for the move or the house.

Excuse me, the farm.

I run my hand across the smooth surface of the bed of the jointer, allowing myself to be pulled in. It's been years since I've been able to play at my hobby.

"I thought you'd enjoy doing your projects again." It's such a new trait for him to make all these decisions without my say. I hope it doesn't become a new habit. "No more furniture graveyard in the garage."

I perk up and gasp. "I didn't know you called the garage that, too!" I say with a light smack on his shoulder. In all truthfulness, this shop is so big that there's plenty of space for all the furniture I've made… and then some.

I don't have a clue how to act right now. I keep quiet, not about to crush his dreams. What can I say? I'm a gentle soul. It takes me a while to take a side on something, and this one, for sure, I haven't even begun to wrap my brain around.

Nick's excitement is palpable as he hops between the well-thought-out floor plans of the machines. Still, I can't get one hot topic out of my mind regarding this gift.

"Five thousand is a lot. I really wish you would have…"

"It's not very much at all when it rolls into the price of the whole house," Nick interrupts.

"But Nick, we could have done something else with that money," I say with worry.

"It doesn't really work like that, hon. It's all added to the lump sum of the loan. Spread over thirty years, it's maybe twenty-five dollars a month. He gently folds my hand into his. His touch couples with his words, working to ease my struggles. "For this first impression, ignore all your worries and *just be*."

I nod with as much excitement as possible and follow him out of the garage. Just be? I'm thirty-four, and I've never been able to 'just be.'

"Come on, boys!" Nick hollers. He closes the garage door and again wraps himself around me, engulfing me in his warmth. I'm in tune with him enough to know that he's in his element of giving gifts, his happy place. "I know this is quite a change for us. I appreciate the sacrifices you've already made for our family. I promise this will work out. Hey, Dillon and Morgan, let's take a look inside."

"Yeah!" they yell, running back to us.

I take a deep breath, allowing myself to believe his words. With us being back together, the initial blow of moving to a farm and the surprise cost of the machinery is softened. How bad can it be since we are finally all together again?

My eyes stay fixed on the house, willing myself to bring an air of hope my way. Everything is dulled by the sight of the two-story wonder, and it's not because it's dusk. In this case, I mean that it's a wonder it's still standing. We'll be lucky if it passes inspection before the bank loans us the money.

"Take your shoes off," I instruct upon seeing the inch of mud caked on our shoes. It looks like extra mud will be a part of my new life.

"We'll start at the side of the house or laundry room,"

Nick says with a hand on my lower back. "There's a shoe scraper right by the door." Under the tiny, flickering light above the roughed-up door, Nick demonstrates how to rub our feet on the bristles to clean our shoes. The boys follow suit, frantically scraping their feet and flinging mud around us. In a few seconds, the chunks of mud have been reduced to a thin layer.

Here goes.

***

I anticipate the worst when I cross the threshold of the door, which looks like a bull has been sharpening its horns on. The boys take off through the house, screaming at the top of their lungs.

"That's exactly what they did at the hotel," I grumble.

"They can't hurt anything," Nick says with an easy smile that discounts what I've gone through to get here.

My first impression inside is the laundry room, which is bigger than our kitchen back home. My mind explodes with ideas for this first room, which is entirely out of character for me.

The musky smell that hits my nose is distracting, however. Unless a dozen dust-scented air fresheners hang around this house, the scent alone means this place will need a cleaning overhaul. Still, a smell of lilac fights through the dust, making me wonder about its source.

The dingy white and lime-green paint is a must-have. Luckily, paint is an easy fix. A shelf rests two feet from the ceiling and runs the entire square of the room above us. It's a style that doesn't tickle my fancy, though I suppose it'll be easy to tear down.

"It looks like we'll need a washer and dryer. Do they have garage sales here?" Our set-back home came with the house we rented. I wasn't sad to say goodbye to the rusty pair that I had spent hours repairing over the years.

"I have one of each coming later this week," Nick says with a wink. I stare at him with yet another look of surprise, one that I hope won't become a default.

"No way!" I smack his arm lightly with this surprise. It's Nick's first good decision in this venture. I've never had a new washer and dryer. "How are we going to pay for that?"

"The sign-on bonus, baby! Remember?" Before I can bask in this new purchase, Nick officially whisks me through the door and into the kitchen. "And here's the kitchen!" he chirps, arms wide.

I take in the entirety of the room, which needs a lot of care but has a spectacularly spacious floorplan. The infancy of the remodel rings clear to my stunned eyes. Parts of the kitchen are new, while others are ripped apart. A partially open floorplan allows me to peer into a hallway and living room that look to be in the same state of remodel.

"These granite countertops are new. Obviously, the floor still needs work," he says, bouncing his foot on the cracked linoleum. "It's not a bad position since we'll get to choose what we want. You name it hardwood or tile, and we'll put it in."

The kitchen is large enough to support an island, with plenty of room around it. Endless, sparkly gold granite countertops with warm cream and gray swirls surround me. A bay window above the sink opens the space further, and though the shelf needs to be repainted, it's a nice touch. A stainless-steel range that would have taken up our kitchen in the last house rests to my right.

"Six burners!" I run my fingers across the stove, envisioning myself making full meals without switching pots and pans out. A large, empty hole awaits a refrigerator, which rests next to… "A pantry!" I breathe, pulling the door open and stepping inside the fifty-square-foot room. Three levels of shelving carry my eyes to canned lights in the ceiling. I look at Nick wide-eyed, trying not to be sold on the entire place by this one room. "I wouldn't have painted it red, but that's an easy fix," I say, brushing my fingertips along the walls.

"Even with this pantry, the kitchen has plenty of cabinet space. I counted thirty-two, and that's without all the drawers!"

"Thirty-two cabinets?" The cabinets appear as old as the house, with each begging for a good sanding and refinishing. My hands practically vibrate from the feel of doing such a task.

I move to the kitchen sink, not caring that the boys run amuck through the house. They're yelling somewhere around here, and I can barely hear them! I admit that this is a huge plus. I peer out into the darkness with the anticipation of seeing what's beyond this window.

"Here's the breakfast nook," Nick interrupts with golden retriever-like peppiness.

"*This is* a nook?" I'm astonished at the area at least twice the size of our dining room back home. It's not much of an understatement that our previous house could almost fit in this kitchen and nook alone. My breath is knocked out of me when I see the table and chairs I made nearly a decade ago. "I hope you don't mind that I put these here," Nick says in a small voice.

I squish my lips together to try and stop tears joining the reunion with this piece. Even though my eyes know every flaw in the table and chairs, it's nice to see them again. I glance into what I label as the living room and see the hutch and end tables I made a lifetime ago. It's Nick's way of uniting me with this move. While it's a sweet gesture, it doesn't work.

"And look, it's the huge hutch buffet you insisted on having in the old house. Remember how it took up so much of the dining room?"

Of course, I remember, that was only last week! Still… "It looks great in here. Look," I gasp, going to the side of the furniture to see the tick marks of the boys' heights.

"Yup, we don't have to turn the whole thing to measure the boys. I think my shoulder still hurts from this solid piece of wood you built." He massages his shoulder with me flashing on helping him move this piece that was squished against the wall.

Nick allows me to be in this moment of silence until I wiggle myself back to reality.

My eyes adjust to the oversized window behind the nook, which has shredded curtains, smudges of dirt, and God knows what else smeared on it. Apparently, acres of land lie beyond this window, but darkness keeps me from seeing them. That twinge of nervousness about being out in the open courses through me.

I hate it, I hate it, I hate it!

It's a mantra I must keep to myself if this adventure will work. Excited, booming voices from Morgan and Dillon upstairs couple with the dimpled perma-smile Nick has given me since we got here. It all glues my feet to the ground, keeping me from running from the house screaming.

"You okay?" Nick asks, resting his arm on my shoulders. Are you kidding me? Doesn't this man know me at all? I nod, overwhelmed by all the new sights and smells, knowing I must continue on this tour. "And we continue…" he says with a silly voice. "Step this way, beautiful lady. Beyond the swinging doors, you'll find the formal dining room."

"*Formal* dining room?" I ask, his comedic ways, loosening my nerves. I shake my head in confusion. On one hand, the house rests in a layer of dust and neglect. On the other, it certainly has the bones to turn into something beautiful if matched with the perfect buyer.

Nick pushes through the swinging door to reveal a dark room with that musky dust scent tickling my nose. Brown curtains that might have been elegant once upon a time desperately need to be washed or tossed. A chandelier and a built-in cabinet with a granite top for serving guests fill this space. I chuckle as I wonder who in this town of strangers I would invite.

"This is to hold all of our fancy China," I joke, running my hand across the surface of the cabinet, which we don't have even one piece for. I flip the light switch, only to continue to be in darkness. "This room needs some work." I eye him with circumspection.

"There aren't any electrical or plumbing issues," Nick says quickly. I give him a worried look. "That's all been upgraded, I checked. It's an old house…"

"Really? I hadn't noticed," I tease, thanking myself for hauling my box of grungy old clothes across state lines. I'll definitely fit in wearing them in this rustic house.

"Very funny. The guy selling it was doing upgrades and thankfully started with the electrical and plumbing before he moved away."

"From all this?" I say with a sideways glance.

My ears twitch when the boys come screaming down the stairs on the other side of the dining room, claiming they've picked their rooms.

"They have separate rooms," Nick says quietly by my side.

"Oh! I hadn't thought of that."

It's another ding, the fact that I didn't ask many questions. I ease up on the criticism, reminding myself I had a million things to do before we left, not to mention deal with the boys and an angry landlord. It's easy to get stuck in our current situations so much that we can't see beyond our immediate bubble of issues.

"How many bedrooms does this house have?"

"Five," Nick says as if he's thrilled to be the one to give me this news.

"Five?" The whirlwind has gone straight to my brain, not allowing it to grasp hold of all the information. Dillon pulls my arms through another swinging door to what looks like a living room and up an oversized staircase. The glance I'm allowed at the living room shows floor-to-ceiling windows, sending me a rush of unwanted excitement.

I look down at Dillon, my first smile spreading across my face since being here. He wants to show me his new room. Me!

Raw cherry wood stairs that look like they once had carpet take me to another spacious seating area. I have yet to see the whole house, and I already don't know what to do with all this space!

The square footage is impressive, though the list of projects grows with every minute that passes. Not one room that I've merely glanced at is put together completely. Floors need to be replaced, holes need to be patched, walls need drywall, and all the doors need to be re-sanded and finished. I foresee a major painter's hand cramp in the future.

Still, the layout is spectacular, with loads of potential once some TLC has been added. The upstairs balcony overlooks a vast living room I can briefly inspect from above. Dillon pulls me along, and Nick explains that three bedrooms are upstairs, each bigger than our master bedroom back home.

The boys whisk us through their rooms with their energy levels set on high. The last moving truck arrived a full day ahead of us, giving Nick and the movers time to bring in the boys' beds and dressers.

"It looks like I chose the rooms correctly," Nick says, having separated their bunk beds. "Do you guys think you'll be able to sleep alone?"

"Yup!" Morgan shouts immediately. "I won't have to listen to Dingus here snore."

"I can't help it if it's a hobby," Dillon shouts back. Nick and I laugh at his slip of words.

"Do you mean 'habit?'" Nick corrects. Dillon isn't having this laughter at his expense and throws a stuffed animal at his brother's face. The action ignites a fit of anger in Morgan. It's a common reaction to be upset when getting hurt; only Morgan flies off the wall.

"That hurt, you idiot!" he screams, lunging for his brother. Nick catches him around the waist just in time.

"Come on, calm down. Let's go to your new room." Morgan is revved up, but Nick easily contains him, having had years of practice.

While I hear Nick talking to Morgan about being nicer to his brother, I take advantage of this time with Dillon, asking him about his room.

"I love it!" he exclaims, wandering around his new space. I mosey to the windows, wondering again about the view the morning light will reveal. Without neighborhood or city lights to cast a glow on the land, I'm kept from even a sneak peek.

"You've never had your own room before. How do you want it decorated?"

"I think I'll put my bed there and my toys there. Can I get one of those net things for my stuffed animals?" Dillon continues to lay out his room in a speed talk that could rival Nick's sister, Brooke's. It's an analytical side of him I've never seen before.

"How did you come up with this so quickly?" I ask, joining him cross-legged on the ground next to a slew of boxes. It'll be a great room once new carpet and paint are added.

"We had to draw our 'dream room' at school one day," he says, leaning on my leg with his good arm. My throat constricts with emotion at the new affection. "I'd want to paint the walls green. Do you think they're still green in the dark?" He continues with a smile that is a younger version of Nick's.

Even at six, Dillon is comfortable with being alone, something I have yet to master in my thirty-three years of living. It's an advancement from him I want to see continue. Here we are, finally allowing my son to have his own space in life. For the first time, my heels ease up from digging in to stop this runaway train.

Morgan appears in the doorway with a sheepish look. "Sorry," he says quietly.

"Why don't you boys unpack your toys," Nick suggests.

"Alright!" Dillon says, digging into a box and unleashing

an explosion of stuffed toys around his new room. Morgan follows suit, with the stuffed animal imprint on his nose being forgotten.

"Okay, don't get too crazy up here. I'm going to show Mommy the master bedroom." Nick turns to me, bobbing his eyebrows up and down before taking my hand and leading the way back downstairs. I follow quietly, fiercely guarding my thoughts. My stomach is sour from all the change, as if I've been eating junk food all day. Nick is like a kid in a candy store with no end in sight for being full. Still, I refuse to allow my analytical side to ruin this moment for him.

"Looks like their fights have crossed state lines," I say with disappointment.

"It's normal. My sister and I used to fight all the time." It's his way of discounting how their behavior affects me, which adds to my list of topics to discuss with him. Now, all I have to do is drum up the courage to start them.

On our way downstairs, I notice the designs carved into the cherry wood railing. I trace the smooth, intricate design with my fingers, impressed by its detail. "I knew these designs wouldn't escape your keen eye. This is the original railing." Nick lowers his voice to match my slowed steps.

"It's nice." It's a reserved answer for the emotions flooding my receptors.

Overwhelm threatens to settle in: the house, the need to unpack, and the myriad of projects, all pushing against my fighting spirit. I have no idea how we will comfortably live here amongst the broken down… everything.

Every step down the stairs reveals the open design of the first floor. I'd be able to enjoy it if the main level didn't resemble a construction zone. The floor is ripped to shreds, and every inch of wall space begs for fresh paint. A living room with vaulted ceilings and equally tall windows shows a ragged portion of a wall that is well out of place.

"It looks like they knocked a wall down right here," I say, running my hand over the section with exposed drywall.

"Nothing gets past you. I went through the house with the previous owner. He said this wall went all the way out to here," he says, taking three giant steps to the left. "There was even a door here to get to the nook."

"It was a good idea to knock it down then. It opens the room up even more. It would look good with a column right here," I say, inspecting the wall. "I bet it can be cut back a few more feet."

I take a few steps from the living room to the kitchen and back again, hands on my hips, formulating a plan. Nick struggles to hold back a smile.

"What?"

"Always a carpenter," he says with his hands on his hips. "I knew this place would spark that passion of yours."

"Yeah, maybe in another life," I say, brushing him off and seeing the living room for what it is. "The ceilings must be twenty-five feet high! Our furniture looks miniature in here," I say, wanting to explore this space.

After a few seconds, Nick pulls me away, leading me down a hallway from the breakfast nook. Looks like the bruises on my hips from our narrow passageways back home will be a thing of the past.

We pass the formal dining room on our right and a guest room on the left before we come to a set of double doors.

"How many square feet is this house again?" If I did ask these questions, they flew out the other ear. Nick stops and swings his head back before answering. This is what I've deemed as *the look* from him. It's one I rarely see and still gives me butterflies.

"Four thousand square feet."

"Four thousand? Did you tell me that earlier? How in the world…?"

"That surprised me too." He grins as if he's done good. I don't have the heart to tell him that this isn't what you keep from someone, especially when she's the one who will be doing projects on every one of those feet from here until eternity. "There's a whole section beyond the living room that I haven't shown you yet with an office and sitting room. Our room also takes up quite a bit of the total."

Nick opens the French doors in one motion as if giving me the grand entrance experience. It's spacious but desperately needs attention in every area. Still, I'm not so naïve that I can't see past the flaws of what this place has to offer.

Our bed lies underneath a window that covers nearly the entire far wall. A bathroom and closet line the whole right side of the room, while the left side is full of windows.

"I know it needs some work, but…"

"It certainly has potential." The positive words fly from my mouth before I can hold them back. My opinion ignites Nick's glee even more.

"Yes! You can see it! Now you know why I couldn't pass this up." He bends to give me a kiss when the doorbell rings. I look at him in confusion. I ordered pizza just before you guys got here," he says with that proud look.

Nick trots from the room, leaving me alone in my new bedroom. I had better get used to it; I'll soon spend a lot of time alone in this house.

Our master room is the roughest I've ever seen in the house. There's a sub-floor beneath my feet, drywall needs to be put on whole sections of walls, wallpaper needs to be stripped from others, a skylight above our bed is boarded up, and window frames need to be installed. And that's just in our room.

"Of course, it has carpet," I sigh upon seeing the bathroom, hating this dirty, dated feature. While the master bathroom is more significant than one needs, the layout is perfect. A thoroughly used vanity leads to double sinks across from a spacious walk-in closet. "I can fit a double-sized bed in here," I mumble, knowing I won't be able to fill my side of the closet with what I own. The back side of the bathroom has the best-hidden gem: what appears to be a new jacuzzi tub. Minus the carpet and general seventies-theme, this will look quite nice.

"Joanie, come eat!" Nick's voice is faint from across the house, but I follow the echo in a daze, hardly realizing that this monstrous house, with equally large tasks, will soon be mine.

"Boys, pizza!" he yells before turning to me. "Two steamy pies, salads, and homemade potato fries. And it's supposed to be pork chop night!" he says with a teasing wink.

"Very funny. How did you find a pizza place to deliver way out here?" I ask incredulously.

"This is the norm around here, baby," Nick says with a quirky smile. Today, I feel like a test subject with him studying my every move and expression.

A sudden dizziness impairs my vision, and I place my hand on the counter to steady myself before taking a seat. That was weird. It must be hunger mixed with the drain only a long drive can create.

"We'll need more furniture. Will your work give an allowance for that?" I joke.

"Yeah, it's called a paycheck," Nick says, playing along.

We sit at my homemade dining table that fills the nook by the kitchen nicely. "I've never heard of anyone being able to use their own plates for the first meal."

"I guess that's one benefit of me getting here early," Nick says with a smile.

"Morgan, don't wipe your hands on your socks. We have napkins." I put one in front of him, which he smears it all over his face to be goofy.

"Well?" Nick asks expectantly.

"I'm going to have a list of things to do from here to the end of the dirt road."

"It's a good thing I married a handy-woman then," Nick says with a full mouth.

"You really think I can do all this?" I ask in honest surprise.

"We aren't in a hurry."

"Not unless we want to dig splinters out of our feet every night."

"Before you boys were born, Mom volunteered for Habitat for Humanity. They grabbed onto her once they saw what she could do, and she ran that place for a few years."

"That feels like it was so long ago. And I've never had to live in one of those places as I built it."

"Our dinner guests will be able to see the potential of this place," Nick says with an expectant look. For years, he's wanted to host gatherings at our home, but it's one thing I always put my foot down on.

"Gosh, I hope we won't have a party anytime soon."

The boys and Nick discuss their favorite parts of the house, spouting off items from their own lists of what they'd like done. It's all muffled in the background as I glance around the kitchen, which has missing cabinet doors and scuffed-up floors. It's exciting and overwhelming simultaneously, the two emotions duking it out to see who will overtake me.

"What do you think?" Nick asks with a hopeful look.

All eyes are on me when it comes to my turn to talk. The pressure to give the correct answer is in full force, and I know this moment will make or break this move for my family.

I do what any mom would: I lie.

Chapter 8 First Impressions

I'm not ungrateful, really. It's not like the house is literally falling down; it just looks like it could at any moment. My honesty about the house not living up to my basic list of expectations would crush Nick.

Everything my eyes have landed on needs work, and I haven't seen the whole place yet! I have to wait for the sun to come back up to check out the barn and whatever else is falling apart out there.

How in the world will I turn this shack into a home? These are mammoth-sized jobs, and I'm only one woman… with big hips.

I feel more like a guest than the person paying the mortgage. Whoa, whoa, that's the wrong thing to say. I won't pay for anything since I no longer have an income.

After dinner, I glance at the back garage through the window in the nook while the boys and Nick run around the house with as much energy as puppies. A soft glow falls on the building full of machinery.

"Pff," I say, spitting the air between my lips. Nick was excited about this surprise. It truly is a woodworker's dream. But that was my past life. I've fixed things in our old house, but woodworking is more encompassing than making a drawer work. I wove a piece of myself into everything I made, and I doubt I can hold that same passion and dedication at the stage of life I'm currently in.

I flick the dingy curtains that will soon fill the garbage can. Unfortunately, Nick has to work tomorrow. That will leave me to explore the house alone, assuming the boys will continue ignoring me. The thought of these truths mixed together brings tears to my eyes. While we are together again, work keeps us apart, leaving me more alone than I was in Fargo.

On my way to my new room, I get a text from Brooke. Nick must have let her know we got here. *Eek! We're in the same time zone! I can't wait to see you after our trip!*

Have a great time! I write with feigned enthusiasm.

A couple weeks ago, I was living out my robotic schedule. A few days ago, I was packing. A couple of hours ago, I was driving. Now, I'm in charge of fixing this place from ceiling to floor. Which version of my life will win my happiest lifestyle award is so far in the air that airplanes are batting it around.

I step out of the shower moments later, my eyes pointing out ten things in the bathroom that need attention. I can't help but begin the process of piecing together a plan. The house screams to be decorated in a ranch style, which scares me to death. Back home, my decorating ideas only reached the nearest yard sale.

"Those definitely aren't items to decorate with," I say to my bag of period pads. I chuckle as I think of how the boys once stuck them all over the walls back home. I throw them under the sink, remembering that tomorrow's the big day. Goody, now I get to unpack while my insides feel like they're being squeezed like lemons.

I brush my long, black hair and twist it into a bun. It's my go-to at night, making me feel like it's in style rather than the long, drab look I've had for years. I open the door to my new bedroom and gaze at my husband as he reads the latest John Grisham in bed, weary of opening my can of feelings to him.

"What's on your schedule besides meeting me at the bank tomorrow?" Nick asks. He sets the book down and switches to his side, holding his head up with his hand. It's funny to see this sexy pose in the dingy room.

Damn. The dreaded signing of the house papers. It's a topic I've wiggled out of until now. Once I've drawn my cursive name on the paper, it's a done deal.

"Is that tomorrow?" I ask now with my back to Nick so I can close my tear-filled eyes. I've been a master at hiding my feelings, the main reason for Nick's ignorance of my distress. Except for that first night when I freaked out after he broke the news of the job, I've mostly kept the uncertainty and unsettled feelings to myself.

Laughter from the boys upstairs filters down to us. I'm on this roller coaster with a new thought: why am I the only one on this ride who hates the sudden drops and spins? I'm the only one who has volunteered to make this difficult; frankly, I'm tired of feeling this way.

I wiggle my shoulders to shed the victim mentality. I make a dull promise to change, to stop being the odd one out and painting myself out of the picture. It's time to buck up and face the fact that there's no going back.

With Nick in bed enticing me, I'm willing to let a piece of my resistance go. I crawl into bed, resting my head on his shoulder, feeling the complete relief of being with him again. I settle beside him, forcing my mind to focus on a different perspective. Now that we're together, I don't care if I have to deal with a house crumbling around me.

Almost.

"I need to take the boys to the school district to enroll them." Another sign that this is a done deal. "It looks like the schools here are good, so we'll see. They've learned a lot this year, and I don't want them going backward. Lord knows they won't learn anything from me."

The words hit against the memory of when the boys hung on my every word in the car. During our countdown of miles left, I explained what coordinates are and how to read a map with them. Dillon joked about it being called longitude because it took so *long* to get to our new town.

"That's not true; they learn from you," Nick replies with the same aloof response I've received for years. I don't press, not wanting to start the circular conversation where I defend my feelings of being invisible. I've always wondered why people try to tell others how to feel for validation. Aren't our feelings alone as valid as we can get? "For real now, what do you think about the house? I could tell you were lying for the boys' sake, so come on, give me the truth."

"I wasn't lying," I respond a little too quickly.

"Joanie, when you fib, your left eyebrow goes up more than the right. I can even see it in the dark. I know you'd do anything to ensure we all have a good experience, even if that means you're being tortured. I hope that's not the case here."

It doesn't take me long to think of my answer, for the truth is ready to come out. "I agree that there's a lot of potential here."

"But?" he draws out.

"I feel the pressure that I'm the one who has to bring it out. I'll be the one completing most of these projects. This is a huge shift for me. I had a job a few weeks ago, where people depended on me. Now I have fifteen scary acres of mud to whip into shape, and you know how much I hate yard work! And the house." My body sinks against him, showing my deflation. "This is a lot of work, Nick. Work I haven't done in years."

Nick nuzzles his forehead against mine. Though our marriage isn't perfect, I've always given us points for being able to discuss a heavy topic without either of us becoming overly upset.

"It's not all on you. I'm here, too. It's not like you need to get all the tasks done at once. The house is still livable, so every little tweak will be a bonus. I'll help after work and on the weekends," Nick sits up. The beige flannel sheets fall off his upper body, revealing the tanned, bare torso I've missed. "I have a little surprise for you," he says with a half-smile.

"And here I thought you only bought me a house." Laughter once again eases some of the tension between us. Nick reaches under his side of the bed and pulls out a teal-colored wrapped box. I sit up and allow myself to feel excited about getting a gift. He moves behind me, pulling me into his bare arms and resting his chin on my shoulder. I love the feel of his unshaven face prickling my skin. I open the box and reach in. "Wow, look at this!"

"I figured it would come in handy."

I hold the brown leather tool belt up, stuffing the lack of confidence away with the curtails sticking out of my jeans. The gift does wonders to cheer up my sullen mood. "You had a design embroidered in my favorite color. This is really sweet of you." I touch the intricate teal flowers with my fingers, turning the tool belt around. "Look, it has the same name as me!" I tease.

I take a deep breath, grateful for the gift but needing to ask a question.

"How can you be so sure I'll be able to turn this place around? The floors aren't done, the drywall has been stripped off in several areas, and the kitchen needs to be finished…"

"I know your resume, baby," he responds, rolling me onto the bed.

Kisses and attention from my husband relieve me from pent-up tension and worry. After some much-needed love shared between us, I lay in bed, listening to Nick's light snore as I ponder the many topics fighting for center stage.

Creaks and pops from the house cooling off for the night keep me awake, even with Nick beside me. I grab my stuffed Annabelle and hold her tight, wondering if I can pull this whole thing off.

✳✳✳

I drearily send Nick off with a kiss early the next morning. Even with the time change being two hours earlier, I'm up before the sun. As my new tasks pull at me, I watch his truck follow the dirt driveway through a dim glow. My eyes continue over the land in the fresh morning flow, barely a shade above dark. I allow myself the luxury of sipping tea and taking in the view as the sunlight slowly illuminates the land before me.

I don't know where to rest my eyes when the sun first peeks out enough to alight the valley. The land before me sparks an image of a young Joanie alone in a field. My brothers have snuck off behind a tree or bush, making animal noises to frighten me.

The stunning scenery before me clashes with the soreness I hold for my mountain lion experience. I'd like to try to get sick of the view from the living room. Here's this town that is taking me away from my comfortable routine, uprooting our entire lives, and dredging up a bunch of childhood drama, and yet, it's beautiful.

I foresee a chaise lounge under the tall windows in this spot. With the view in front of me, I could spend hours here.

The neighbor's animals come alive with the arrival of the day. Horse tails swish as they graze in the fields, and puffballs of sheep dot the hillside. I lean against the windowsill, smiling at the bunnies hopping in my yard full of weeds. A doe with her two fawns lazily walks by, confirming that I'll spend a lot of time in this room.

The bloom of dawn inspires me to get started on… something. "Piece of paper," I say, scrounging through the box labeled *stationery*. It's a fancy word for the box that held our junk drawer items of pens, papers, and whatever else we were tired of looking at on the counter.

I'm being granted a fresh start, which was in my cards anyway since I got fired. I've been thrust into a palette of opportunities!

"People start over all the time," I whisper. I grab the salmon-colored notebook and rip out the pages with to-do items of my old worries. "Won't be needing these anymore." I ball up the papers and notes from our previous life, getting a fresh piece for this new chapter we are in. I write *kitchen* on the top of the page and get started on my bulleted list.

Since I'm in charge of transforming this house into a masterpiece, organization is needed. That, I can do. In the kitchen alone, there are over nineteen things to be done, with the most time-consuming being re-sanding and staining the kitchen cabinets. I do my best to prioritize as I go, leaving the painting and cosmetic items for last.

"There," I say, looking over my list, trying not to panic after seeing its length.

I take my notepad to the laundry room next. It's not a bad room with less to spruce up, but it's not at all my style.

Is messy a style?

I riffle through the stationery box again, looking for a colored pencil to match the color I want to paint this room. "Green is nice," I say, finding one in my stash. But a sage would be pretty, not this lime green that matches Dillon's cast.

I scribble my last note for this room when a noise from the other side of the house straightens my spine. I jump, freeze, and stare in the general direction of where I heard the sound.

Silence.

I would think it was in my head if not for my ears being pricked and my heart pounding. Noises upstairs drift down, indicating that the boys are up.

I release a long puff of air, the tension thankfully easing. I'm not used to this house or the racket it makes. I am, however, used to this scaredy-cat type of reaction.

Dry cereal and leftover pizza are on the menu this morning when the boys come down for food. "This house is the best!" Dillon shouts when I deliver our meal. Nick may have unpacked, but a visit to the grocery store is a must.

The boys chatter about playing outside all day, something I feel bad putting a kink in. "You'll be able to play when we get home. We have some things to do in town today, so…"

"Come on, Dill, let's get ready!" Morgan screams, dashing upstairs. Dillon follows, his cast not slowing him down for one second.

What in the world was that? Usually, I have to light a fire under them to get them to do anything I ask, and it never happens with the first request.

The boys barrel downstairs before I'm done with my minimal makeup routine. I admit I want to make a good impression on my first day in town. In a small place like this, I assume the news of a new family will travel fast. I hop into jeans, throw a purple fuzzy sweater over my head, and call it good.

The boys are digging through the remaining boxes in the living room when I come out.

The boys run to the van while I grab a bag of snacks for them. An odd banging noise in the back of the house stops me before leaving through the laundry room door. "What the heck was that?" I say, wondering if this noise really is in my head. I shrug it off, guessing there's a breeze or something I'm not yet used to.

I brace myself for a rush of cold air but am greeted by a light morning chill with a hint of lilac scent.

"Oh, Van, how I've missed you," I say with a hug to the side. The boys eye each other as if I'm weird, which they're right in this case.

"Hello!" The new voice makes us turn around to see a woman power walk up our driveway. She appears a bit older than me and looks like she could run circles around the valley. "You must be the new family in town, the Nelsons."

As I assumed, news travels fast in rural areas like this.

"I'm Alice. I live over that way," she says, pointing to a field that bears no house. "What do you say I come in and we chat?"

Her forwardness takes me aback, especially since we're obviously leaving. I figure she wants to be the first to gather the drama of a new family, boasting to have the scoop. "Nice to meet you. I'm Joanie, and these are my boys, Morgan and Dillon. I'm sorry, we have a few errands to run right now," I say, grateful for the truthful response. I'm nowhere near allowing anyone to see this house in its state.

"Maybe some other time then. I'd like to hear about these carpentry skills I've heard about. How about tomorrow?"

"Oh, um, I don't know. I have quite a bit of unpacking to do. You understand." Her return of a frown most certainly shows she does not understand.

"Well, I guess I'll ask the welcoming committee to hold off," Alice says in a snarky tone, raising her chin. "You boys be good for your mom, you hear?"

"Yes, ma'am," Morgan says, surprising me with politeness. "Get in the car, Dingus!"

Alice turns back to me with wide eyes of surprise. I smile sheepishly back before hopping in the van after them. I pull out of the driveway and glance in the mirror halfway, expecting Alice to be peeking through our windows. To my relief, she's speedwalking away from our house, no doubt formulating a story about her first impression of me.

"It says to turn left here, Mom," Morgan says, pointing with one hand while holding my phone with another.

"Thanks, Morg," I say, willing my fingers to relax their grip on the wheel. Though it's inevitable, I hate having the spotlight on me. I also hate getting lost, something I never had to worry about back home. This is a tiny town, though. It's not like I'm going to get permanently lost.

The grocery store called Food 4 Less is clean and relatively empty this Tuesday morning, with a large selection of items that suits me. With my laminated list of food for the scheduled week of dinners, I'm ready to tackle this chore with the boys.

The dinner list was in my bag of necessities that rode in the truck's front seat. It used to be that there was nothing worse than figuring out what to make for dinner. Now, I'm afraid the entirety of the new house and fifteen acres have taken that slot.

The boys throw every junk food item in the cart with sugar as the first ingredient, with me unloading most of their chosen items. I follow Dillon around a corner, look at a couple of things, and then notice that he's no longer in the aisle.

"Dillon?" I call, doing my best not to yell. It's too early to panic. He's probably around the other corner. Only, he doesn't come back. "Dillon?"

My mind spins out of control, seeing headlines of a missing child. My heart speeds with the fear of losing my son. My legs feel like they are immersed in water. The faster I try and walk, the more resistance I create.

"Morgan, run ahead and see if your brother is up there," I bark with a harshness that is really a lashing at myself. I rush my cart to the end of the aisle, which never seems to end. This is precisely why we never should have left North Dakota! I always knew where to find...

"Dillon, what are you doing?" Morgan scolds, interrupting my racing thoughts.

"Talking to my friend," Dillon says, looking up at us with irritation. He and another boy are sitting next to the fruit snacks without a care in the world.

"Oh, yeah? What's his name?" Morgan challenges, his hands on his hips.

"I don't know. What's your name?" Dillon bluntly asks

the boy.

"Lucas. I'm six," the boy with blonde hair answers.

"Lucas, there you are!" says a mom who frantically joins us. "You know you're not supposed to leave the cart. Sorry," she says, facing me with her billowy red hair framing her beautiful face. "I'm afraid I've let my helicopter mom out."

"It's okay; I just did the same thing. Scared the heck out of me," I say with my hand on my chest, still trying to gain control of my breathing.

"I'm Annette."

"Joanie. This is Morgan. And the guy who likes to perform the disappearing act is Dillon. It's all I need is to lose him on our first day here."

"Oh, you're the new family in town!" Annette says, her green eyes lighting up. "I hear you're a carpenter."

"Yeah, we just got here yesterday. I'm signing the boys up for school today."

"There's only one: Glenbrook Elementary," Annette says. "It's a good school."

I smile down at Dillon with ease at this statement. "Maybe you two will be in the same class!"

"There are only two kindergarten classes, so there's a good chance," Annette says, taking her son's hand. "It's nice to meet you, Joanie. I'm sure we'll be seeing you around."

We part ways, and I finish up, forcing the boys to keep a firm hand on the cart.

I drive below the speed limit on the way to the school so I can eye the town. "It's clean and green," I say with a little chuckle.

"That rhymes, that rhymes," the boys say in chorus.

We pass what appears to be the center of town, which holds a huddle of stores. Everything is cleanly painted with welcoming flowers and signs boasting the best knick-knacks or pastries. Old-fashioned wrought-iron lamps line the streets. Cobblestones cover the ground in what looks like the oldest part of town, giving an even more inviting feel than the usual black top I'm used to.

Quaint brick storefronts with colored awnings and carts of merchandise outside invite me to explore, but I ignore the pull and steer toward the school district office. "We should do a family outing soon and explore the town. What do you think?"

They shout in agreement. "Can we get ice cream when we go?" Morgan asks as we pass an ice cream shop.

"Absolutely," I say through a smile. We hardly did anything as a family back in North Dakota. Our schedule didn't allow for fun adventures besides the occasional park or movie theater trip.

Our stop at the school district is easy, and to my surprise, the boys behave. While this is a big step in solidifying ourselves in this town, it's the next stop I've been dreading the most, the one that will make me sign my name in blood.

The fresh smell and décor of the bank do nothing to ease my squirmy stomach. It's not like it's the bank's fault that Nick has sprung all this newness on me, but I hate it all the same.

"Are you okay?" Nick asks, taking in my sour expression that matches my mood.

"Fine. I just hate all the bank lingo. Makes me feel stupid," I mutter.

We wait on couches in the nicely decorated waiting room, each minute weighing me down more than the next. My anxious body is convinced that I'm waiting for a doctor's appointment where they'll perform some kind of procedure.

"Boys, please don't bang your army men on the table like that."

"Hey, stop," Nick says as a follow-up when they don't listen to my soft command.

"Hello, Nelson family. I'm Sasha. I'll be your loan officer. You two sure look like your dad," she says to the boys.

Dillon looks up at Nick for a second before responding. "I don't look like a man."

Sasha laughs and starts for her office. "Follow me." The tall, round woman has a pep to her step that irks me. What in the heck does she have to be so excited about? I dig my feet in again, despite my promise to go with the flow. Once my name is scrawled on a dozen or more papers, I'm fully committed. All those projects will be plopped squarely on my plate. In a few short days, the whole town will know what a joke I am when it comes to my so-called carpentry skills. Nick has been bragging about me, and from what I've seen, every one of his words has already made a trip around town.

After two minutes, Dillon throws himself on the ground, roaring in laughter at something Morgan did. Sasha flinches at the volume of their laughter. Judging by the photos in her office, she doesn't have kids to give her this experience.

"That office right across the hall is our entertainment room. You guys can go check it out if it's okay with your parents," Sasha suggests. The boys don't wait for our approval before dashing across the hall and jumping into the beanbag chairs.

After Sasha finally finishes the introduction about the closing of a house, she opens a folder that has no less than fifty pages for us to sign. I lose my breath upon seeing the stack. My eyes fix on the dreaded pen on the desk before me, wondering if I can run from this office like the boys did down the hotel halls.

"Shall we get started? I hope you've been practicing your signature," Sasha jokes. Nick laughs and looks at me. I lose my will to join him, even with a fake guffaw. "Yours is next," Sasha says, holding the pen out to me.

I conjure up the ability to take hold of the thick felt pen that I will definitely be stealing from this place. It's an odd thought I contemplate before obliging to what this woman thinks is an innocent request. Shouldn't Nick and I have discussed moving, oh, I don't know, *before* we sat in these cushy chairs with the paisley design?

The note of positivity I brushed on this morning flies away, leaving me only in contempt for being in this position.

"It's your turn, hon," Nick prods with a broad smile that reveals slightly crooked, white teeth.

"What? Oh. I do know my signature," I say, my voice full of nerves.

Nick and Sasha's chuckles do little to relieve my stress. Yup, I'm definitely going to sign. Right… now.

I lean forward in slow motion, praying for something to interrupt like a fire alarm or for Dillon to have another laughing fit. Something needs to save me right now before I go through with this.

But nothing does.

A glance at Nick reveals his widest smile yet. That broken-down house is his dream come true. He thinks he's bringing me back to happy memories in the country while reuniting me with my tinkering hobby.

"Signing my life away," I mutter, putting pen to paper. Nick and Sasha laugh again, not realizing that I'm speaking the truth.

The first signature is the hardest mentally. After that, I swear my pen gets scratchier with every scrawl of my name. An hour and two hand cramps later, Nick squeezes me to his side after signing his name for the last time.

Once back at our vehicles, Nick throws his hands in the air. "We did it!" he shrieks to the surrounding mountains. "We just bought our first house!"

He hoists Dillon up on his shoulder and runs around his truck, with Morgan following. I watch from the sidelines, taking in the happiness that my family is emitting.

It's a proud moment for my husband, and I feel nothing of his joy.

Chapter 9 Working Together

The day after the signing, I feel a mixture of regret and anxiety similar to a hangover, complete with a queasiness I can't shake.

The refrigerator Nick ordered is scheduled to arrive today. He has assured me it will meet my standards. "As if I'm picky," I mutter. The refrigerator doesn't have to be as good as a table saw in my book.

Now, there's a strange comparison.

I'm actually not particular about most things in life. Maybe this is why Nick has been bulldozing over my opinion when making decisions. Perhaps he's trying to save me from fretting about the details.

"Buying a house is *not* a detail," I say to remind myself of this enormous decision. I don't need to make a note on my calendar to remember to talk to Nick about his new behavior. My resentment towards him has been building like sand in an hourglass with every minute that goes by.

I look over the vast living room, which is my favorite so far. The balcony railings above and the exposed natural wood beams are nice touches. The rest of the room has exposed wooden walls, naked of baseboards, and missing and chipped rock pieces around the fireplace. The foyer is blocked off from the rest of the room with an unsightly half-wall that I am totally going to destroy with a sledgehammer.

Maybe I can release some of my anger by doing that right now…

A tapping noise in the room to my left snaps me from the fantasy of tackling the ugly half-wall. I chalk it up to the house settling… when the tapping happens again. A chipped white door stands between us, keeping me from the source of the noise. Hopefully, it's also keeping me safe from whatever is making the sound.

I hear the sound again, and my heart beats faster. The rest of my body freezes. I've never been one to have enough courage to see what's on the other side of the door, so to speak.

I tiptoe to the door and turn the lock, feeling a sense of security. It's probably just a cracked window making the blinds wobble about. Or maybe there's a weird pipe that's clicking. This is an old house, after all.

I peek at the boys playing outside for the tenth time. They got up early today, even on their spring break, and flew out of the house to play in the yard before chewing their last bite of breakfast.

Is it considered a yard with so many acres to it?

I figure now is a good time to inspect the living room more thoroughly, which desperately needs help. There are no lights, the windows aren't framed, and the carpet should have been ripped out ages ago. Then, there's the wall on the other side of the room that awkwardly stands between the living space and the kitchen. The previous owner had the same idea as me to tear this sucker down.

After an hour, I'm done dedicating a page in my notebook to this room. It won't be cheap to do all the remodeling, but I guess it's good that I can't tackle everything at once. I'll save us a ton of money doing the work myself. It feels funny that it is my job to fix this place.

It's a reminder that I need to have a better attitude. "No turning back," I whisper. Really, how can I fail when almost everything is in shambles anyway?

I quickly peek at the boys again before rushing to my room to find the box I'm looking for.

"Yes!" I yelp after scrambling through a couple of boxes. I look in the mirror and tie my hair back in the green and blue paisley bandana. I change into a pair of grubby jeans and an oversized shirt, a uniform I assume will be my usual from now on. I grab my pocket knife from a drawer in my jewelry box and cinch it to the waistband of my jeans, feeling the more positive effects of this fresh start. This monster-sized job is going to take daily dedication.

And I'm ready to get started.

The boys run into the house from outside, screaming that a truck is coming up our driveway. Their enthusiasm to tell me only jumps-starts my ready-to-work look.

"It's the refrigerator!" I yell back, joining them in the kitchen.

"Whoa, Mom, you look different," Morgan says.

"I sure do," I say with certainty. I look down at them, one tiny step closer to accepting my fate.

✳✳✳

A rainstorm this afternoon dampened their outdoor time. We've replaced our snowy, frigid weather with rainy yet warmer days. While the boys happily play upstairs, I investigate what's hiding under the kitchen linoleum. It's my first project, and with the refrigerator temporarily in the laundry room, there's no better place to start. I pull up a large chip, anticipating discovering what's underneath.

"You don't say." It's the best-case scenario to see hardwood floors. "Yep, there they are." The sliver of missing linoleum reveals a pine wood that probably has more years than me. I scrounge for gloves to pull up the old, crumbly floor.

Memories of doing this same thing at my brother's first house curve my lips into a smile. Owen is eight years older than me, and the fixer-upper that he moved into across the street from my parents' house taught me a lot about house remodeling.

I soaked up all the information about demolishing a house down to its studs before rebuilding it. I learned that I not only liked this craft but was also good at it.

After mere minutes, the rewards of my labor pay off. A spacious area around me reveals what I assume will be a glowing, polished floor one day. It's not the most fun thing to do in the world, but it's a good feeling to see the progress I've made all on my own.

My garbage can is nearly full of the old scraps when the boys bounce downstairs.

"We're bored," Morgan whines. He drags his feet under his dangling arms but stops when he sees me. "What are you doing, Mom?"

"Are you sticking your tongue out?" Dillon asks.

Darn. This habit has followed me all the way to Oregon. It's something I've always done; stick my tongue out when I'm working like this.

"Look what's under here! It's hardwood!" I say with enthusiasm, excited to share this with them. It sounds silly, but this one thing has bumped the house up a few notches in my book. I've always loved the clean look of natural wood. It makes me feel like we've brought the outdoors inside.

"It looks horrible," Dillon says, trying to dig under his cast.

"Does it itch, honey?" I ask before giving Dillon a look of sympathy. "Here, try this." I hand him an unsharpened pencil from the stationery box. "It looks bad now, but it'll be great after being sanded and stained. Let me show you a magic trick." I grab a rag from the mudroom, run it under water, and swipe it across the floor. "See?"

"That looks better," says Morgan with a nod of honesty.

The dust tickles my nose, and I tuck my mouth in my elbow to let out a monster sneeze. "I can't wait until this place is at least halfway put together so I can clean," I say triumphantly with my arms out wide. "Hungry? I'm starved!"

I wash the grime from my hands before making sandwiches while the boys pretend to pull up more of the dingy, off-white linoleum in the kitchen. I cut the sandwiches into cloud shapes and use the crust as raindrops to emulate the day. I finish off the dish with grated cucumber for grass and blueberries as flowers. I haven't done this for them in years, and I doubt they will remember.

"Oh my gosh! Are you actually pulling up the linoleum?" I say when I see what the boys are doing in the nook. I make a big deal with my praises since they made significant progress.

"Look at lunch!" Dillon yells.

"Neat," Morgan says coolly, sliding into the booth seat. "Didn't you use to do this for us when we were little?"

"Yes!" It gives me a sense of gratification that he remembers. It feels like a lifetime ago when I shared a stronger connection with my two sons. They have slipped away from me over the years. Once Dillon was about two years old, he and Morgan tucked themselves in their room and I fell like I haven't seen either of them since.

I join the boys at the table. "You know… I made this table."

"No way!" Dillon exclaims.

"You mean, you bought it at the store?" Morgan challenges.

"No, I mean, I made it with my own two hands."

Morgan inspects the table further but shows no sign of being impressed. Why would he? That would mean he would relinquish some of his standing in this family. "It looks good," Morgan says with a nod.

Within minutes, my sandwich is gone, and my milk is drained while the boys aren't even halfway through. "Mom ate like a piggy," Dillon says with a glance at my empty plate. I gasp, pretending to be hurt by this description. This is an old joke. I used to call the boys piggies in fun when they were younger and I'd tickle their toes.

"I know, and I'm still hungry. I could eat more!" I reach for Dillon's plate, snorting and grunting while pretending to steal his food. He guards it with his fingers spread out, giggling the whole time.

"What are we doing after lunch?" Morgan asks with seriousness while swinging his feet underneath him.

"We?" I ask, perplexed. I try not to get my hopes up about being accepted into their boy's only club, but my heart soars like a balloon. I rush ahead with an answer, not wanting Morgan to change his mind. "I want to look under that dingy carpet in the living room and see what's under there."

"I'm on it!" Morgan says, rushing to the other room.

"Um, sure, we can look now." I leave the dishes on the

table and follow the boys. I pull out the pocket knife my dad gave me when I was ten. I push the button, and the blade springs out with a clicking noise.

"Whoa!" Dillon cries with interest in the knife. The boys look at me with wide, amazed eyes, asking every possible question about the tool.

That's right, Mom is kind of a badass.

"My dad gave this to me when I was about your age," I say with a look at Morgan. "I first had to prove that I could handle it." It's the severe tone I bring with this statement that I hope will make my point.

I dig into a piece of carpet in the corner of the room, easily prying it up.

"It's an ugly green-speckled floor," Morgan sulks. I smile, thinking it's funny how they've adopted my desire for hardwood floors.

"That's just the padding. See, if you pull this up… yes!" I yelp. The boys jump a little before looking at each other with small smiles. "It's the same hardwood!" I hop up and give a wiggle of excitement. To my surprise, the boys join in with their own dance. Their investment in this discovery is minimal compared to mine, but I love how they copy me.

It was always a struggle to keep the carpet clean at the other house. Floors and paint are easy ways to spruce up a home without much effort.

"Can we pull all this up?" Morgan asks, his light brown eyes glimmering with intrigue.

"I can try with my good arm," Dillon says, holding his right arm in the air.

"Sure!" Shock and thrill fill me. I can't remember when we've spent this much time together without me telling them not to do something destructive. I fail to keep a laugh in.

Doing this type of work *is* destructive. "Do you think you have enough muscle for this job?" The boys flex their arms in a routine they've playfully done with Nick. "Those will do," I say with a hand on my hip. "I wish you guys had gloves. There are nails on the ground by the walls that are sharp."

"We have our snow gloves," Morgan says, his face filling with delight. "They are still in our bags from school. Come on, Dill Pickle!"

I stare after them, hardly believing how they want to spend time with me. They run back at record speed, ready to help. Dillon squeezes his good hand into a glove while Morgan slides his on like a pro. I position them on each side of me, slowly rolling the carpet with their help. "There's a lot of carpet in this big room. It'll get heavy soon," I say.

Instead of ditching me with a half-done job, the boys help me roll the carpet to the middle of the room.

"We might have to stop here with the couch in the way." I get behind one end of the couch and push with all my strength, but I am only able to move it an inch. Sofas aren't usually this heavy, but I personally made this one with a solid wood frame.

Dillon and Morgan come to my side and push the couch with all their might. Together, we build momentum and push it into the kitchen nook. I cut the carpet at the floor so we can start on the new roll since the old one weight more than the three of us combined.

"Look at you two go!" With the three of us working together, we have the nearly disintegrated carpet rolled up on the opposite side of the room in just under an hour. "I'll need Daddy to get this big hunk of junk out of here," I say with a kick to the roll.

"*Daddy*," the boys sing, drawing out the word in silly

voices to tease.

"Very funny. We can keep going and rip up the padding if you want."

The boys have a blast ripping the soft pads from the ground. As they throw pieces at each other, an atmosphere of peppiness surrounds us. While they work, I grab the mini shop vac stashed in the laundry room.

"Can I suck it up?" Morgan asks.

"I want to do it," Dillon pouts.

Who are these kids?

I turn the vacuum on low so we don't have to cover our ears. I let them take turns as I grab an empty box and toss in the larger scraps. It's quite a mess, but this is usually a side effect of progress made in any project.

"What are those ugly things?" Morgan asks, pointing to the nail strips. "It looks like the living room has teeth."

"Those are nasty little boogers," I say, and the boys laugh.

"I'll say," Dillon says, lifting his arm to reveal a small nail strip dangling from his cast.

"Oh, no!" I gently pull the strip from his cast, turn it towards me, and pretend it's alive and trying to attack me. The boys let out the desired belly laugh, giving me a high that I'm sure stand-up comedians get while on stage. "I need a pry bar to get them up." The boys give me a blank stare. "I can get one and show you," I say slowly. I walk from the room to search the back garage, surprised they follow me like little ducklings. "Sure, you can come."

"What are we going to do with all this junk?" Morgan asks after we run to the garage with our shoulders slouching from the rain. He uses the same blunt manner he's had since he started talking.

"Junk? This equipment is old, but it's actually in good shape. This will help me fix up the place." I show them around, pointing out every machine and describing its use.

They hang on my every word. What I first labeled as a ghost of my past is bringing the boys closer to me in this moment. They aren't quite as interested in the machines as in the pry bar, but they might switch to my side once I demonstrate everything.

When we're back in the living room, I show them how to lift the nail strips, answering their questions along the way. Before long, I'm in an easy groove, quickly making my way around the enormous room with their company. When I reach the window, I pause to admire the views radiating through this rainy day. A downpour in the distance spreads water over the hillside, making the greenery pop with a fresh dose of moisture.

I'm brought back to reality when Dillon tugs at my shirt. "Now what, Mom?"

"I think that's all we can do for now in this room. I better start something for dinner. And then I might continue with the linoleum." I make a fist and stretch my arm like a superhero. The boys copy me with a power yell.

I pull the slow cooker from a box and get started on an easy stew recipe scheduled for tonight. A noise behind me makes me turn to see what is going on. Once again, the boys are pulling up the linoleum!

"Wow, look at my helpers!" I praise. "Wait until Dad gets home and sees what we've done." I throw the ingredients for dinner in the pot, kick off an upbeat playlist on my portable speaker, and join them. A warmth surrounds me with our time together today, making it one of my best with them. I haven't had to scold them once!

"When will it look like that?" Dillon asks, pointing to the wood I wiped with the wet rag.

"It needs a little cleaning up first, huh? I'll need to vacuum up all the dust."

"I'll do it!" Morgan declares, jumping up to drag the vacuum cleaner in.

The three of us work diligently, with me soaking up this quality time as if I'll never see it again. Morgan and Dillon have morphed their palpable energy into eager helpers. Who knew that a few fun tools were all I needed to bring them to the party?

Boys and power tools; that's a hard one to figure out, Joanie.

The jab goes straight to my stomach, scolding me for not putting this together sooner.

"What's on your floor, Mommy?" Dillon asks.

He's only six but hasn't called me mommy in over two years. I take too long to answer, and they run to my room to inspect the floor.

"This one is already wood," Morgan says with irritation.

"This is the subfloor," I say with a smile, coming up behind them. "They only got the floor pulled up before moving out." The boys stare at me in confusion, so I explain. "This is what is under the hardwood floor. There must have been something wrong for them to get down this far. I'm not sure if we'll put carpet or hardwood in here."

"Are you going to do that?" Dillon asks in amazement.

"I might. I haven't thought that far ahead."

"Mom doesn't know how to do that," Morgan says in the snobby tone he picked up at his old school. Heck, for all I know, he's the one who has taught it to the other kids. It certainly won't hurt for him to be in a smaller school district where it'll be easier for the staff to monitor him. His popularity at the last school went straight to his head.

"I've installed all kinds of floors, including hardwood," I say, puffing myself up.

"Oh yeah, where?" Morgan tests.

"I was pretty young when your grandma and grandpa moved us into a large house that was a fixer-upper like this one," I answer, touching Morgan's nose with my finger. "We tore everything up and rebuilt it. It was a lot of fun. We slept all over that house as we moved through it and refurbished each room."

It feels like a lifetime ago when I was a kid. I often wonder if it feels like this to us adults over time as more memories and life stack up in between.

I look at my boys, hoping they are having a good childhood like I did. For the first time, I'm siding with Nick on moving here. It's an odd feeling to not want to be here but to also be grateful.

Because of the house, the boys have paid more attention to me than they have in years. Because we are here, they can play outside and have their own rooms. And because we are here, I might have reignited my old passion.

Chapter 10 The Coop

My eyes pop open in the middle of the night to a new creaking sound. "Nick. Did you hear that?" I whisper. Of course, he's sound asleep. A freight train could go through the middle of the room, and he wouldn't wake up.

The sound repeats, and I do what my definition of bravery is: I turn towards it. It's several shades darker here in Garden Valley without outside light pollution, but with the aid of the nightlights I've plugged in, I spy a small figure by my dresser.

"Morgan, is that you?" I breathe. He turns toward me and moves his hand by my dresser. Whatever he had in his hand clangs down before falling noisily to the floor.

"Never mind. Go back to sleep," Morgan blurts before darting from my room.

After a restless sleep, I say goodbye to Nick in the morning. My bedside lamp shows my pocket knife on the ground beside my dresser. I get ready for the day with the company of disappointment in my son. I can't believe he would take my knife after I told him how important it is to me.

Nick was impressed with the amount of work we got done. The boys chattered about the flooring project, stroking my ego as they used the technical words they heard me say.

It ended with several conclusions: the boys chose to

spend their time with me and had a good time. While we are far from finished with this project, we accomplished a lot in just one day. And it was fun.

A loud noise resembling someone kicking the house outside my bedroom window interrupts my thoughts. "What the heck was that?"

The large window to the left of the bed is covered by an old blanket, which will obviously be replaced by curtains one day. I lightly pull the blanket aside before my scaredy cat awakens and pulls me back. Whatever it is, it's safely outside.

It's not the first time I've had the heebie-jeebies from these house noises. I do my best to get over the adrenaline rush, starting dinner early so it won't interrupt me midway through a project. I cut vegetables and chicken for kabobs and leave the ingredients in our new stainless-steel refrigerator that offers plenty of space for a family of four.

The glow of the day starts to brighten the kitchen. A glance out the kitchen's bay window shows movement outside. I'm frozen still until I notice a dusty old country cat.

Gosh, Joanie, lighten up.

A flutter of love and excitement erupts in my chest at the site of the mangy-looking animal. We never had pets in Fargo. We simply weren't home enough, but let me be clear: I love animals!

Even if this is someone else's pet, I make a note to pick up food and maybe even make a snuggly place outside for the animal. My nurturing instincts overtake the red flag warnings to not add another thing to my plate.

Checking my notebook, I peruse my bulleted list for the day as I devour a piece of toast. Our new washer and dryer should arrive sometime this morning. I give Nick credit for surprising me in this department. We've had hand-me-down everything that has constantly needed tweaking, so I'm looking forward to this new adult step: brand-spanking new appliances!

I don't want to blow through Nick's promotion, living paycheck-to-paycheck like we did until we moved here. I'd like to think we've learned a thing or two about budgeting over the years, sticking to our payments, and not buying shiny new things. The long list of projects, coupled with my zero income, will be a test to show if we can live within our means.

A rag and cleaner are my companions to tackle my first chore of the day: wiping down the entire pantry before I stock it. I look forward to loading up on non-perishable items now that I won't have to shove them in a hallway closet. If I chip away with one step at a time like I'm doing now, I'll be crossing my last item off the list in no time.

"As if that will ever happen."

My words want to diminish my enthusiasm, but I won't allow it. I'm reminded that I won't have to be away at work all day and will have much more time to complete tasks. That'll take some getting used to.

"Challenge accepted!" I say out loud, remembering the stressful parts of my job instead of allowing myself to miss my patients.

I whip up pancakes for breakfast while the pantry dries with a fresh lemon smell. I add blueberries and strawberries to the plates and stir up frozen orange juice. The boys follow the aroma of food and stampede down the stairs the minute breakfast is ready. Morgan pushes his little brother down at the last step, continuing like nothing happened. Before I can correct the action, Dillon jumps up as if no harm has been done.

I gasp when they get closer to me. "What did you do to

your hair? Oh boys, not again." They run their hands through the jagged, uneven chunks that are missing.

"We were getting ready for school, but it didn't turn out very good," Morgan answers casually. He pauses, and his eyes grow large for two seconds when he spies the beautiful food on the plates. Though he doesn't express his appreciation, I know it's there.

"It looks like a haircut is in order before school. How did you sleep?"

"With our eyes closed," Dillon says. We all laugh at my dad's age-old joke.

"Pretty good," Morgan answers. "It was nice to sleep without hearing dingus here grind his teeth."

"It was nice to sleep without hearing you snore!" Dillon retorts.

"I think I, uh, was sleepwalking last night," Morgan says without making eye contact.

"Uh, huh," I say, keeping my eyes on him. "You know that knife is mine, right?" Dillon snaps his head to his brother, understanding our conversation. I quickly continue, not wanting the tension to scare Morgan away. "I have a lot of things like that. I plan to pass them down to my sons, but they need to prove they can handle them. Sneaking into my room at night to steal them is the opposite of this."

Morgan is all ears. He nods frantically in understanding. "I can do that!"

"Me too!" Dillon adds.

"Okay then. Let's dig in. I think it will be warm enough to play outside today."

"I'm going to figure out where the spiders are coming from," Dillon says casually.

"Spiders?" I ask.

"Yeah, I've seen a couple of spiders in my room. It's okay, I like them."

"I guess if there aren't tons of them, that's okay."

"How do they even get in there?" Dillon asks.

"Maybe they climb up the house," Morgan answers with a huge bite.

"To the second floor?" Dillon asks with huge eyes. I stay quiet as I bask in their conversation. This small interaction is more than we used to have back home.

A glance outside from the kitchen nook reveals rays of sunlight streaming through the maple trees in the backyard. I'll get to enjoy it every morning if I so choose. It's like my life has been black and white, and here I've been touched with color.

My eyes blink upon seeing the rotting curtains. "I've had enough of them!" I hop up, grasp hold of the curtains, and pull. They are so old they nearly disintegrate in my hands, easily pulling from the rod. "There!" I say when they are crumpled on the ground. I wave the dust in the air and open the screenless window. "Care to get that side?" I ask, pointing at the other half of the curtain debacle. The boys revel in this burst of spontaneity, hop up, and rip them from the window. "There. Now we can see outside!"

We scarf down our breakfast so fast that the plates practically spin by the time they dart outside.

"We don't care if it's cold," Morgan states as he runs out the door. I'm left with the dirty dishes, but at least it's an easy cleanup with the dishwasher.

My ears perk again with that darned rapping noise at the back of the house. I set my lips to a straight line and slam the door behind me. Today isn't the day to tackle my over-imaginative tendencies. I'm sure it's just the house warming up in the morning sun.

It's easy to see that the outdoors will take up several pages of my notebook that is tucked under my arm. As with any yard, I expect it will be a never-ending list of cutting and pruning.

"Can't wait," I mutter.

I keep an eye on the boys, willing my mind to remove the connection between them being outside to my incident with the mountain lion. It took me a while to return to the fields after that. I eventually did, and even after spending hundreds of hours outside, nothing like that ever happened again. That was when my dad gave me his knife, which I had clipped to my belt every single time I stepped foot outside the threshold of my childhood home.

I let myself into the back pen, which I'm guessing was once used for goats and chickens. The gray cat I saw earlier sits on the back porch, swooshing his puffy tail as he keeps his squinted eyes fixed on me. I focus on inspecting the outside, keeping myself from bonding with him.

I've been staring at the chicken coop area through the kitchen window for the last two days, wanting to explore it like a kid in a new treehouse. Beyond this area, a healthy stream trickles music to my ears. It flows between full-grown maple trees, sprouting new growth for the season. Being immersed in nature is a serene experience, and it's on my property!

A well-trodden path weaves as far as I can see through the trees, begging me to go on a walk. Lilac once again drifts to my nose, pulling me further into nature.

A black crow flies over the house before dipping down in my direction. It flaps its wings and throws its feet and body forward to slow down enough to land on the chicken coop.

It's a nice touch until he eerily looks at me with intentional yellow eyes, bobbing his head to look at me from every angle. He holds an eye contact better than I have in regular conversation.

"What are you lookin' at?" I challenge.

"Walton?" the bird chirps back. What in the world? I back away slowly, with the creeps spreading throughout my body.

"Hey, boys!" I yell, setting my notepad on a fence post, all while keeping my eyes on the bird who won't keep his head still. It keeps me in his vision, and I'm not about to stick around and see what he does next. They hesitate momentarily, not wanting me to interrupt their game, as usual. "Want to explore that path with me?"

"Not really," Morgan says before returning to their game. Dillon doesn't even glance my way.

"Fine, I'll go by myself."

I start on the path with my hand firmly grasped around my pocket knife, just in case. Apparently, I need daily pep talks before tackling this whole place. I visualize the air cleaning out my pent-up anxiety. I have a seemingly never-ending to-do list but a lifetime to complete the items. That's good news! This is my job now!

A twig cracks behind me, mixing with footsteps pounding against the earth. I spin around to see the boys following the path. I breathe a sigh of relief and slow to allow them to catch up. A few moments later, they come alongside, again choosing to be around me!

"Dad bought fifteen acres of land. Can you believe it?" I say as a conversation starter.

"How much is that?" Dillon asks.

I stop and spread my arms out wide, turning in a circle.

"This. Everything on this side of the white fence is ours. It's a sturdy one if you ask me," I say, jostling the white posts on the edge of our property. At least there's one thing I won't have to fix.

"Look, Mom!" Morgan screams, pointing ahead of us at two tiny bunnies. Their ears twitch, and they hop off, their legs flying behind them.

"Their tails look like cotton balls!" Dillon chuckles in excitement.

"I'm sure we have a lot of wildlife around here. I saw deer in our front yard yesterday."

"Cool," Morgan says with a little nod.

The path comes to a right angle that continues into what could be mistaken as a forest.

"Why do people need fences around their yards?" Dillon asks.

"So their animals don't get out, duh." Morgan snaps.

"But we don't have any animals, dummy." Dillon retorts, kicking at the dirt.

"It's more than just that," I say with a strong voice, narrowing my eyes at them. "People pay for their land and want to see what's theirs. The animal thing is true too," I wink at Dillon, understanding that much of his behavior is due to the irritation his bossy brother causes.

We walk up a slight hill until we reach the back of the house by the driveway. This area shows our entire fenced-in yard. It's a breathtaking view of the hundreds of acres beyond our space.

"Look at this place," I breathe. It's not only the green pulling me in. Pockets of spring colors decorate the town. Country houses are nicely groomed with their own areas of trees, bushes, and flowers customized to the owner's preferences.

I compare the perfect country homes with our own yard and house that somehow looks like it's tilting. I'm sure it's the unfinished status that's causing the house to even appear crooked.

"Yikes, ours needs some help, huh?" I say to the boys, who surprisingly haven't run off. "These earwigs aren't making me happy," I say with my foot kicking in the dirt.

"Can you work on the outside too, Mom?" Morgan asks. His little face expresses admiration, a look I've never seen from him.

"I've done a lot of yard work in my time. We used to live on a couple of acres growing up. Grandma and Grandpa didn't have a lazy bone in their bodies. We were always working on something." As I think of these memories, I wonder why such trepidation has overcome me in this move. It's not like I haven't lived on land before. I know the responsibility involved, but my parents were in charge of maintaining it, not me. This leveling-up is what being an adult is all about.

"Why would someone have a lazy bone in their body?" Dillon asks innocently.

I laugh in response as we walk back to my starting place by the coop. "It's just an expression, silly. It means they aren't afraid of hard work."

And neither am I.

"What's this little building? Is it a playhouse?"

"No, this is a chicken coop. It needs a little work, which I think will be my common saying around here," I say, inspecting a few rotted pieces of siding.

"Can we get chickens?" Morgan asks.

"Can we get chickens?" Dillon repeats.

"I hope not," I say before seeing their hopeful expressions fall. "Maybe after being here for a while. Growing up, we had chickens. And a milking cow and goat."

"Can we get goats?" Morgan begs, clasping his hands.

"What's a milking cow?" Dillon asks.

Morgan and I look at him first and then at each other before sharing a smile. "You know that milk comes from a cow," I say as a gentle reminder, knowing we've had this conversation.

"Milk comes from the store." Dillon corrects.

Now it's time for Morgan and me to chuckle. We look at each other, fully sharing the moment. "Don't you remember reading that book about milk coming from cows?" Morgan asks with more curiosity than a slant of rudeness.

"I thought they were kidding. That's gross!" Dillon scrunches his face and sticks his tongue out.

A rumbling sound and crunching tires alert us to the black SUV pulling into our gravel-filled driveway. A woman's voice mixes with chatter from kids that filters to the side yard. When she sees us, the woman throws her arm straight in the air with a wave.

"Hello! We're your neighbors!" she yells with spunkiness.

I wave back and start their way. "Come on, let's say hi. And be good!" I warn. We all know it's a hollow threat, as I've never given them a strong enough punishment to curtail their behavior.

"I will. I have my dog to take care of," Morgan says, bringing his hand out of his pocket to reveal a little beagle from one of their play sets. "You know, to prove that I can have your knife," he says to my blank stare.

I laugh and tousle his hair, which is horribly uneven. I'll never stop being amused by the workings of his mind.

"I have one, too!" Dillon says, holding his own dog.

"You two are so funny!"

We join the woman behind her SUV as she messes with something in the back. She pulls back with a basket wrapped in cellophane, revealing a warm round face with dimples in her full cheeks. It's hard to believe that she's shorter than me, but I quickly notice that she shares the same darker features as I do.

"Hi there! I'm Cinda. I hope you don't mind us stopping by like this. We wanted to drop off a welcome gift. We rarely get new neighbors, but we share a street, which means we're second families." She blurts this as if needing to rush off, only she stays put while holding the basket out to me.

Her high-pitched voice is enough to reciprocate a smile of welcome. Dark curls frame her face perfectly, and I love how she paired a green flowery vest with a long-sleeved shirt. Her jeans have a few smears of dirt, mimicking my own after our walk and inspection around the yard.

"How nice of you," I say, taking the basket from her and eyeing what's inside. My stomach rumbles at the sight of a loaf of bread that has my name on it. Since I've had these changes in my life, I've almost constantly had grumblings of hunger. "I'm Joanie, and that's Dillon and Morgan," I say with a point to my boys, who are already playing with her three.

"Aww, poor guy with a broken arm," she says, sticking her lip out. "Last year, each of my kids was stuck in a cast at some point."

"Yikes! And…" I press my finger against my lips, "he doesn't need any more attention for being bad." It's only half a joke.

"I know how that goes," Cinda says with her hands on

her wide hips. "What does your husband think of that shop? I remember asking Glen, the man who used to live here, to make me a table once. It turned out amazingly. I still haven't been able to find matching end tables. Maybe one day a decent furniture shop will open up in town."

"Yeah, or maybe I could make you something." It's a hollow response that has come out of nowhere, like when someone offers to watch your kids sometime or have tea with you. Cinda's eyes light up nonetheless.

"Really? Are you the handy person in the family?" she asks with excitement. I nod, and she practically jumps at me. "It's so cool when a woman has these skills. I always wanted to do stuff like that, but if I can't push a button, I don't even try."

I smile despite being on the spot. I can't help but be proud of these skills I used once upon a time. Still, Cinda never knew that I always made mistakes. "I used to build furniture but haven't in a long time," I say, shying away from the subject.

"I'm sure you're great. It's probably like riding a bike or something; you never forget. If you're interested in starting back up and want to make extra money, put my end tables on your list, will ya?"

"Sure. This loaf of bread looks amazing," I say, changing the subject. I'm not about to take on other people's home projects when I have a million of my own.

"Yup, everything in there is homemade. Oh, and here," she says, once again dipping into her car to pull out a mason jar filled with white liquid. We didn't have breakfast long ago, yet here I am, ready to eat again. The work I did on the floors yesterday must have kicked up my appetite. "I almost forgot the milk from Clarice. That's our cow," she says, eyeing the kids showing each other their GI Joes.

"I'm never drinking milk again!" Dillon shouts.

"He just discovered that milk comes from a cow. That's a mom-fail if you ask me," I say with a tight smile and a jiggle of the jar.

"All of us are in that boat, Mom. I'm sure you told him at some point. I swear I repeat myself dozens of times, and my kids barely remember my words of wisdom," she says, fanning herself dramatically.

"Three boys, huh?"

"I have a four-month-old baby girl at home, too. My mom lives with us and helps babysit. Otherwise, I'd be way outnumbered. Danny," she says with a more forceful voice, talking to her middle child, "was that the nicest thing you could have done? Next time, don't just grab the toy; ask if you can see it."

"It's not really a toy; it's an army guy," the boy responds. Cinda purses her lips, and her eyes grow large simultaneously. It's an expression that makes even me want to confess something. "It's a toy, I know," the boy quickly says with a quick nod.

"Our boys should play together sometime," Cinda says, switching from mom mode and facing me again. "We're just a few horses down that way," she says, not correcting herself.

I laugh at the description of how our houses are just down the street, but she only smiles at me. "That would be great."

"If you don't mind me saying, we look like sisters from another tribe."

"Oh yes, I thought the same thing," I reply.

"I'm not nearly as dark as my brothers." She pushes her sleeve up and strokes her skin with her fingertips. "I swear my siblings got all the Indian DNA."

"That's so funny; that's exactly what I say about my brothers."

"Oh, I almost forgot," she says, ducking back into her SUV to pull out another jar of creamy liquid. "It's a sourdough starter. It looks like glue, but this has been in Garden Valley for hundreds of years and is our heart and joy. Well, for those of us who cook and bake, it is. I included instructions on how to care for it. Everyone in town has a piece of this starter, and I figured you need some since you're a part of us now."

I take the jar with trepidation, having never made homemade bread. "Well, there's no going back now," I only halfway tease about being here. "Thank you."

"Did I mention that our husbands work together?" she asks with her hand on her chest. I shake my head, and she continues. "My husband, David, was on the committee when they hired Nick. I remember how much he raved about him when he came home that night."

"That's good," I nod, proud of my husband while feeling the sting of betrayal from that time. "Oh my gosh, don't look at their hair!" I say, covering Morgan's curls when they come up to us. He pulls away aggressively as if it's the worst thing I could have done to touch his head. "They were getting ready for school on Tuesday."

"Life is never dull when you have kids. If you're looking for a salon, there's one on Cotton Street. They're great with kids."

"I'll keep that in mind," I say, happy for the tip.

"We'll let you get back to your day. We're on our way to the store. We're out of veggies, even though our garden will overflow with them soon. I'm glad I have a new neighbor to share them with. Let me know what I can bring to your dinner party."

"Dinner party?" I ask in confusion.

"Yeah, David said Nick invited everyone at work to show off your house, so let me know what I can bring. Boys, time to go." I stare after her in stunned silence by the dinner comment.

"Wow, obeying after asking just once," I say quietly, unable to keep from being impressed.

"Dessert is on the line," Cinda says with confidence.

"Now that's a good one."

"Looks like you have more company," Cinda says, pointing at an approaching truck.

"My new washer and dryer!" I shout, shelving the dinner party worries. "Sorry. I've never had brand new ones before."

"Don't apologize to me. With as much time as we spend on laundry, having two working machines is a luxury."

"Yeah, if Morgan stops wiping his hands on his socks, I'd be in better shape."

"It's the perfect napkin. It's always there," Morgan says in defense.

Cinda giggles before hopping into her rig. Rig? Am I getting into the country scene or what? I did just get welcomed into the valley with a sourdough starter and everything. Does that mean I'm part of the club yet?

"Nice to meet you and your boys!" I say with a wave.

Cinda pulls away just in time for the truck to take her spot. I instruct the men where to set up my new beautiful gray machines that have a pile of clothes waiting for them. They hook them up, show me the fun buttons, and are off within an hour.

I've never been so excited to stuff dirty clothes into a

machine. I push one of the buttons with the boys standing next to me. "Ooh," we all say to the fun, blingy noise that rushes through the room.

"I'm hungry," Dillon says forcefully.

I take a mothering tip from my new neighbor and speak up. "Dillon, is there a nicer way you can ask me to feed you?"

The boys glance at each other before Dillon looks down and mumbles his following sentence. "Can we eat?"

It's a small step up for him, so I give him points for trying.

"That's still rude, Dill," Morgan chastises. "Mother, can we please have lunch?" Morgan says with an English accent.

I clutch my belly and laugh. "Let's see what Cinda brought us!" I say before pushing the power button on the dark gray machine. It chimes another jingle for us to enjoy. "Gotta love that. Daddy did good."

We dig into the gift basket on the kitchen counter to find cookies, muffins, a loaf of sourdough bread, and… "Oh my gosh, Cinda made us split pea soup! It's my favorite," I say in amazement, holding up the transparent container with the green liquid. A note is taped to it with 'Welcome to the neighborhood!' in beautiful script. Hearts and smiley faces surround the words, filling me with as much warmth as I'm sure the soup will.

"It's green," Dillon says with a scrunched-up face. "What kind of soup is split pea, anyway?"

"It's the kind that matches your cast. Let's try some!" I heat up the soup, toast the sourdough bread before slathering a giant heap of butter, and read the instructions about caring for the sourdough starter. "Sounds like fun!"

The boys hesitantly take sips from their spoons before their eyes light up. "This is good!" Morgan says, shoving the whole spoon in his mouth and looking to his brother to copy him.

"Let's try the milk," I say, filling three glasses with the thick white stuff. The boys have never been shy about trying new foods, which has always been on their list of good traits.

"This tastes like ice cream." Dillon sags down in his chair in a moment of indulgence.

"You know, there's plenty of room for a playground out back," I say with the soup satisfying my ravenous stomach. "We can either buy one, or I could try to build you one."

The boys look at me with the same confused expression they gave me with the floor project. "You can do that?" Dillon asks in amazement.

"There's only one way to find out."

Chapter 11 A Haircut and Chicks

I spend an absurd amount of time getting the boys to wash up to go to town the following day. Why is it so hard for someone to step under a shower? "Just do it so we can go!" I scold, having reached my limit. I stomp downstairs, figuring that the boys showering together in their swimsuits is as good as it will get.

I rush to my room with a mixture of irritation and guilt. Even though the boys hardly notice, I hate yelling at them. As usual, I burn off my anger by absently hanging clothes in my nearly bare walk-in closet before picking my bunny Annabelle up and sinking into my bed.

Why can't the boys just take a shower? I text Nick, wondering why I scheduled their hair appointment first thing this morning.

I'll take a shower with you. Nick

At least I don't need to make sure you clean yourself. Joanie

What if I'm a dirty boy? Nick

Geesh, it seems like someone needs attention.

That's nothing that water can cleanse, honey. Wish me luck at the salon. Joanie

School starts for the boys on Tuesday, and I realize I will have all day to myself for the first time in nearly a decade. I glance at the house with worry, knowing it alone will be my source of company. I recall the strange noises that have sent chills down my spine, still not knowing the source. I'll be alone with whatever is causing that noise all day.

But that's not all that's bothering me; something is missing, and I can't quite put my finger on it. I don't think it's my fear of loneliness or even the absence of floors in my bedroom.

"Gosh, it's right on the tip of my tongue," I mumble, ambling around my room. "Oh well." I shrug, figuring that having a million tasks will do this to someone. I brush my blah hair out that is lacking style. I haven't gotten my long, straggly hair done in ages. Maybe I'll make an appointment with the stylist if all goes well.

I give up the hope of having a good hair day and meet the boys at the bottom of the unfinished stairs. They run and hide when they see me, something they think is fun. Calling out to them is pointless. I rein in my frustration to gain control of the situation.

I find Morgan in one of the lower kitchen cabinets, grinning from ear to ear. After he crawls out, I rest my hands on his shoulders and bend to look into his eyes. "We have things to do today," I say firmly yet respectfully. "I need you to get one toy to bring with you. You have thirty seconds to return here, or I won't let you bring anything. Same goes for you," I say, pointing at Dillon when he emerges from his hiding spot.

It works!

The boys rush off with me counting down from thirty. I run to my own room to get Annabelle. Their clomping gets louder as I approach number ten, and soon, we are in an all-out race to the laundry room. I win, holding my bunny up in victory.

"Not fair! Your room is downstairs," Dillon whines.

"It's not Mom's fault you're slow," Morgan teases. "I have my beagle," Morgan says, holding his toy like a trophy.

The creepy noise in the back of the house halts their bickering. The three of us crane our necks in the direction of the sound.

"What was that?" Morgan asks.

"You heard it too?" I ask with surprise.

"Of course, we heard it," Dillon answers. "What was it?"

"I don't know! I've heard it a couple of times."

"Let's go see," Morgan shouts before both boys run through the house.

"Wait, no!" But it's no use. Before I can stop them, the boys storm through the kitchen to the living room as if we've lived here for years instead of days. Without hesitation they fling the door to the mysterious room.

It's only my second time in this room. The side door that leads outside is wide open, lending a peek of the tall weeds in our back yard. Only the long windows and dingy, off-white, stained carpet await. There's no furniture in this room or anything else that a mouse or rat could hide in. Other than needing a thorough scrubbing like the rest of the house, I see no evidence of funny business.

"Why is this door open again? I closed it from the outside last night!" I stomp through the breezy room, slam the door, and turn to see two sets of surprised eyes. "I've been hearing that noise since we moved in. It's driving me nuts!"

"I'll say," Morgan says with a glance at his brother. "It's probably just the open door."

"It shuts tight though," I say, pulling on the knob and

then inspecting it again. I run my fingers across the scuff marks on the frame, but the markings aren't ones I can identify. "I should probably get a new lock."

"Maybe it's the cat!" Dillon yells, pointing out the window. Morgan and I look; sure enough, it's the gray cat from yesterday.

"Can we keep him?" Morgan asks in his high voice. It's a sight I rarely see: the boys giving me pleading, sad eyes to win me over.

"I don't need something else to take care of right now," I sigh, hearing the weakness behind my voice. It's not my first time wanting a pet in recent years. Growing up, I spent most of my time with my many four-legged friends. I would run with the goats and sheep, ride our neighbor's horses, and sometimes sleep with the pigs. Heck, I was Dillon's age when I got a job mucking stalls.

"We aren't going to solve this mystery right now. Let's go. We're about to be late."

"The house has a mind of its own," Morgan says spookily, his fingers dancing in the air.

"Not funny!" I tease, shooing them to the kitchen. It's not the first time I've thought of there being a ghost in the house.

Our only stop today is the salon on Cotton Street. I'm dreading this visit. Usually, haircuts are a nightmare for the boys. Still, as we get closer to our appointment time, it's easy to settle into the serenity of the slower cadence of the town.

Every house we pass has the same theme: beautiful yards with shrubs, flowers, and animals. If I didn't know better, I would think we are the only family without at least one farm animal.

We pull up to the red brick building with flowers in

bright blue pots out front. A glance down the street has my exploratory side going crazy. I text Nick before we get out of the car.

Can we explore the town this weekend? Joanie

Sure! Anything you want! Nick

I exit the van amongst a crowd of people gathered outside the salon. The murmur circulating is about an item on the next ballot to put in a housing development across the street from where we are downtown.

"Maybe we could have moved there," I mumble when we walk by, thinking how nice it would have been to have a turnkey house. Unfortunately, a woman with keen ears overhears me and points her serious stare my way.

"What did you say? Do you mean to tell me you're in favor of them building here?" she snaps. The rest of the crowd turns my way with equally stern eyes.

And there's Alice, the lady who wanted a tour of the house on our first day here, front and center.

"Oh, I just mean that we moved into a house that needs…"

"So, you're new in town?" a man asks in accusation. Murmurs erupt again about me not having the same stakes as they do since I'm an outsider.

"You don't care what they do with our land. You're probably one of those city folk who thinks we need to build on every acre we have," another person shouts. Alice smirks, not offering one word of defense for me.

"Whoa, I didn't say any of that," I say with my hands up. "We're just here for an appointment." I quickly shuttle the boys into the salon before things escalate. People continue shouting negative remarks that couldn't be farther from the truth.

"Tough crowd out there, isn't it?" a woman comments once we enter the salon.

"Gosh, all I meant is that my husband could have picked a less broken-down house. You guys okay?" I ask the boys, who accept my arms as comfort. They each nod with shocked expressions before settling into the waiting area.

"They've been out there heckling people all week," the tall woman continues. "I merely *looked at* the open field this morning on my way in, and they started harassing me, and I've lived here my whole life! My husband owns a building company and said no one plans to develop the area they're talking about."

"Good luck telling them that," I say, still peering at the group from the safety of the salon.

Most of our town isn't like those guys. There's a handful of stinkers, just like anywhere else."

"I should have told them I took care of my Garden Valley sourdough starter this morning," I joke.

The beautiful woman who greeted us rests a hand on her flat stomach and leans back for a laugh. "Good one," she continues, pushing her thick red hair from her face to dab at a tear. Her beauty would be intimidating if it weren't for this warm welcome. "I'm Monica. I'm guessing you're here to see Bailey?" I nod and take a few steps into the salon, quickly feeling comforted by my surroundings.

I'm impressed by the cozily decorated salon in blues, grays, and yellows. Low lighting and cushy-looking couches invite me to sit back and relax for a while—as if that will be possible while the boys terrorize the place!

"Hello! You must be the Nelsons. I'm Bailey. I'll be doing your hair today. This is Monica, our makeup artist slash manager slash wedding planner." The woman's curly blonde hair is as bouncy as her voice. Bangs round out her look, giving her a soft, inviting feel. "Let me guess who is who," she says, turning to the boys with her finger up to her lips. "Morgan," she says, pointing to my oldest, "and… rambunctious." The boys look at each other and laugh.

"No, I'm Dillon."

"Dill pickle. Got it. I'll be coloring your hair green and making it spikey on the ends, right?"

"I don't want my hair green," Dillon responds with a worried glance at me.

"You don't?" Bailey teases. "But pickles are green. Look, even your arm is turning green. I'm just teasing," Bailey says, tousling Dillon's hair. The boys laugh at the interaction as I look on with envy. "What's the plan, Mom?" she asks.

I instruct Bailey that I want a simple shortcut for both. She starts with Morgan while Dillon spins in the next empty chair. I back away slowly as they chat with Bailey.

"Take a load off," Monica instructs, holding her hand to the cushy floral chairs in the lobby area.

"Shh, they're being good. Don't distract them," I whisper in honest surprise.

Monica laughs. She's entirely done up as far as makeup goes and towers over me with long limbs. It goes along with the poised way she holds herself in white denim skinny pants and a trendy jean jacket. "So, you guys are new in town?"

"Yup, we haven't even been here a week," I say. I clutch my purse to my stomach, waiting for the boys' first slip-up. They laugh again and seem to hang on to every word Bailey says. "She's good with kids."

"She sure is," Monica answers easily. "She has a little one of her own."

"It's a relief. Salons and dentists aren't our best places to visit." I shake my head slowly. "I'm surprised they didn't get banned from school in Fargo. But things have been different since we've gotten here. The boys have been hanging out with me around the house!" I confide.

"Seems like a good move. Sometimes, we need something like that to shake things up. Have you found a place?"

I nod while keeping my eyes on Dillon as he scratches at his cast. "Dillon, stop itching!" Morgan instructs in his ultra-bossy tone.

"Dude, I'm sure there's a nicer way to say that," Bailey says with her eyebrows up. I know nothing about this young woman, but she has the mom's voice down pat. A glance around her station shows pictures of her and a little boy.

Morgan responds with a sheepish expression while looking down. What do you know? He *can be* shamed for being bossy.

"My husband bought an old house on a hill that just went up for sale. It's..." I think for a second as I point across the salon, "over that way."

"Tranquility Hill? That's not too far from where I live. Let me know if you ever need a cup of sugar."

"Dillon, stop messing around!" Morgan shouts, this time gaining the attention of everyone in the salon. Only one other client is getting her nails done, but still, his tone brings fire to my cheeks.

I stand to correct him when Bailey jumps in yet again. "He's fine, I promise," she assures.

Dillon responds by standing on the salon chair, no doubt testing Bailey's bounds for how far she'll vouch for him.

"Dillon, get down!" I whisper-yell, jumping out of my seat. I take Dillon by the arm and help him down, with

Morgan looking on with a smug grin.

"It's not funny!" Dillon says to his brother.

"I'm not laughing," Morgan says with a snarky tone.

I hold Dillon back as he attempts to rush at his brother. He grabs a comb from the station beside Bailey's and throws it at Morgan. He knocks several things to the floor, sending a loud clang across the salon. It's a disappointing display of sibling rivalry. Disappointing because there's an audience to watch and because they've been getting along so well lately.

"I have juice boxes for whoever is good after their appointment," Bailey entices, holding the boxes in the air. Dillon instantly stops wiggling and sits in the empty chair. Morgan stops cold, not saying a word for once.

"That worked," I say, wide-eyed to Bailey.

"Food and drink normally do. Relax, I've got this, Mom," she says with a wink.

I clutch my purse as I make a walk of shame back to my seat, eyeing the nail technician with Leslie scrawled on a nameplate in cursive. My shame is of my own doing, however. The nail tech and her client aren't even looking our way anymore. Leslie laughs and continues on with what sounds like a story about her date.

Another woman enters the salon and makes herself comfortable, leaning against the tall reception desk. Monica compliments her outfit before turning my way.

"Joanie, this is my sister, Amy," Monica introduces, flashing a perfectly straight white smile my way. "Joanie and her family are new in town,"

Monica should be upset that Dillon made a mess. She should be scolding me for being unable to control my sons, yet here she is, still including me.

"Welcome to town," Amy responds with a sweet smile.

Judgment is void from both of their faces, throwing me off guard. "That crowd is still out front, huh?"

"They're making the rounds. I'm sure they'll shuffle off to Gordon's shop tomorrow."

"You should sick office McDonald on them," Amy suggests.

"Nah, they're harmless, even though they are nondiscriminatory. Every person who comes in here gets harassed."

"Hey, there's a market this Saturday over by the lake," Amy says to me. "It's a good way to meet some of the locals. Will you be there, sis?" she asks Monica.

I look between the two women, not seeing an ounce of resemblance to each other. Monica is tall and thin, while Amy is shorter and resembles me with more of a curvy figure.

"No way. I've had my fill of those things," Monica responds.

"I love them. All those crafts and goodies to sample get me there every time. Jason and I are looking for a new coffee table, but I'm probably getting my hopes up. What do you think of the town so far?" Amy asks.

"It's nice. I haven't gotten a tour yet, but I like it," I say with a little nod and a tight smile. There's so much bothering me about this move that it's hard to keep it all in. "Except, I have no idea what to do with our land. We don't even have a lawn mower. Our place back home was small. Like small, small." My hands form a square, making the ladies laugh. "I have so much to do," I say, slouching into my chair. "When I think of all the projects I need to get done… it makes me want to sit in this cozy chair forever."

Their laughter helps me forget some of my seriousness. "One thing at a time, right?" Amy encourages.

"I always have to wait until Brandon is off on the weekends before we get anything done around the yard," says Monica.

"We?" Amy says with a mocking tone.

"Yeah, fine, it's mostly Brandon doing the work. I'm there for moral support and to watch him work with his shirt off. I can't do ninety-nine percent of what he can. It'll all get done," she says to me. "Even if you have to wait for your husband on the weekends."

I shake my head and purse my lips, with every fiber of my being pushing against my following sentence. "It's mostly on me, I'm afraid." Am I, though? Don't I love to fix things? "I've got the handy work down. It's the decorating that freaks me out. Right now, I'm in the process of stripping the house down to bare bones, which I'm actually looking forward to. But once I piece it back together, I'll never be able to do anything like this," I say with my hands out to indicate the beautifully decorated waiting area.

Monica's eyes light up as if someone handed her a dozen roses. "You call me when it gets to that point, and I'll be there in a heartbeat. Seriously, this is my jam!"

"Mine too!" Leslie yells from across the salon before joining us to ring up her client. She's a petite woman with the most gorgeous straight brown hair I've seen. "Don't steal all the fun from me, Mo. I'm Leslie," she says with a little wave.

"Nice to meet you." My chest swells with the sense of belonging to their club. We've only just met, and these nice women are offering to help with my projects!

"It sounds like fun, bringing a house back to life," Amy says, sitting with me. "Maybe you can make the table I'm after," she laughs. "With you knowing how to do all those home renovations yourself, that would be gratifying."

I shy away from the compliment, once again feeling out of my league. "It's just slightly stressful," I say, holding my thumb and index finger an inch apart with a glance at the boys.

"I don't even know how to swing a hammer." Monica looks at me with sudden confusion. "Is that the right way to say it?"

Leslie stands beside me after showing her client out and laughs as I nod. It's a pep talk I desperately need, with these women making me feel like I've known them for years. Nick has been giving me these, but it means something different when it comes from an outsider.

"I've got my work cut out for me. We had a nice walk around the property, the boys and I. I noticed a bunch of earwigs," I say, remembering the bugs with a little shiver. "I don't think I've seen an earwig since I was a kid."

"Chickens are good for that," Monica replies. "They love earwigs."

"Chickens!" the boys shout in unison.

I look at Monica with wide eyes and lips in a straight line. "I made a rule for myself to not take on any animals until I've at least detailed out all of the projects." I stop and sigh yet again. "That might take two years with the state the house and property are in."

"Chickens are pretty easy to take care of," Monica says.

"Chickens!" the boys yell again.

Amy claims it's time for her to pick her kids up from swim lessons and says goodbye to us all. Monica flits around their display of products to add flower decorations that jibe with the spring season.

"Chickens just want to peck and scratch. Throw out some seeds and give them water, and they're happy," she says, returning to our conversation.

I keep my voice low so the boys don't hear me. "I remember that from growing up with our farm animals. We have a coop and everything. A barn and stables, too. The people before us must have had the whole shebang."

"Yup, Glen and his wife were full-on farmers. Looks like you're set," Monica whispers back. "Bailey's pretty fast, so I'm sure she'll get to you soon," Monica says.

"Oh, I'm not getting my hair done today," I say, running my hand through the scraggly strands that desperately need moisturizing therapy. "She'd probably find a whole bush buried in this mess."

"I have time if you're interested," Bailey says from her station. I look at the boys and back to Amy and Monica. "The boys can play in the kid area. I've been wondering if the games we got are good enough. They can be my testers," Monica says as if reading my mind. These women, who don't even know me and have already witnessed my lack of parenting skills, my biggest flaw, welcome me as one of their own.

"Go for it!" Amy encourages.

"I want my hair to look hers," I say with a point at Leslie. The women laugh with Bailey saying it's no problem. A little pampering might just be what has been missing.

Chapter 12 New Additions

Call me crazy for driving to The Grange after our salon treatments to take a look at chicks! The boys and I go completely ga-ga over their cuteness. It doesn't take much persuasion to cave to their peeping, which is now our background music as we drive home.

"Can we put them in their house? The lady at the store said to throw in hay and the heat lamp, and they'll be fine," Morgan says, already planning ahead.

"The coop needs a little work," I say, something I've repeated like a record since we've arrived. I find it humorous that the chick's house and mine have this in common. "Maybe you two can help me spruce the coop up?"

"Alright!" Dillon says, running toward the coop the second I stop the van. Morgan trots after him, shouting warnings to be careful of his arm. I hadn't even asked Nick about the chicks, but he always goes with the flow. Heck, lately, he's been creating the direction we flow. Considering he barely asked if we could move or buy this house, I think buying chickens on my own will be fine.

Zing!

Dillon fills the coop with handfuls of hay while Morgan sets up their food. I am surprised to find an electrical outlet on the side of the coop, and wonder if the barn down the hill also has power. This farm used to be the real deal. I inspect the small building again, noting the boards that need replacing.

I run inside to grab the new tool belt Nick got me, threading it around my waist it on as I rush back. To my surprise, I'm on one of the last holes in the belt, meaning this will cinch around me quite flatteringly. I check our dinner in the slow cooker, make three PB&J sandwiches, and rush back outside, feeling like I'm late for a play date with my boys!

With a sandwich in one hand, I go through a scrap wood pile in the back garage. A few pieces will work perfectly for the boards that need replacing.

Within minutes, I'm on the ladder to pry the first board free from the roof, ignoring the voice in my head telling me I'm going to mess up. "It's a simple fix, not a huge project," I grumble back, putting my negativity in its place.

The reignition of this ambition sends flutters to my stomach. I haven't wanted to get back to my carpentry side, yet here I am, on a ladder, rebuilding a chicken coop as if it's no big deal.

Gosh, Joanie, it's not like you're creating a piece of furniture here. It's just replacing a couple of boards!

"What are you doing?" Morgan asks in a near panic.

The boys run my way with the first crack of wood coming loose. I started without them, figuring they would want to keep playing their game.

"I'm sprucing up the coop for the chicks. A few of these boards looked cracked and need to be..."

"You're ruining it!" Dillon shouts from the ground.

"I'm not, you'll see," I chuckle. "All I have to do is take a few boards off and nail in new ones. They'll be a different color, but the whole thing needs to be painted anyway. Those boards down there will work fine, but I'll have to cut them to size." Their confused faces stare back when it hits me: they have no idea how to do any of this stuff. "Hey, um, would either of you like to try this?" Morgan steps forward in a second, not showing a smidgen of hesitation.

"I do," he says confidentially.

I invite him to stand with me on the ladder, only a couple of feet off the ground. "If you turn the hammer around, you can pull up the nail with the claw. Like this." I start one for him and hand him the tool. He struggles initially but realizes he needs to leverage the head against the roof for more strength. "That's good!"

"I did it!" Morgan exclaims, holding the piece of wood in one hand and the nail in the other. Dillon cheers for him from the ground, turning in circles like a happy dog. The moment settles in well with me, with the boys sharing this basic woodworking task.

"You sure did," says a male voice. We turn to the source in surprise. In our excitement, we didn't hear or see that we had a visitor. The man stands tall and is as thin as one of the fence posts. "I'm sorry to barge onto your property like this. I'm Fred, your neighbor across the way. I'm looking for my goat, Glenda. She likes to wander and visit the neighbors."

I shake my head. "I'm sorry. We haven't seen her." I feel slightly silly on this ladder with my toolbelt paired with a head of perfectly styled hair. Bailey gave me the works with a new layered cut before blow drying and straightening every strand. Monica even put a layer of makeup on my face, making me shine like a star.

"If you see her, let me know, please. I'm a horse or two over that way." I smile broadly at hearing the description again, thinking Fred will correct himself, but he doesn't. "I'll leave my number on your doorstep. That's a fine-looking coop you have there," he says to Morgan.

"Mom is showing me how to fix it up. We got chicks today and everything!" Morgan responds with a cheery voice.

"Are you getting this ready for your husband?" Fred asks.

"Nope, we're doing it ourselves," I reply, keeping my smile in place. This isn't the first time I've been asked a question like this. People see a hammer in a woman's hand and assume she's getting it for a man. It's nothing against his assessment. The last time I checked, only fourteen percent of women do this craft. Still, the feeling of pride that the boys want to spend time with me overshadows any stereotype.

Fred stays put with his hands on his hips and a confused expression. He looks from the coop to the boys and to my toolbelt but not at my face.

It must be the hair.

Surely, with this being a farm town, at least a few women are proficient in carpentry.

"Chicks are a good start to a farm," Fred says, snapping out of his funk, now finally flashing a smile. "Well, good luck with that coop. Let me know if you need any help."

I nod politely. "Thanks, but we've got it handled. The boys are great students." The fact that people didn't believe in me used to fuel my ambition to keep going with this hobby. It wasn't even a sexist thing. It was about proving that I could do it on my own.

"I'm in need of an upgrade to my coop as well if you all are interested."

"Sure!" Morgan shouts while I notice Dillon's shyness. He has stayed on the ground while Morgan and I have been on the ladder. As for me, yet another opportunity has come up to either help fix someone else's house or make a piece of furniture.

"We'll see, huh?" I respond with a tip of my chin.

It was an odd encounter but one that has me wondering if the people in this town have a fixer-upper business to help with this sort of thing. Cinda and Amy are looking for furniture, Monica has untended projects at her home, and this guy needs help with his coop. Sometimes these projects get shrugged by the wayside. I shake my head against it, figuring everyone in town has handled it on their own before I got here.

I return my focus to the coop, pointing out the other boards that need to be pulled up. I ask Dillon if he'd like to join in.

"I don't want to do any of that stuff," he answers quietly.

"Why not, sweetie?" I ask.

"I'll hurt myself," he says softly, holding his cast in the air. He's barely complained about being bound by the cast. When I think of his comment, I realize he has been slightly tamer after getting it. Maybe getting hurt has actually scared him into calming down.

"You won't get hurt if I'm here to help you." I climb back on the ladder and lay a board in place. Dillon climbs to the ladder's lowest rung, allowing him a better view. I show them how to pry up the nails as I did before. "See? Easy-peasy."

"Maybe for you." Morgan's sass clashes with his wide smile. It's an interaction that mends the heart they've left sore for years.

"This piece of wood is actually the right size," I say, grabbing one from the ground. "We can nail it in. You can watch me do a few and see if you want to jump in." I finish nailing in the first board and the second before Morgan looks more comfortable trying it. I show him how to hold the nail with a set of pliers so he doesn't hit himself when pounding it in. "Some people call it cheating; I think it's common sense." He gives it a try and, sure enough, hits it on his first try. "See, you did it! Go ahead and hit it a few more times until it's flush with the board. Make it flat like this." I run my fingertips over the nails to emphasize their smoothness with the boards.

Dillon laughs freely from his position. "Morgan, you're sticking your tongue out like mom does." Morgan and I make eye contact in an instant.

"I guess that means you're good," I reply with a shoulder shrug. He agrees with a nod and his bottom lip sticking out.

"My beagle is helping me," he says, holding the dog up again to give himself another point of responsibility.

"That's good. These two last spots need to have the boards cut. Want to help me with the table saw?" Once again, frozen, blank stares return. "Come on, I'll show you. We'll measure and use the old boards to mark where to cut these new ones."

They follow me to the shop when we're done measuring, a location increasing in familiarity. I lay the boards on the table saw with envious eyes watching my every move.

I've got to admit, it feels good.

"These are safety glasses," I say, handing two old pairs to the boys with a commanding voice. "You absolutely must wear these when operating any of this machinery. A piece of wood can fling out at you; for some reason, it always goes straight for the eyes."

The boys quickly fix the glasses on their faces, astonishingly paying attention to my words.

"This is a table saw," I say with my hand on the

equipment. "The blades can oscillate, or spin, at a speed of four thousand rpm, or roughly one hundred miles per hour. It won't stop if a finger or limb gets close to it. Understand?" I say, mimicking the same voice as my instructor had. The boys nod wide-eyed when I hold my hand with my index finger folded as if I've lost half of it. "Now, when I'm using this, you need to stand behind this line." I draw a line in the dust on the ground with my foot. The boys shuffle behind it like they're about to be a part of something spectacular.

You better deliver, Joanie.

I flip the switch and bring the saw to life. I keep my hand out to remind the boys to stay put as I inspect the machine. The machine starts and turns the saw at an impressive speed. You never know how an old machine owned by someone else will work. It easily cuts through the two pieces of wood I marked, sending familiar vibrations through my arms. I bask in the feel of the wood being ripped by the machine. It's powerful, yet I'm the one in control.

"I'm sure the blade needs a good sharpening, but it's a nice clean cut. See?"

The boys look at each other before timidly touching the wood. "That was awesome!" Morgan shouts.

"The wood is warm!" Dillon yells in amazement.

"Yup, she did a pretty good job, didn't she?" I say with a smile, giving the machine a small pat. It felt more than good to be doing something crafty again. I take a moment to savor the feeling. "Just to be clear, you are *not* to use anything here on your own," I caution with a stern look before softening. "Over time, I'll teach you how to use everything."

I will?

"Come on, let's see if these fit." I use the sudden burst of energy to run to the coop. The boys follow, and we soon make it a fun race, with Morgan smacking the coop with his hand in victory.

After Morgan and I nail in a couple more pieces, Dillon steps forward. "Want to try your hand with the last board?" I ask.

"It's literally your one hand," Morgan says with a laugh.

"Now, now, we don't want to discourage him. You really only need one hand to swing the hammer. I can help," I say, stepping aside to make room for Dillon on the ladder.

Morgan jumps on the roof of the coop, lurching my stomach into my throat. "Don't worry, I won't fall."

The naming of the action propels him to do just that: fall. Luckily, after only a second or two on the ground, Morgan pops up and looks down at his body, brushing the dirt and mud from his shirt and jeans.

"I'm okay!" he says with slight surprise. I remain quietly relieved while Dillon laughs, though I give Morgan the stink-eye for being so cocky.

With Morgan on the ground, I have one-on-one time with Dillon. I hold the nail with the pliers, angling my body back with trepidation, trying to ignore my hand that's in a vulnerable position. Dillon swings the hammer way above his head, ready to strike down.

"Whoa, whoa! It doesn't need to be a Herculean effort," I say, pulling my hand back with fear. "Just… lightly tap on the head." Dillon follows my instructions and taps on the nail. "There, see, that's good."

"It's not doing anything!" Morgan teases with a laugh.

"Oh yeah!" Dillon shouts. He swings the hammer back and over his head. I swing my head to the side, dodging the claw just in time, but the action distracts me from what's to come.

"Wait, you don't need to…"

Crunch.

It happens in an instant: the blunt hammer meets my hand, sending a rush of agony to the area. The progression of pain rushes up my arm, circles around my heart, and back again.

"I'm sorry!" Dillon says, jumping off the ladder.

"What did you do?" Morgan asks, rushing to join us.

"It's fine. I'm fine," I say as quickly as Morgan did after he fell, not wanting to ruin the moment. I cradle my left hand, afraid to look at the damage. "This wouldn't be the first time I've gotten hurt. I've actually hit myself with the hammer before," I say. My words rush out, helping me deal with the throbbing pain.

The boys stare at my hand with worried expressions. I slowly take my right hand off my left to reveal my wounded area. The boys gasp before I can see anything.

"See, it's not that bad," I say as a coverup. The space between my index finger and thumb has already begun to bruise and swell into a knot, pulsating with the beat of my heart. "At least you didn't get a finger!" I chirp.

Dillon drops the hammer and runs for the house, leaving Morgan and I watching behind him.

"Let him go," I advise Morgan when he starts after him.

"He hit you with the hammer and…"

"He feels bad," I say softly with my good hand on his shoulder. "That's why he ran into the house. Let's leave him alone for a few minutes and see if he returns on his own."

"We can get the chicks!" Morgan suggests.

"Let's finish up the coop first."

I stall Morgan as long as possible before we are ready to bring the chicks out. Just as we head to the van a few minutes later, Dillon's little face peeks out from the window at the nook in the kitchen. I wave him forward to no avail.

"Come on," I say with a smile. Dillon shakes his head but stays pressed to the window. I jump up and down like a monkey, trying to get him to loosen up. He laughs lightly but tucks his lips in to stop himself. Morgan gets wind of my goofiness and joins in.

"Come on, Dill-weed," he shouts, running in a silly circle. "We want to show the chicks their new home." He continues with silly moves, such as smelling his armpits and falling over. Dillon finally moves from his spot when Morgan starts peeping like the chicks.

"Do you think he'll come out?" I ask.

"I don't know. He's pretty stubborn," Morgan says smartly.

The door opens slowly, and Dillon comes out with his head down. "Not a negative word about my hand," I growl to Morgan. "Honey, I'm fine, really," I say, giving Dillon a side hug. "I've been able to use my hand and everything." It's one hundred percent a lie. It's been killing me every second since it was slammed by the hammer.

Dillon gently takes my hand and pulls it close to inspect with his red, puffy eyes. I never knew my son to be so protective over me! He brushes his hand lightly over my own.

"See, it's fine," I assure.

"It's big and purple," Dillon squeaks.

"Come on, let's get the chicks!" Morgan yells before running toward the van.

I drape my right arm around Dillon's shoulders for a few seconds before he runs to join his brother. I take this time to inspect my injured hand while they aren't looking. It doesn't appear broken, but it looks terrible, with an egg-sized lump getting bigger by the minute. I'm not about to tell Dillon.

"I hope it isn't too cold for them in the coop," Dillon says.

"That's what the heat light is for, dummy," Morgan says. His eyes snap to me, awaiting my disapproval.

"That wasn't nice, was it? You don't like being called names. You ever hear of the golden rule?" The boys look up at me in wonder. "It means that you treat others the same way you wish to be treated. Remember that the next time you think about saying something nasty." I pause for a moment to allow my words to sink in, knowing I've beaten myself down a few times regarding my ability to fix this place up.

With my hand out of commission, I instruct Morgan to go slow with the chicks. He gently picks up the box and walks to the backyard at a snail's pace.

"Maybe you can go a little faster than that," I laugh.

Once at the coop we tilt the box on its side, allowing the chicks to explore their new world. The three of us have a blast watching the little birds acclimate to their new surroundings. At first, they hesitantly run around in their new home, pecking, peeping, and flapping their wings.

"They're kind of like us, aren't they?" The boys look at me like I've gone crazy, so I explain. "We moved here, just like they are being relocated to their new house in our backyard. And, we fixed up their house, just like we're doing to ours."

"Are we supposed to be doing this?" Morgan puts his hands on his hips and swings his elbows to his sides. He scratches at the ground with his feet while walking around, peeping like the chicks. Dillon laughs and copies him once I start giggling.

"Too bad one of them doesn't have a little green wing,"

Dillon says.

"That's a good idea!" Morgan says with excitement.

"Remind me to hide all your green markers," I tease.

A familiar visitor flies by, once again landing on the coop. "Walton?" the big black bird says in a perfect dialect.

"Whoa, that bird can talk!" Morgan says with a thrill.

"Oh, I know," I say wryly. Don't get me wrong, it's incredible when birds learn to talk. I just think it's a bit odd when seemingly wild birds have taken to our language. Something about them learning enough to take over the world has always stayed in my mind.

"That's cool. Maybe we can keep him, too!" Dillon says, walking up to the bird.

"Let's just leave him alone," I suggest. "Make sure he doesn't pester our chicks."

"Chicks?" the bird repeats. The boys laugh before doing their ruffled feather dance again. The move scares the black bird off, much to my pleasure.

After spending another hour outside we head inside so I can finish dinner. Dillon plops in the chair at the dining room table and flops over with exhaustion.

"Man, I need to retire," he says with a breath of air. Morgan and I laugh.

"You crack me up."

"Like an egg," Dillon returns.

My cheeks ache from smiling so much. These must be a different muscle group than what crying uses, which had been my standard response to having the boys around.

"Time for me to feed my sourdough starter," I say, measuring equal amounts of water and flour. "From what I read, it'll start bubbling when it's active. It will be fun to make our own with as much bread as we eat."

The boys color pictures in the kitchen nook, a delightful company while I make dinner. "Look, Mom!" Two proud faces smile at me as Dillon and Morgan hold up the pictures they drew of the chicken coop.

"What's this? These are great, boys!" I take Morgan's picture from him, pointing out the chicks and showering him with compliments. "What are we doing here?"

"That's you teaching us how to hammer the boards," Morgan says proudly.

"I have one, too," Dillon chimes in, not wanting to be left out. His picture is of him hugging me with a big heart around my huge hand.

"You drew my owie," I say with a hug.

My head swarms with so much sentiment that I can't fight the tears stinging my eyes, but these are different than the ones that frequented my life back home. My sons, who have hardly included me in anything over the last few years, are drawing pictures of our time together.

"This is so sweet of you. I'm going to put these right here." After dabbing my tears, I promptly hang the pictures on the refrigerator in the kitchen and stand back to admire them. "I absolutely love them!" Dillon and Morgan each accept a hug as if sealing an initiation of our bonding. There's no going back in our relationship, which I had feared would head to ultimate estrangement.

This isn't a perfect house, I have a million things to do, and I'm not quite used to their company yet… but these are all tasks I'm now ready to accept.

Chapter 13 Date Night

Hours later, after playing with the chicks and doing light cleanup in the yard, I take off to the bathroom to see if my hairstyle from Bailey has held up. I turn this way and that, feeling like a princess with my haircut and styled curls. Bailey chopped four inches from my head, giving me a lighter look and feel. Heck, with everything else changing in my life, why not spruce up my dark chocolatey locks while I'm at it?

After popping a couple of Tylenol to settle my left hand, I dig under the counter for my hand mirror to check the back of my hair. I brush up against the package of pads.

"That's what I've been forgetting!" I say with a snap of my fingers. Oh well, I'm only a day behind, which is my usual.

Dirt is under every one of my fingernails from digging around in the coop. I push the pump for my bathroom soap, and instead of it being white, an odd blue liquid pools in my hand. At first, I'm irritated. The boys love putting food coloring in the hand soap as a prank. Instead of being annoyed, gratitude instead fills the space in my heart. The boys are including me in their joke! It's their way of showing their love.

"Shouldn't Dad be home soon?" Morgan asks from behind me, plopping on my bed.

I've spent all day with him, yet Morgan is in my room!

"Is it that time already? Goodness, where has the day gone?"

"In our memories," Morgan answers like a wise old man.

"True," I chuckle. "Dad sent me a text earlier saying he'll be off work early today," I'm happy to report. I'm excited to see my husband, even though my days have been so packed that I haven't had time to miss him.

The boys go nuts when Nick's black truck pulls in twenty minutes later. "Dad, wait 'til you see what we did!" Morgan shouts, running through the mud to greet him.

"Come and look at what we got!" Dillon screams with a bounce once we get out to the driveway.

"Hey, guys! Whoa, Joanie, you look amazing," he says before letting out a wolf whistle. He leans over to kiss me as the boys shout, "Eww."

"Thanks. I'm not covering this hair-do with a bandana today!" I respond, hiding my wounded hand behind my back. I'll show him my injury later, but I want the focus to be on the chicks instead of making Dillon feel bad again.

"I should take you to dinner," Nick offers, bouncing his eyebrows up and down.

The thought percolates in my mind, and suddenly, I want to go on a date as bad as a kid wants to go to Disneyland.

"What's in here?" Nick asks, peeking in the coop after Dillon has dragged him to the area. "Chicks? As in chickens?"

"That's usually what happens when they get older," I tease. Nick tilts his head with a smile as serene as they come. Sure, these chicks were mainly for the boys, but this has also fulfilled another of Nick's desires that he's talked about for years. With all my qualms about not wanting a big plot of land, I'm seeing the effects of his dream of having a farm come true.

"Look what we did with the roof," Morgan boasts,

tearing his dad away from the chickens to show him the work we've done. He's more excited to show Nick the boards we replaced than our new animals! "I did these ones. Mom got new boards, and she measured them, and then Dillon and I watched as she cut them. I nailed some on. Mom showed me how and everything." I smile with a pride that stems from more than the new boards.

"You don't say?" Nick says with a wink. "It looks great! So much for a couple of haircuts in today's plan. Did you get to help even with your gimpy arm, buddy?"

Dillon's demeanor shifts as he looks first at me and then to the ground. "I hurt Mom," he blurts. I squish my lips together to keep the tears from flowing from his cuteness.

"What?" Nick asks, darting his eyes up and down my body.

"Oh, I'm fine, it was just…"

"Dillon whacked Mom's hand with the hammer!" Morgan shouts, coming to my side to hold my hand up to show Nick.

"Ouch, Morgan!" I flinch.

"That looks terrible!" Nick says in reaction, bending over my hand in worry. I give him a 'shut up' look, and he stands straight. "I mean, with some ice, it'll be like new in no time." He puts his arm around Dillon and wrestles him around to get him out of his visible funk. "What are we going to name our new pets?"

"I'm calling that one Peep," Dillon announces. "That one's Cracky because he ate my cracker. Mr. McPuffy is over there. He looks like he got zapped by lightning."

"Hey, you can't name all of them," Morgan protests.

"Maybe we should each name one," I say cautiously, unsure how my suggestion will be received. Nick is usually the idea guy in these circumstances.

"I call that one!" Dillon says, pointing to the puffy one.

"Who will name the extra one?" Morgan asks, ever the pragmatist. "There's five of them and only four of us."

I stay quiet until I realize that all eyes are on me to make this decision.

Me!

"Maybe we can drop the names in a hat and pick one. Or maybe we can have a 'name tournament' or something. We can each submit a few names and take a vote to see who makes it to the next round."

"No voting on your own name," Nick chimes in.

"That sounds cool!" Morgan shouts. He runs inside and gathers the materials before rushing back in less than two minutes. "Write your names down and put them in the hat," he instructs, dropping a hat on the ground.

"We're doing this now?" Nick asks with amusement.

"Yes!" the boys say in unison as they scribble their names on the paper. Within minutes, we're pulling names and casting our votes, and before I know it, the chicks are named.

"I'm not sure I like the name Petunia for mine, but what're you going to do?" Nick chuckles.

Nick and I mosey to the house hand-in-hand as the boys play tag in the yard. It's still early, with the afternoon sun sending highlights over the trees and tall blades of grass. A crisp breeze rustles new leaves on the eucalyptus tree by the house, catching my eye. "I've always loved that kind of tree. When the wind blows, it looks like it's clapping."

"Maybe we'll get a few. We can plant a whole row of them by the fence line if you want.

"I might like that." I nuzzle into Nick's neck, giving him a sniff. His new scent of wood from being at the mill all day surrounds him. "At least I know you're at work during the day," I laugh.

"Or maybe I just roll around in sawdust and come home," he winks.

"Nah," I smile. "Hey, do you mean it about going out to dinner? It is Friday night."

"Sure. I'm always up for a date with my beautiful wife," he says, switching positions so his arm is around my shoulder. It does my body good to have his touch on me. "We don't have a babysitter, but I can call a couple of people from work."

"Our neighbor from down the street came by and gave me her number the other day. Cinda. I could ask her. She has boys of her own. Do you think it's too late?"

"The worst she can say is no," Nick responds.

I text Cinda, resting my phone on the counter to tap the message with my right hand. I told her I'll repay the favor by bringing the casserole that's replacing the dusty smell in the house. She responds right away that she would love to have them over but not to bring the food since she's already made dinner. "She said yes!" I say with surprise.

"I'll go wash up!" Nick says, trotting into the house.

I round the boys up and let them know our plans, warning them to be on their best behavior for Cinda. We are ready in no time, with me in a flowery blue, floor-length skirt, and an old blouse with sparkles down the mesh long sleeves. Nick dresses in khaki pants and a button-up green long-sleeved shirt that seems to change his brown eyes to hazel.

Nick formally opens my car door and holds his hand out. I play along and use my right hand to swing myself into the truck easily, aware that Dillon is watching my every move.

The rolling hills and green pastures offer a pleasant view

as we roll down our dirt driveway. I haven't bonded with this town yet, but I hope if it ever does happen, I never take its beauty for granted.

No matter how much fresh air has blown through me, I'm still fighting the changes in my life. Moving and losing a job are two of the major changes that can happen to a person. For now, I allow myself the excitement of the night ahead.

Cinda's white house is up the hill around the corner from ours, with its own long dirt driveway. A two-story farmhouse with a wraparound porch comes in view, complete with two boys playing catch out front. Their view of the town offers different angles than ours, which are just as beautiful.

Her house is a cleaned-up version of mine. It reminds me of the before-and-after clips on one of those house fixer-up shows.

The immaculate front yard has me wishing for a duplicate of my own. With the warm days, I've been finding it refreshing to be out in nature. Still, I wonder how my yard will go from mud to this.

A set of swinging porch chairs sits next to the front door. I immediately begin turning this into a woodworking project of my own soft lines and smooth wood.

The calculations and angles slow my steps at first, taking me off-guard. I know how this goes. Once bitten by the bug, I become obsessed, wanting to woodwork every second of the day.

Geesh, all I did was replace a few boards on the chicken coop!

Cinda welcomes us into her home, which reminds me of a finished, much more polished version of my own. It's equally significant in size, with high ceilings and an open floor plan. Every inch is impressively decorated in whites, pastel blues, and greens. Faux barn doors enhance the entrance from the living room to the large kitchen. Figurines of chickens, pigs, and horses lay next to silk flowers on distressed white end tables and shelves on the walls. Cinda and her husband, David, are full of smiles and welcome our boys with open arms.

"Joanie, I'm so glad you're here!" Cinda says with a hug, even as she has her little girl in a wrap around her chest.

"Dillon, don't touch!" Morgan scolds.

"Oh, it's okay, sweetie. With three boys and a baby girl, I've kid-proofed every inch of this place. I'm not kidding. I've either glued the valuables to the tables or put them high in a cupboard," Cinda says sweetly.

"Dillon, stop touching stuff!" Morgan says again, disregarding Cinda's message.

She leans over to me and whispers, "I have one of those who wants to be in charge. It's fun, isn't it?"

"What, to have a Bossy Benny in the house?" I laugh as the boys run off to play. "He challenges my passive personality for sure." I've always wondered if I've been up for the challenge of raising a strong boy such as Morgan. To this day, I'm quick to put myself down for not being able to stand up to him. "Thank you for watching them. I can't remember the last time we went out to dinner."

"I can," Nick pipes up. "It was when my parents came to visit four years ago." We share a look that encompasses our sad romance story. We've wanted to spend more time together over the years, but the rush of life has swept it from our grasp.

A deep breath brings in a mixture of pleasant spices and coconut candles. "I hope I'm not dumping them on you. I gave them a snack before we left, but Morgan and Dillon have quite the appetite."

Cinda brushes her hand my way. "I said not to feed them, and I meant it," she says confidentially. "Oh, and Joanie, I wanted to show you…" She rushes to the kitchen and picks up a round loaf of bread. "We made sourdough today!"

"How cool! I've been feeding my starter, and today it started to bubble," I say excitedly.

"I have a ton of recipes if you need them."

"Thanks! Aww, look at how wide-eyed your little girl is," I say, offering my finger to her baby, squirming around like crazy. "What's your name, little cutie?"

"This is Shyann, named after my great-grandma. She'd be so proud that I'm raising the kids with her Indian heritage. She'd be less proud that my husband has red hair and freckles, but what she doesn't know doesn't hurt her."

"That's true in my court, too. Nick doesn't have the red hair, but I'm sure our guys burn at the same rate when they're in the sun."

We laugh and one of her sons runs by with a water balloon, screaming that he will get his brother. "No, you don't," Cinda says calmly, stopping him with a hand on his arm. "We've talked about not having water balloons in the house. Remember, Brian?"

The little boy does his best to wiggle free while complaining that she's ruining his plan. Cinda remains cool and simply takes the balloon from him. She holds his arm as if it's no bother while the boy flails around. She shows zero embarrassment or shame that he's misbehaving while, at the same time, owning her position as the parent.

"Brian, you're showing our guests your naughty

behavior."

The boy looks our way sheepishly. "Sorry," he says after a moment. Nick and I share an expression that shows how impressed we are by how she has dealt with the situation.

Cinda releases Brian, who promptly trots away and screams playfully in the distance. "We're having stuffed bell peppers, Spanish rice, and roasted veggies for dinner."

"Sounds fancy. How in the world did you have time to make all that?" I ask, trying to not sound too envious. "If it's not in the slow cooker, I usually don't make it."

"I have a mail-order food system, honey. Plus, my mom lives in the mother-in-law suite next to us, which is a fancy way of saying we converted our back garage for her. She helps us out a ton, and so do the boys. You should give the mail-order thing a try."

She flits to a drawer in the kitchen and pulls out a brochure. With her back to me, I check out her organized kitchen, noting the pot rack hanging above the island. I've always loved this idea and hope she doesn't mind if I steal it.

"You still need to go to the store for a few things," she says as she hands over the flyer, "but I love how it takes the guessing out of what to make. I get a box every three weeks and double the recipes so they last a few nights."

"Pff, like my kids eat leftovers," I say with a roll of my eyes. "I don't know how you get yours to."

"Um, mine don't have a choice," Cinda says matter-of-factly.

I feel the sting of embarrassment from allowing my boys to run the show for so long. Cinda shakes me from my thoughts when she grabs my arm and whispers in my ear.

"You look great, but if you have a minute, I have a top that will go perfectly with that skirt. Want to see?" I nod vigorously at the thought of wearing something new, even if it's just new to me. "We'll be right back," Cinda says to our husbands, engrossed in a conversation about work.

Cinda shows me through her home, moving easily with her baby strapped to her front. Each room is more beautifully decorated than the last. Windows line every wall, allowing natural light to enhance pops of color. I mentally take a picture of Cinda's blue pillows here and yellow flowers there, loving the contrast. The theme is clean and quite the opposite of how I've labeled my dusty home.

Cinda's bedroom suite is wide open with large windows on every wall. It follows the white and light blue color scheme, which gives it a fresh look. I envy her completed house, wishing I could snap my fingers and have the same when I walk into mine.

"I love your room," I say, eyeing her many perfectly aligned pillows on the white down comforter.

"Thanks," she says, heading straight for her walk-in closet that's as large as mine. In fact, the layout of Cinda's bedroom is quite similar to my own. I stand a little straighter, realizing I have exactly what she does, just in the 'before' stage.

"Both of these blouses will pair nicely with that skirt and your skin coloring," she says, holding different variations of silky blue shirts for my choosing. "I don't know if you're into your heritage, but there are some tribal groups in town."

"I haven't connected with my roots in ages. It's one of those things that fell by the wayside when I had kids, but maybe I'll check it out once things settle down a bit. These blouses are beautiful," I say, loving the soft feel of the fabric on my fingertips. "I've been wearing scrubs for the last eight years. My fashion savvy is about as drab as my house decorating skills."

Cinda gasps and lightly takes my left hand in hers. "Joanie, what happened to your hand?"

"Dillon accidentally smashed it with a hammer today when we were redoing a few of the boards on the chicken coop. He felt so bad!"

"That's really cute, but this looks bad," she says with a sideways head tilt.

"I thought so, too."

"Here, let me send you the contact of our family doctor in town. It's Doctor Thompson, and she's fantastic."

"Thanks!" I say, uncertain whether I should let her in on something personal. "My boys don't show much of that sentiment towards me. It came with some pain," I say, holding my hand up, "but I must admit that I liked the attention this got me."

Cinda laughs, showing she understands my meaning. "Boys are like that sometimes. I swear I have one of each personality. It goes to show that all types fall into the normal range. It takes some creative parenting, but it gets easier once they know who the boss is." It's the first response I've gotten about my boys that's helpful.

"I bet you're curious to see how different your little girl is," I say, taking one of the blouses from her.

"She's already been more easy-going and less difficult than the boys were at her age, but we'll see. Do you like that one?" she asks about one of the blouses. I nod and hold it to my body, wondering if it'll fit. "That one's a bit tight on me, so if it fits it's yours. Go try it on!" she says with a warm smile.

It's funny that Cinda's blouse fits *and* looks good on me. Here I've been, constantly criticizing my size when Cinda has a fuller, yet totally flattering figure. I would never say such things to her as I've thought about myself.

"You look great in that, Joanie!"

"It does look better than this frumpy thing, doesn't it?" I say with a chuckle at my blouse. "The next time I go shopping, I'm taking you with me!"

"I'll show you all the great places in town, honey," Cinda says, turning toward a built-in vanity lined with glass bottles. "You want a squirt of perfume?" I chose a bottle with a daisy on top and am pleased to find the scent is light and flowery. Once dressed and smelling like lilac, Cinda briskly leads me back into the living room.

The couple practically shoves us out of their house, demanding we have fun and take our time. Nick gives me a sultry grin on our way back to the car.

"What's that look for?" I chuckle knowingly.

"I like that shirt," he says with a wink.

"It's a blouse," I say playfully. "I'm surprised you can recognize me in these nice clothes and new hair."

He opens the door for me and holds his hand out. "This is a long overdue evening, hon, and I intend to enjoy it," he says with a pat on my behind.

"It feels like we're breaking the rules by going out," I laugh.

We hop in the truck, where he promptly takes hold of my left hand as usual. "Ouch!" I say with a flinch, pulling my hand back.

"I'm sorry!" Nick says, eyeing me with worry. "You should go see a doctor about that hand."

"I know, darn it. If it's not better by next week, I'll make an appointment for when the boys go back to school. I don't want to make Dillon feel worse about it. He was trying so hard with the coop.”

“It sounds like the three of you had a good day.”

“We did,” I say with a simple nod. Nick glances at me several times before forcing his gaze to the road.

“What?” I ask sneakily.

“It seems like you’ve had much better days with the boys since we’ve been here.”

“We’ve only been here a few days,” I remind. He nods vigorously in return. “What’s your point, sly sir?”

“Maybe the move wasn’t such a bad idea after all.”

I quickly turn to the windshield, not wanting to broach this subject now. I’m still quite sore about Nick bulldozing me into this move, and I’m not about to ruin our date with the topic.

“Where are you taking us, anyway?” I say, my voice taking on a light tone.

“Somewhere that everyone at work talks about.”

I nod and settle in for the drive. It’s relaxing as can be, especially after such a busy day. Miles of hilly countryside drift by my window. My eyes take in the scenery as I memorize street names and landmarks.

“This place is so perfect that it looks fake. Are you sure that’s not a screen?” I say, pretending to grab at my window. Nick’s laugh fills the truck before he continues that squishy, sideways glance at me. “What?”

“This will be our view during dinner,” he says, pointing out my window. The break in the trees reveals glistening water.

“A lake? I saw it on the map but didn’t realize we were this close! We need to tour the town!” Nick pulls into the resort that sits on the waterfront. “This lake is huge!” I get out of the truck with my eyes glued to the water.

Small waves brush the shore lined by Douglas fir trees that sway in the evening breeze. The water reveals a ripple from the wind that's rushing our way. A refreshing gust sends my bouncy hair flying behind me.

"I could sit at that picnic table all day," I say, keeping my gaze on the lake while following Nick inside.

We walk through the log-style lodge and up a grand staircase. A table by the window awaits us with a perfect lake view. Nick orders a plate of bruschetta with a homemade tomato and mushroom topping, and I get myself a sweet iced tea.

"Who knew it would be this easy, huh?" Nick says, sipping his water and gazing upon the small waves on the lake.

"It is?" I casually sip my tea to show I'm not upset. "That's not very good," I say, quickly putting my glass down. The tea has an odd flavor, so I switch to water.

"I know it's an adjustment, and I've been worried for a while. Since back when I was doing my interviews."

My stomach erupts in nausea when he mentions the secret he kept from me. It's stayed as sour in my mind as old milk in the refrigerator. Having barely confronted him about the topic, it still feels like a betrayal that he didn't include me in this process.

"I didn't think I'd get the job. That's the honest truth," he continues as if reading my mind. "A part of me wondered how you would do with the move if I were to get it."

I sit quietly, allowing this to sink in. Hearing these words eases the resentment that has built up against him. "Why's that?" I ask, testing how well he can think on his feet.

"We both know how strict you are with your schedule," he says, eyeing me as I snatch a roll from the basket as soon as it's delivered.

"But look," I say with my finger up, "people can change, as evidenced by how late we're having dinner tonight. I'm starving," I say, spreading a huge chunk of warm butter on the bread. It's true. I haven't been on a schedule one day that we've been here.

"I want you to be happy, Joanie. I know I kind of messed up with the job thing." I keep staring at him, having wanted to hear the words for a month now. "I'm sorry."

I look down at my place setting, filled with an overwhelming urge to forgive him on the spot. And why shouldn't I? It's something to be proud of to be able to forgive someone and move on. It isn't like I had to carry our belongings on my back or make it across the country in a covered wagon. My experiences since we've been here have been far from terrible.

"Okay, if I'm telling the truth to you and me, it hasn't been all that bad. I'm not thrilled about having to do all of the house projects by myself; I'm going to say that out loud. You know I put that side of me away years ago, and I'm hesitant about getting back into it."

"Joanie, you're amazing at that craft…" Nick starts.

"That's the thing, I'm not!" I retort with slight irritation. "I'm not even being modest here; I mess up on everything I do." Nick sits back and chews his bread, keeping his eyes fixated on me but letting me speak. "You know why I haven't done my woodworking in years, and yet here you are, pushing me into it."

Nick looks at the table as if it's guiding him on what to say next. "Don't take this the wrong way because I do hear what you're saying, but you are always too hard on yourself."

"Nick, none of my stuff ever came out straight! I sawed

off a whole corner of a table one time. My chairs were lop-sided. And those weren't even the big mistakes!" I put my head in my hands, still feeling the disappointment of my failures. "Now, you want me to practically rebuild a house that's falling to pieces. A chicken coop is one thing, but a whole house?" I rest my head on my good hand, feeling the sting of the damage to the other. "And now I only have one and a half hands to do it with."

He leans back with a feigned smile, keeping his eyes on me. "I know I've been working since you got here. I'm sorry. I'll be more like your little helper," he says, tapping my forearm playfully.

I look down with a smile of my own. It has always been difficult to be mad at my husband when he epitomizes boyish charm. "Well, the house is a tinkerer's dream." I put my hands on my chest and look up with my eyes closed before turning more serious. "It's starting to grow on me, I guess." Still, he looks at me as if he's not convinced. "The boys and I have been having a good time together. They start school next week, and I'm thinking at that point, I'll be able to dive in and make a lot of progress. I was thinking of putting a window in that area in the hall before our bedroom."

"It's a little dark," we say together before his eyes light up. We always have had the same taste in everything from food to furniture. After fifteen years together, knowing we still have this is more than a comfort.

I shrug. "Maybe after dinner, we can stop by a store and look at flooring for our room."

"There's a place on Maple Street," Nick says enthusiastically. "We still have a few thousand left from the moving allowance." Seeing him in this light, relaxing, and having this conversation feels good. Our lives were so busy before that we rarely got this type of interaction.

"It's funny. I've had a couple of people ask me to help them with their house or make their furniture. Isn't that weird?"

"I don't think so," he laughs. "You've always been super approachable, and that hand-brain combination makes you great at your trade."

"Yeah, but they don't know that. I don't know either anymore," I say nervously. It's more than just a statement. This is me spilling something that has been eating away at me. "How do I know I can cobble a house back together?" I reach over and squeeze Nick's hand, sharing with him my worry through my expression.

"I have complete faith in you," he says, looking into my eyes. "It's like I've said, it doesn't have to get done all at once. Allow yourself to have fun with it"

"Yeah, but we are walking around on subfloor and unpainted walls. We're in a construction zone."

"The boys aren't noticing a thing if that's what you're worried about. I know it will be amazing," he says again with confidence. "A few people at work want to see the house when it's ready."

"Cinda mentioned something about that. Maybe next year or something," I say with a shake of my head.

"I'm sure a month or two will be a good time. Then maybe they can come to see it in a year and see all the progress you've made."

"Yeah, sure." I can't tell if he's serious or not. I hated having people over at our other house and still have the residual negative feelings of being a party host. I can't imagine how self-conscious I would feel having strangers see our house now!

The waiter comes for our orders, allowing me to ignore this subject. After we order, we easily fall back into a discussion about the house.

"I have so many pages of my notebook filled with things that need to get done." It's odd; instead of this being a negative statement, I can feel the anticipation of getting started.

"That's my girl! You like it!"

I shrug, repelling my negativity. "Except for one thing," I say with a finger in the air.

"What's that?"

"Okay, don't think I'm crazy, but I think we have a ghost." Nick barks a laugh in response before quieting down.

"Oh, you're serious?"

"As serious as the knocking noises I've heard. The boys heard them, too! I've even checked it out… nothing. I don't have any other explanation," I say with my hands out.

"The previous owner didn't mention anything." He cocks his head and squints suspiciously.

"I'm not making it up! One morning, it sounded like someone dropped a brick in a metal bucket."

"That doesn't sound 'ghosty.'" I jump a foot when our waiter arrives behind me to deliver our salads. "Gosh, you are extra jumpy. I'll check it out with you." Nick reaches out to touch my arm, giving me extra support.

It's a date full of free-flowing conversation and laughter as Nick tells me about some of the characters at work and me recapping the experiences the boys and I have shared. "That's called bonding," Nick says proudly.

"They've been helping out. I mean, really helping, not just kid help." Nick's laugh pulls the whole night together for me. We've been through ups and downs, as most couples have. I know I'm a bit needier than him, wanting more time with him than he can give. He has been working a lot, but it's been okay so far, with the new things stemming in my life. Still, I'm not ready to admit that this change in a new home has benefitted me.

Home.

It's a thought that grounds me. I still consider our tiny house in Fargo our home. I wonder when my opinions will change and catch up with the times.

I text Cinda after we finish eating, asking about the boys. "She says they've been upstairs since dinner and to take our time."

"Good. Sounds like we don't have to rush back."

I smile, thanking the stars that this is turning out okay so far. I mean, our house is almost falling down around us, but shouldn't our happiness stem from the relationships in our lives, not the four walls that surround us?

Nick pays the bill and excuses himself for the restroom, giving me my first alone time of the day. I dink around on my phone, clicking on my period app, when I see that Nick has found someone to chat with on his way back.

Seven days late.

"What?" I sit to attention. That can't be right; I thought I was supposed to start yesterday. I shake my head as I disbelieve the app. I click back to the previous month, counting the days by hand since my last period. The stress of the move must be getting to me, messing with my natural cycle.

My mind flashes to when I was pregnant and how hungry I was. I look down at my empty plate that held at least two dinner servings a few minutes ago. I also remember that when I was pregnant, tea tasted like acid.

Nick touches my arm from behind, causing me to jump yet again. "Do you think you're the only one here?" he teases with a kiss on my neck. "Ready?" I nod, not giving any indication of the thought he's interrupting.

I take his arm with a forced smile, happy our date isn't over. As we leave, I glance one last time at the table that holds my full glass of tea.

Chapter 14 Reigniting an Old Flame

A knocking noise stops me from dabbling with the makeup Monica sold me at the salon. There's a room between ours and the one off the living room, but the unmistakable noise travels quickly to my ears.

"Nick! It's the noise!" I yell, running into our dingy-looking yellow bathroom. Nick sticks his head out of the shower door to hear me better.

"What?" he yells over the sound of the shower spray.

"I heard the noise!" I hold a towel out for him, hopping up and down to hurry him along. He obliges, and a minute later, we are at the door to the spooky room. "Okay, here we are," I say, breathily. "I haven't heard it in a minute or two, so…" Nick's face breaks into an amused smile. "It's not in my head!"

"I never said it was, you're just cute. Here goes." He turns the knob and walks in as if it's any ordinary door and room. As for me, my stomach and heart are in a race to see which one can jump out of my body first.

We step inside and find… emptiness.

I rush into the room and walk in a big circle to scope it out. "I heard it; I know I did! The boys heard it the other day," I say as I sulk through the room with another disappointing inspection. It's not like I want to find something scary. A logical answer would settle my nerves, though.

"Joanie, maybe this is it," Nick hollers from outside. I join him to find a pipe dripping, creating a small mud puddle by the door.

I look from the mud to my half-naked husband and back to the ground again. He's trimmed down a few pounds since we've been here, barely giving me something to hold on to around his middle. It's probably due to his full days at work, complete with the hours of yard work he's been putting in.

"You think that little dripping noise would be making a loud tapping that I can hear from across the house?"

"I don't know what you've heard," he says with a shrug and a smile that shows he feels sorry for me.

"Let's get going. You might want to wash the shampoo out of your hair first." I dab his head with my hand, loving that he could care less about being outside in just his towel. "I'm sorry to drag you out here."

"Anything for you, hon."

I slowly walk back to the bedroom with a sinking feeling. The boys will start school in a few days, and I'll be here alone with the noise!

While allowing my achy left hand to rest in my lap, I stay attentive during our drive, trying to memorize street names and landmarks. We first visit the shops on Cotton Street, where I had the run-in with the angry crowd.

"Talk about visiting the combat zone," I say, pointing out where the confrontation was. The space is empty now, the crowd probably darkening someone else's doorway.

"People are passionate about this town," Nick says cooly.

"What are there, a hundred little stores in here?" I ask in amazement, shifting my gaze down the cobblestone road. I must have had tunnel vision when we were here before, worrying about how the boys would behave at the salon.

"Let's see what the brochure says," Nick says, lifting the top of a wooden box with city maps. I hungrily take one, wanting to see all this town offers. This is where we live now, and I want to know this place as well as I knew the last one.

"Would it be an oxymoron to describe this as a historical strip mall?" I look down the street, feeling the coziness from the different colors of buildings amongst the trees and hanging flower baskets. The storefronts blend together with their awnings reaching out over the sidewalks.

Nick and I stroll hand-in-hand down the wide sidewalks. The boys enjoy window shopping as much as we do, peering into the boutiques and stores with homemade soaps, trinkets, or any type of knick-knack you could want.

"It's nice to be squeaky clean for a change and not full of dust or mud," I say. "Hey, those are the shops on the Garden Valley website!" I announce, pointing my finger with as much excitement as spotting a celebrity.

We visit several stores, getting a sundress and a few blouses for me and a couple of outfits for the boys' first day of school. With his beagle figurine in tow, Morgan picks a decorative set of clay chickens that resemble our little chicks. He's excited when I suggest that these can be used to decorate the bay window in the kitchen. A couple of people sign Dillon's cast, adding to his list of friends he's made since we've been here.

We are so busy sightseeing that we forget breakfast and opt for an early lunch outside a cute café. With our bellies full, we lazily roam through the rest of the town, taking in all the sights. "I feel like royalty walking under these petunias," I say, admiring the overflowing flower baskets on the black decorative street lamps.

I'm engulfed in the cozy charm of it all, slowly falling in love with the laid-back feel and warm smiles of welcome from the locals. It all goes well with the greeting Cinda and the salon ladies have given us, a nice change from the angry people who confronted me the last time I was downtown.

We hear news of an outdoor market near the lake that we all excitedly agree to check out. "That's what Monica's sister, Amy, told me about the other day."

"Already name-dropping, huh?" Nick says with a sideways glance at the truck.

"Lake in the Woods," Dillon says when we pass the greeting sign fifteen minutes later.

"It makes sense. It is *in* the woods," Morgan says seriously.

"This is where we went to dinner the other night," I inform the boys as we pull in.

The lake is much bigger than it seems on a map and bends off in the distance into another large segment that we cannot see from where we stand on the shoreline. A chilly breeze slides off the water's surface and blows my hair back, taking more of my pent-up worries.

"We should try kayaking sometime. I'm sure the boys would have fun," I say, watching the people paddle in canoes. Nick threads his fingers in mine, looks out over the lake, and takes a deep breath.

"I love it here," he says.

I'm beginning to understand the allure. We've always wanted to slow down and do family outings like we are today.

At the market, we gaze upon the booths of handmade

pot holders, wax sculptures, paintings, and goodies. Morgan and Dillon join the other kids as they freely run about the meadow without any parental reprimands.

"Hey, hey! I see someone familiar," Nick says, hugging his parents. They are a welcome surprise. Having been busy since we arrived, we haven't had a chance to visit them yet. The boys go nuts when they see Grandma and Grandpa and shower them with hugs.

"Joanie, it's so good to see you," my mother-in-law, Marge, says with a bear hug. Having them nearby solidifies that I'm no long alone when it comes to family.

"Are you whipping that house into shape?" asks Phil, my father-in-law. He towers over all of us with his thin frame, something that skipped over my stocky hubby. My face must show worry, and he lets out a little chuckle. "I was friends with Glen, the previous owner. I helped with some of the demolition, but he didn't get far on his repairs."

"Yeah, I'm living with that now."

"I'm sorry about that," Phil says, taking responsibility for my worries. "Call me, and I'll gladly help whenever you need me."

"Thank you," I say sincerely. Phil worked at the same mill as Nick does now for a few years before he retired. Having an offer of help takes some of the load off.

"Now that you're here," Marge starts, "I get to share my sourdough starter with you. It's a thing here and means you're a part of the town." I miss her eye contact with the blues that match Dillon's. I even remember the hair dye number she uses in her thick light brown hair.

"One of my neighbors beat you to it. I've been feeding it daily, and it has already started bubbling."

Marge holds her hands out wide in welcome. "Then

you're already part of Garden Valley. Joanie, my goodness, what happened to your hand?" she asks, gently taking my left hand in hers. Marge is a retired nurse, which is why I became a CNA in the nursing home years ago.

"Dillon accidentally hit it with a hammer," I say quietly, ensuring my son is far enough away to not hear me.

"You should get that checked out."

"That's what I keep telling her," Nick agrees.

"I'll go Tuesday if it doesn't look any better," I assure. "That's when school starts."

"Go Monday. We can come to watch the boys," Marge offers.

Besides Cinda, it's the first time in years that someone has stepped in to lend us a hand with… anything. A glance at Nick shows he shares the relief I'm feeling.

We enjoy ice cream from the local creamery, which I learn is famous nationwide. Homemade waffle cones satisfy my sweet tooth, and I rest on the benches by the lake. I ignore the questioning behind my insatiable stomach, allowing myself to feel this simple joy.

We snap a few amateur family photos with our phones with and without Nick's parents. I send some to my family with the captions *wish you were here,* and *let's plan a get-together!*

I sneak away and make another loop around the booths while Nick and his parents watch the boys. I mosey by the Indian tribal table and take a flyer, not receiving any pressure from the smiling faces manning the booth.

As much as I've been fighting it, my hobby is at the forefront of my mind with all the crafts we've seen. The only woodworking I saw today was handmade jewelry boxes and the place I'm currently visiting.

"Figures that you'd be drawn here," Nick says, sneaking

behind me. "These are pretty cool," he points to the homemade kid stools shaped like animals. "I bet you could sell your furniture here," Nick says. "I haven't seen much of your style so far in town. I know where you can get the wood," he says with a sneaky grin.

"The thought has crossed my mind." I take Nick's calloused hand with my right and continue walking around the various booths. There's so much to see that one lap wasn't enough to take it all in.

"It isn't like you were an amateur. You have thousands of hours into it."

"I'm hardly enough of an expert to be able to make things for other people."

Nick pulls his face back in surprise. "Why would you think that? You made some of our furniture."

"I wouldn't want to pass my messed-up pieces off on someone else, especially if they spend their money thinking they are getting store quality."

It's a story I've told myself for years: I make too many mistakes. For the first time, I wonder if these statements are valid anymore. Who knows? Maybe all those inadequacies are in my head after my years of hiatus. Yeah, because that's how it works. People get better at something by *not* practicing.

"Store quality," Nick says with a puff of disapproval. "You know that's not perfect either. The flaws you say you make only add to the sentiment of a handmade item."

It's good advice but not enough to give me the confidence to take on projects like Cinda's ottoman or Amy's table.

"It's funny that people are selling farm equipment here," I say to change the subject.

"I guess when that's your market," Nick says with that

sideways grin. There's always another thought behind that smirk, making me connect the dots to my craft.

After a few hours, we say goodbye to Nick's parents, planning to meet with them next week before heading to the mill. I have yet to lay eyes on this place that uprooted our entire family.

The manufacturing plant takes up an entire street block on the outskirts of town. It has a log yard, equipment as big as a house, and a mill that would take a whole day to tour.

"This is a plywood mill. We make boards to sell to construction companies, and they use them to build houses," Nick tells the boys.

The 'we' in that statement shows how invested my husband is with the company. It's bitter-sweet for me. I'm proud he's so dedicated to his career and part of a team, even when they get to see him more than I do. I am grown up enough to know this is how the working world goes.

"We run twenty-four, seven," he continues, "but it's a lighter crew on the weekends. I'll show you some of the machines and where my office is."

The whiff of freshly cut pine fills my nostrils and stops me in my tracks. I'm flooded with memories of woodworking, and I don't hate it. I thought I wouldn't take to this part of my life creeping back, yet here I am, running my hand over the wood, visualizing it turning into a chair or end table. "Is this wood local?" I ask with interest.

"Most of it comes from Oregon, but some trees come from out of state," Nick replies.

"This place is cool!" Morgan says, loving the noisy equipment. Everyone we pass gives a friendly wave or hello and knows my husband by name. It tells a lot about a boss when the employees appear genuinely happy to see him.

"This is my wife, Joanie," Nick says with pride, introducing me to a man in slacks and a button-up shirt. Most people we've met are in hard hats and bright orange safety vests, but not this guy. I assume this tall, grey-haired man is one of Nick's bosses.

"I'm looking forward to seeing your house in a few weeks," the man says as he greets me. "Nick has really talked up your skills."

I look at Nick in surprise, hoping he hasn't nailed down a date for the ridiculous dinner gathering that has been brooding. "Well, Nick does like to exaggerate," I say, hoping the guy will take a hint that he isn't welcome at my house yet. No one is!

The man continues with the burning question of how many people Nick has invited to our house and when they will appear. For all I know, I'll open the front door to thirty people next Thursday.

"That over there is our scrap wood pile," Nick points out casually. "You okay?" he asks. I nod, not wanting to bring this up at his place of work.

I do my best to pay attention to what Nick is saying, trying to ignore the questions stirring about the party. Has Nick formally invited people? When is this supposed party? How many people are we talking about here?

These worries flee when we come to a large area with piles of wood pieces in a scrap bin. It's a woodworker's dream.

A woodworker like me.

I feel quite privileged to have access to all this wood, now seeing through Nick's plan of bringing us here.

"Is all this up for grabs?" I ask as Nick nods. "How much do they sell it for?"

"It's scrap, so it's free."

"*These* are scraps?"

"Yup. It either goes to a good home or gets thrown in the furnace." He comes up close and whispers the following statement in my ear. "I'm a man with an ample supply of wood… and a wife who knows what to do with it."

"Nick, shh," I say with a playful smack to his chest.

"The boys can't hear me. And they'd have no idea what I'm talking about anyway," he says in my neck with a quick nuzzle.

I pick out quite a few pieces that I can't bear to see go through the chipper or be incinerated. We soon lay them in the back of the truck, with me hoping to give them another chance at becoming something amazing.

***

"I'll be inside in a few," I say with a touch to Nick's arm when we get back. I meander back to my garage full of machines, telling myself I'll just take a peek. Before long, I'm separating the salvageable pieces of throwaways from Nick's work with my good hand. It's all usable and up to my standards, even though the beefy surface planer in the back corner could bring almost anything back to life.

This garage is stocked with all the machinery necessary if I decide to start building again. With Nick giving me his work scraps, I'll be set.

While the boys play in the yard, I flip through my old furniture sketchbook. "Because I need more to do," I mutter sarcastically. A wooden chair catches my eye. It's a cutout I've taped in here from a wood-crafting magazine I used to read.

This design has always been something I've wanted to bring to life with its low seat and angled backs. The wood in the picture is quite bland and, in my opinion, needs more variation in the colors. It would work perfectly with a mate out back.

It's one thing this house and land have to offer: plenty of spots to put my pieces. I could make anything and everything I've ever wanted and never run out of room.

A hop enters my step as I rearrange the tools in the garage to make more sense. I sold my tools long ago when I gave up my hobby. I turn on my speaker, blasting away any doubt that is not welcome.

I have a million things to do to spruce up this place, but without a job, I have at least an extra fifty free hours than I had before. I've had the mindset to use all of this on the house. I don't have to go full-blast with everything around here. Why shouldn't I allow myself a few of those fifty hours on something for… myself?

⁎

Last night sparked a side of me that I haven't felt in a while, and I want more. I tiptoe to the back garage early the next day before everyone gets up, tucking my shirt into my jeans with the holes in the knees. "First things first," I say, linking my portable speaker to my playlist, starting with The Weeknd.

My worries want to creep up like a hot flash on a woman in menopause, but I don't let them. Right now, this time is for me.

It doesn't take long to determine that I have more than enough wood to start a project. The teak chunks leftover from the last resident makes up half of the wood I need for my chair, and the pieces from Nick's work *almost* make up the rest.

"No biggie," I say, mentally preparing to return to town and see where I can pick up more specialty-type woods. Cherry or Birdseye maple would look beautiful in this chair. It's my style to lay in a different type of wood into my pieces to break up any monotony of color. In this way, I put my own stamp on my creations.

I quickly fall into the groove of organizing the wood so it flows together in the piece. I individually run the pieces through the surface planer to get the proper thicknesses.

There's more to making furniture than nailing something together and throwing paint or a finish. I flow with the machinery and tools, transforming what was once a tree into something that has a use and usually holds a sentimental value.

"Looks like you've already made progress," Nick says, coming in at dawn. "You haven't lost it. The boys and I are unpacking," he says with a kiss and a smile before running through the rain on the way back to the house.

I ignore my achy left hand as I continue to move as I once did. I lay the beautiful pieces of wood on the machines, using finesse to guide them through the process. Familiar scents bring me back to the countless hours I've spent losing myself in these movements.

After dozens of tummy grumbles, I call it quits with enough progress to feel satisfied. I never expected to finish the project today. I've done more than just start the chair; I reignited an old side of me. It's a side that hasn't been used in a while, but I'm pleased to say it hasn't been forgotten.

Chapter 15 A Trip to the Doctor

But I can still use it," I whine to Nick in defense of my hand. "I don't have time to go to the doctor. The boys start school on Tuesday. I'll just go then."

"My parents can come over and watch the boys, Joanie. That knot hasn't gotten any smaller, and you know it," Nick reminds me, kissing my hand on Sunday evening.

It's not a bad idea to get established at the family doctor's office. Dillon will soon be going there for his arm.

After another one-handed shower, I decide to call the doctor first thing Monday morning. Luckily for me, they have a spot open that very morning.

"Whip this place into shape for me, will ya?" I tease my in-laws on my way to the van. The boys are already dragging their grandparents to play with the chicks, something they have been doing for hours every day since we got them.

I love how I feel in my skinny jeans and red blouse that I haven't worn in ages. It's a nice change from the clothes that I swear looks like I've rolled in dirt all day. "This is my life now," I say teasingly, not missing the scrubs I wore almost daily.

I rush to the doctor's office with an underlying feeling of needing to get back to work. My projects seem to call to me at an audible hum, trying to woo me back to the decrepit house as a Siren calls to sailors. If I don't complete some projects soon, I'm afraid my brain will vibrate out of my head!

The office is tucked away in a corner of the downtown area. A community college is spread out at the end of the block. The size of the school surprises me with how small the town is. I pass a huge park that the boys would love and pull up to a one-story office that looks like it could have been a farmhouse once upon a time.

"Can I help you?" the receptionist asks as soon as I walk in. Her smile matches the bright décor of the office.

"I'm Joanie Nelson. I called this morning to be seen about my hand."

"Oh yes. Here are some papers to fill out," she says, handing me a clipboard. "Can you use your dominant hand?"

"Yes, it's the other hand that got hurt. Thank you for squeezing me in."

"No problem, Joanie," the young woman says warmly.

The waiting area is full of magazines and has a few televisions showing relaxing scenery. The piano streaming through the speakers has a drowsy effect on me. My eyes scan the list of symptoms and land on the word *fatigue*. I check the box next to it, feeling like I could nap on this couch. I'm lucky to be healthy and can skip past the health history section. I realize my denial when I ignore the question about my last menstrual cycle. I flip through my app and fill the answer out truthfully, still chalking it up to all the changes in my life. So far, I've ignored this little hiccup.

I don't have to wait long before a woman pops her head out a door and calls my name. I promptly stand and follow her to a cozy, clean exam room.

"We'll take a quick x-ray here," she says with pep. "Which hand is hurt?" she asks, looking from my right to my left, where her eyes stop on my purple bruise. "Ouch, that looks like it hurts. Can you move it?"

"I actually can, which is why I didn't get it checked out sooner. I figure it's not broken or anything if I can still move it, right?" I say, knowing I'll fail to persuade her not to take an x-ray.

"You could have a high pain tolerance," she says, expertly readying the X-ray equipment. "Or, it could be in a spot that isn't bothering anything else. Go ahead and sit here. Is there a chance that you could be pregnant?" she asks as a routine question.

I hesitate before answering, causing her to stop fiddling with the machine and look at my face. I grit my teeth together into a *maybe* type of smile and shrug my shoulders slightly.

"Oh," she responds, facing me. "Is that a yes?" she sings.

"It could be," I whisper.

"Would you like to take a test?" she asks in a whisper. I nod, and she flies into action, showing me to the bathroom.

This isn't exactly how I thought this appointment would go. It's a doctor's office, so I figured the question might come up. But it's my hand that's hurt, not anything that's even close to a reproductive organ.

After washing my hands four or five times, I nervously step out of the bathroom with the warm, embarrassing yellow cup in hand.

"Okay, let's try again," the young woman says, showing me back to the x-ray room. "We can still do this, but I'll use a different technique."

The one good thing about being seen for a hurt extremity is that you don't have to wear one of those thin gowns. As I wait for the doctor, I play "Would You Rather," wondering which news I want to hear first.

Would you rather have a broken hand or be pregnant?

Would you rather rebuild a house or be pregnant?

Would you rather have a boy or a girl?

This last one piques my interest.

Having a daughter would allow me to tap into my feminine side. Growing up, it was me and my brothers. I did everything with them. Everything I did was boyish: mucking stalls, playing ball with my brothers, riding horses, and running with the sheep in the field. Everyone called me Jon, and I loved it.

A soft knock on the door is followed by a woman about my age and an assistant in tow. She turns her head and gives me a smile that I try desperately to read.

The doctor sits her tall, thin frame on the stool before pushing a few buttons on the computer. Her trim body is a match to every runner I've ever met. "Joanie, it's nice to meet you. I'm Dr. Thompson. I hear you're new to Garden Valley," she says with an easy smile. Her brown hair is swept up in a messy bun, revealing simple gold hoops, an accessory that matches her forearm full of bracelets.

I'm nervous as hell, and it has nothing to do with my hand.

"We are. We've been here about a week," I reply. "And I already have the sourdough starter," I say, loving this icebreaker.

She laughs. "Looks like you've been inaugurated then. I'm glad you came in. It's good news; your hand is just bruised, I think," she says, using her ringless left hand to inspect my own. "There is a possibility of an undetectable hairline fracture in there. Give it a couple more days with ice and acetaminophen, and the swelling will decrease considerably. It's funny that pain can be caused by swelling, but once that goes down, it should start feeling better. Now, the other news," she says, looking into my eyes with her bright, beautiful blues.

I wait for her to continue, but the pause extends past the usual second or two. I lean forward slightly, waiting for her following words. "Yes?"

"Do you really not know?" she asks with a sideways glance and a squint.

"If I don't say it out loud, maybe it won't come true," I whisper, tears pricking my eyes.

"Well, I know we've just met, Joanie, but," she claps her hands and smiles, "you're pregnant."

I squeeze my tear-filled eyes closed, my most intimate secret splashed out in a way I can no longer ignore.

"I'm happy, really," I say through a few sobs.

"Did you not know?" she asks gently.

"I knew," I say with an angry tug at my jacket. "I mean, all the signs were there. Eating like a pig, feeling nauseous, tea tasting like turpentine." The doctor simply smiles back.

"Does your husband know yet?"

"No!" I say in a voice that comes out as a bark due to the crying. "I hadn't taken a test yet, even though I suspected. Nick has no idea I'm two weeks late."

"Do you think he'll be upset?" Dr. Thompson asks with a tilt of her head.

"Not at all. Nick loves babies," I say with a shake of my head before covering my face with my hands. "This is a horrible time for a pregnancy. I want this baby, don't get me wrong, but what am I going to do, put a play pin on the subfloor? Maybe the lack of drywall will allow him or her to climb the walls better. Dillon and Morgan would have loved that!" I snort, and the two ladies look at me like I'm crazy. "We just moved into a fixer-upper. How am I going to get everything done with a baby?"

"You're up on Tranquility Hill, aren't you?" the doctor asks innocently, looking at my paperwork. I nod, and she continues speaking as she wheels to the computer. "That's a beautiful place to raise a family."

Seriously, has the whole town been on a tour of my house? Do they all know we are living in a dump?

"If we all waited for the perfect time to have babies, our population would be in trouble," she says, handing me a note with the type of hand brace to buy. "Use caution if you start hurting, but you can moderately use your hand when doing your renovations," she says with a gleam in her eyes.

"Yeah, because I'm Ms. Fix It," I say sarcastically.

"Then what's the problem?" the doctor asks with one eyebrow higher than the other. I stare at her, not knowing how to answer. Dr. Thompson slaps her hands on her thighs and stands, ready to solve her next patient's problems. "Well, it was nice to meet you, Joanie. I look forward to seeing you for your prenatal checkups! My practice is for primary care, but I also specialize in obstetrics and gynecology."

"You must have been in school forever," I reply, gathering my purse and swallowing the frog in my throat.

"I was one of those child prodigies, so I got started early," she chuckles.

"Thank you, doctor," I laugh.

"And don't worry, your secret is safe with me. But I always find that the best relief is the honest one," she says with a wink before leaving the room.

I drive to the pharmacy in a daze.

What's the problem?

The question circles in my mind as my car seems to find a parking spot all on its own.

"What's the problem?" I repeat again.

I walk through the pharmacy aisles until I find the hand brace I need, wondering if I've been building a monstrous mountain with all my new experiences. Are these serious problems that I've been worked up over just mere bumps in this thing called life?

"Just this," I say a few minutes later, setting the brace on the counter before the cashier. She holds her hand up with an irritated expression while the other hand taps her headset. "Oh, sorry," I say, not realizing she's on the phone. The woman's eyes flare at me as if saying she can't believe I'm interrupting her again. She looks familiar, and though I want to study her face to connect the dots, our awkward encounter warns me this isn't a good idea.

I do my best not to analyze her from the outside, but what else am I supposed to do while I wait? A short hairstyle and thick red-rimmed glasses accentuate a pointy nose and thin lips. Sunken cheekbones and small shoulders indicate a petite person behind the tall counter that hides her body.

She says goodbye a moment later and begins to ring up my brace without a word. It hits me where I recognize her from: she was one of the ring leaders of the small rally outside the salon that day. I definitely don't want to bring up that connection!

"Sorry," I say again. "I didn't realize you were on the phone." More silence. Apparently, not everyone has taken a bite out of the Garden Valley sweetness. I perk up seeing her name tag, hoping this topic will help brighten her day. "Your name is Joan. I'm Joanie. Just add an 'E,' and you get me," I joke. Of course, it's dorky, but sometimes this knocks the chip off the other person's shoulder.

It doesn't work in this case.

"I'm hoping this will help with my home projects," I continue, holding my left hand up, thinking maybe she'll come to my side with a sliver of sympathy. I stand awkwardly and say thank you without a response. I'd love to say I'll never come here again, but I'm guessing this is the only pharmacy in town.

"What's the problem?" I ask with a small laugh, shrugging off this interaction on my way to Daisey's Hardware Store.

The biggest eyesores in the house are the walls that were knocked out between the kitchen and the living room and the wall in the foyer that obstructs the view of the house from the front door. I'll need to cut the walls out and smooth them out before finishing them, and to do that, I'll need a Sawzall. I had one in the past but sold it when I traded my toolbelt for scrubs.

I find the Sawzalls and pick one up with my good hand when a round man in a red vest approaches me. "Can I help you, ma'am?" He's only an inch or two taller than me and reminds me of a rosy-cheeked elf.

"I've found what I needed, thank you."

He hesitates. "Are you looking for a Father's Day gift?" It's a funny way of asking if this is for the man in my life. Father's Day is still over two months away.

"Nope, this is something I need."

"What will you be using it for?" he asks, flashing his cherub smile.

My shoulders beg to slouch, only I hoist them back. It's not like people mean to place women in one bucket and men in another. Men usually do the repairs. Still, I'm an expert with this power tool, and I *can* fix just about anything whether I'm out of practice or not.

What's the problem? I ask on repeat.

"I need to repair a wall that has only been knocked down halfway. Before I can put the drywall on it, I need to round out the edges. Actually," I say, stretching on my tip-toes to compare the tools, "I'll need something more powerful than this since I'll be cutting out whole sections of wall. I've inspected them, and there aren't any electrical wires in there, so it'll be fine. I haven't done drywall in a while, but I'm sure it's like riding a bike." The words rush out with a new spark of gumption and confidence. I'm buying a Sawzall!

I haven't been able to shrug the scent out of my nose since Nick showed me his scrap pile. It was the spark I needed that got the fire in my heart smoking. Now more than ever, a new, burning enthusiasm has set my soul ablaze. A determination to finish our house has come unleashed. With a garage full of premium tools and a house begging for my know-how, nothing can stop me now.

"Okay," the guy says with a quick shoulder shrug. He dives into the different models, explaining their usages, which I listen politely to, refraining from correcting a few of his slip-ups. I decide on the best, which is also the most expensive.

I text Nick, asking what my budget is for home repair tools and equipment.

For you, the sky is the limit. Nick

How's that for an open ticket?

Eighteen items and four hundred dollars later, I'm ready to tackle the world of dust and drywall that awaits me back home.

"What's the problem?" I repeat again once I'm unloading

the goodies into the van. I give myself a few beats before turning the key. I'm in a new town, a new house, and… I'm pregnant! I not only recognize this 'new' theme, I'm living it. And, at this moment, I'm ready to tackle it.

"Time to go *home*." I sit back with the impact of this word, liking the feeling of a positive view of my life. I don't have to rush through my projects. I can take my time, live in the house for a while, and explore my style. It's not like we're going to throw a God-awful party anytime soon. It sounds like the whole town has already been through my house anyway.

Driving through the historical part of town, I'm seeing this place through a different lens. A feeling of pride fills me as I pass by perfectly trimmed lawns and well-kept wooden and iron fences. Neighbors chat outside, and people walk their dogs down wide sidewalks. A farmer bales hay off in the distance, sending the smell wafting over the entire town. For the first time, it feels right to be here.

I pull up to my house, feeling less contempt for it than usual. I get to bring this place back to life! A feeling of ownership is slowly taking over. That happens once you've slept in a place for a few days. Your body quickly gets used to the sights and sounds, adopting it as your own with as much defense as a guard dog.

My eyes flash when I see the work my in-laws have done in the front yard. Even a stirring of the newly cleaned-up flower beds by the porch looks worlds better.

"I've only been gone for a couple of hours!"

"You know we love yard work. Phil has taken over our outdoor projects without consulting me," Marge says the last part while giving the evil eye to her husband.

"Must be where Nick got his 'take charge' attitude

from," I say in understanding.

"This place is a blank slate!"

"Feel free to do what you want. As you know, my specialty is *inside* the house, not out. I don't have much of a green thumb. With my left one being bandaged up for now, you can do all the yardwork you want." I give a rundown of the doctor's assessment, mindfully leaving out the day's biggest news.

"I'll help as much as you want. The only requirement I have is getting hugs from these two little monsters," she says, pulling Morgan to her as he and Dillon run by.

"I've been tackled by the kissing queen!" Morgan says, laughing as his grandma plants one on his cheek.

Dillon slows to a crawl before he gets to me, keeping his eyes glued to the brace strapped to my hand. "It already feels better with this on," I say, holding my hand up for inspection. "The doctor said it'll be much better in a few days."

"Is it broken like mine?" Dillon asks, his eyes pointed to the ground while his right hand attempts to scratch under his cast.

"No, it's not. Oh, and I liked the office," I say. "I made you an appointment for a couple weeks."

"Is that Valley Family Practice?" Marge asks as I pull Dillon in for a hug. I nod, and she continues about how much she likes the office and how long they've served everyone in Garden Valley. "Doctor Thompson took over the practice a few years ago when Doctor Meyers retired. She's from Eugene, a bigger town about forty-five minutes from here. It took her a while to be accepted."

Oh, goody.

"Well, come on! We need to play!" Morgan demands of his brother.

"I'm seeing if Mom's hand is okay," Dillon replies as he hides behind me.

"Hey!" Marge says, standing for authority. "We talked about this, Morgan. You don't own your brother. You need to *ask* him to play." Her voice stays calm but firm.

Morgan shifts his weight from one foot to another. "Dillon, I want to play with you. Please," he says between tight lips.

I look down into Dillon's pleading blue eyes, the only pair of his shade in the family. "Hey, Morgan, maybe you can help Grandma a little, and Dillon can help me bring everything in."

"Fine," Morgan says, stomping past Marge toward the back of the house.

"Let him be," Marge says. "I don't care if he's angry with me. The little stinker needs to be challenged every now and then. He's been on Dillon's case all day." The confrontation doesn't get under her skin one bit, something I take note of.

"What'd you get back here?" Phil asks, opening the back of the van. "Ooh, I've wanted this one for a while," he says, lifting the Sawzall and carrying it to the house. "Shall we get started on the walls?"

"Sure!" I say I am happy to have a partner, even if it is for the day. Heck, I'll take a half hour of help.

I barely grab a bag from the van when Dillon zips to my side to take it from me. "I'll help!" he says, grabbing another, balancing it on his cast.

"Okay, thanks," I say slowly.

When Phil and I start talking about our project, Dillon soon runs back outside to play with his brother. Our planning to saw at the wall is undoubtedly dull for a child, while my insides flare excitedly.

We have a plan in no time, with the kitchen wall marked where I want it to end. With our eyes shielded and earplugs in place, we power up my new tool. I use the utmost caution when cutting into the wall, with Phil standing back but watching with interest. I'll give him a turn once my left hand becomes achy, but I want to live in the moment of doing this work again.

It feels more than good to be back. I didn't know how much I've missed the instant gratification of working on projects like this. Within minutes, I'm yielding a noticeable difference.

I turn the tool off, bringing the room to silence. I stand back to view my work. "Perfect job, Joanie," Phil says with a pat on my back. When we lived in Fargo, we did quite a few of these jobs together and are familiar with each other's strengths and weaknesses.

"Thanks." I turn to the ugly wall in the foyer. "You're next, buddy." Phil laughs. "Do you have time to stay and help me knock it down?"

"Sure!" he says, his face lighting up as much as the boys' did when we got the chicks. Before he starts, he turns to me with that look of wisdom. "One day, you will look back on this house and be grateful that you didn't give up." He does this occasionally, stirs up a piece of advice, and can deliver it in one thought-provoking sentence.

The cutting doesn't take long, and we finish in under an hour. "It's the drywall that will take a while," I say gloomily, not particularly liking this task.

"You never have liked that, have you?" Phil says with a laugh.

"It's a messy job," I say, preparing our supplies.

"I don't mind taking the lead if you'll be my assistant,"

Phil offers.

I accept, happy that I spent the time and money to purchase all the supplies necessary for us to check this big one off the list. We spend the rest of the afternoon zipping through the processes, chatting along the way.

"Looks darn good!" Phil assesses.

"It sure does," I say, noting the room's openness with the two wall portions missing.

This confidence is one I haven't felt in a while and one I welcome. Slowly but surely, this house will come together. My previous doubt melts away, though it's replaced with something bigger, something that really does have a stringent timeline. Soon, baby number three will join the Nelson family.

Chapter 16 A Day on My Own

What's the problem?

The question has circled my mind dozens of times since Dr. Thompson stitched it there. Before we moved, I thought the problem would be that I'm unemployed. This has actually been a solution to my problems. With the boys starting school today and my left hand feeling like it's on the mend, I can dig in and start making progress.

What's the problem? My attitude has been the problem! Well, that and the monster secret I'm keeping from my husband. Sooner or later, I'll have to tell Nick I'm carrying baby number three. As for now, I'm not ready to shift my focus, not when I've finally come to terms with my new fate.

My morning walks give me a moment of silence, allowing my brain to slow down. I've been able to plan my days on my walks, slowly formulating a strategy instead of frantically attacking my day.

A noise on my walk cuts into the cadence of my feet crunching on the rocks. My heart jumps into my throat and nearly has me sprinting back to the house until I see the gray cat again.

"You again," I say with a pant as my heart rate decreases. The cat meows and arches her back as she walks to me. She flows between my ankles, rubbing her sides against my jeans. I bend to pet her, my fingers feeling clumps of gray fur.

"Poor thing. Do you have a home around here?"

She meows back. My hands run over the bones that are masked by her thick fur. "I don't speak 'cat,' but I can see you need food!" The cat silently follows me back to the house as my feet crunch against the rocks. "Stealthy, aren't you?"

"Walton?" The strange voice rings from above, turning my gaze to the sky.

"Not you again! Keep flying, buddy," I scold, quickening my pace so the bird won't land on my shoulder.

The cloud overhead releases its contents just before we get to the house. The sun gleams through the raindrops and sends a rainbow across the sky. My plot of land and the valley beyond is a picturesque scene that is an artist's dream.

It's like the town is begging for my approval. I shake my head lightly and roll my eyes. I'm not yet ready to demolish the wall between this town and me and fully accept this new life.

"A little at a time, okay?" The cat meows back in a way that says she understands. The sound of my laughter hits me. Besides the few tears I shed at the doctor's office, I haven't cried here like I used to in Fargo.

"That's strange for this Cancer sign." The town and all the shifts that have come with it have replaced the crying and hopeless feeling I used to ignore.

The cat saunters into the laundry room as if I'm opening it for her. I laugh and allow it for now. I pull the leftover chicken out of the refrigerator and throw a few pieces to the stray before soothing my insatiable stomach. At least now I have an answer for my extra hunger. The cat wolfs the chicken down before licking her lips in approval.

"I guess now that I've fed you, I should give you a name. I've never been good at naming things, you know." I put the chicken back, seeing the name Dahlia on one of the containers. "That's a pretty name. How about Dahlia?" The cat meows in approval as I scratch behind her ears.

Soon, I'll have someone else to name.

I stand and dust my pants off, pretending to shrug this obstacle away as if it's one of the specks of dirt on my jeans. I know full well that I'll have to face this issue, but I need time to process it for a few days.

I start on a breakfast of cheesy eggs and toast, loving the sound of the rain as it taps a soothing song on the bay window.

I move freely in the kitchen now, having organized the cabinets to my liking, even though every door needs to be redone. I sneak glances through the window, drinking in the scenery that turns my dish duty to one of luxury. Well, almost.

An argument upstairs trickles down with the boys when they finish getting ready. This first morning of school feels different from our carefree weekend. I pray that they'll be good and adopt new habits as I am.

They trudge downstairs with shirts halfway tucked in, messy hair, and school bags strung haphazardly around their shoulders. "It *is* my folder. Mom bought it for me," Morgan shouts, shoving his little brother.

"Hey, what's going on?" I turn off the eggs and give the kids my full attention. I take another tip from Cinda and crouch to be at their level. "You know," I say, straightening Dillon's collar first and then fixing Morgan's hair, "I would always throw up on the first day of school. This isn't your first day of the year, but it is for this school."

"Ew," the boys say in unison, their typical response to puke.

"Yup, and then I'd do this to everyone." I open my mouth and blow out air as people do when they want others to smell their breath. My fictitious joke works to snap them from their funk. "Who wants toast and cheesy eggs?" I ask, with a trot to the kitchen. The gray cat follows my every move, bringing the boys' attention to her.

"It's the cat!" Dillon says, falling to his knees to pet her. Morgan follows suit. My parents used to distract my brothers and me with enough animals and chores so we would forget about our petty arguments. At the moment, it's working wonders for my boys.

"She followed me in."

See, it's not hard to add to the family, Joanie taunts my inner voice.

"You're sweet, aren't you?" Morgan says in his animal tone.

"It seems like there are more animals in this town," Dillon observes. It's funny how I agree with his statement. Since we've been here, I've seen my fair share of four-legged friends.

And then there's that pesky-winged friend who keeps calling me Walton.

"I've never had an animal adopt me before. You two don't count," I say with a slight shove to Morgan's shoulder.

"Are you calling us animals?" he replies in shock.

I give him an exaggerated sniff and pull back with a pinch to my nose. "It sure smells like a zoo in here." I tousle his hair and jump away when he playfully reaches for me. His smile indicates he understands my teasing.

"What should we name him?" Dillon asks.

"I think 'he's' a girl, and I've already done that," I say proudly. "I've always liked the name Dahlia."

"Ooh, that's pretty," Morgan says, uncharacteristically.

"I guess that works," Dillon says with a twist to his face. He crouches closer to Dahlia and meows. The cat arches her back and saunters away from him. "Did I say something offensive?" he asks seriously.

Morgan and I laugh. "Maybe she likes her name and is upset that you don't."

"I take it back! I like it!" Dillon says, chasing after Dahlia and scooping her in his arms. The cat obliges and rolls her head under his chin. It's new for me to see the sweetness in my boys. They've had my heart in a vice for years, and it feels good to have finally found the keys to loosen its grip.

"This is a good breakfast, Mom," Morgan says after I serve their meal. It's one of his only compliments regarding the meals I've made.

"Thank you," I reply, noting the beagle figurine beside his plate.

"With five chicks, we'll soon make quiches and anything else with eggs as the main ingredient," I say, remembering the information we researched over the weekend. It all came back to me, how I would reach under the hens to steal their eggs. Growing up we always had a basket of fresh eggs on our counter.

"It'll be a feast every day!" Morgan comically shouts, holding his beagle in the air.

"Ew, I don't want to eat a feast," Dillon says in disgust, sticking the end of his fork down his cast.

"A feast is a big meal, stupid," Morgan says rudely.

I'm being tested by his remark, something I don't let pass by me this time. I squish my lips together and give him the same stare that Cinda gave her boys when I first met her. Morgan slows his eating, glances at the dog figurine, and then looks at his brother.

"What did you think I said?" Morgan asks. It worked! I didn't have to be mean!

"A feast," Dillon responds.

"Yeah, but what do you think it *means*?" Morgan asks as I return to the kitchen for my own meal.

"You know, one of those birds we see with the funny mohawk on their heads." Dillon fans out his hand and clumsily puts it on his head. Morgan and I share another laugh behind our smiles.

"You're thinking of a pheasant," I say, wanting to inhale my eggs.

"Yeah, pheasant," Dillon says like there's nothing unusual about this conversation. "What were you talking about?"

"Feast," Morgan answers with another laugh. He adds a description of what it means. It feels as though we've been doing this for years, having these easy conversations over breakfast. I bask in the glory of connecting with them, proof that it's never too late unless you give up hope.

Twenty minutes later, I shuttle the boys out the door. "Look, it's grandma! Is she doing yardwork again?" Morgan asks with his face mimicking my surprise.

"She is! Marge, what are you doing here so early?" I ask with a laugh as I shout out of the car window.

"I'm glad I didn't disturb you, Joanie. I've been here since the sun came up. I'm getting my greenery fix. You said you don't mind..."

"And I don't! Have at it!" I saw quickly before waving goodbye.

I can practically feel the boys' nerves in the back seat as I drive them to school. "I got an email on Friday with your teacher assignments. Cinda said that Justin and Adam are in your classes with you. Isn't that great? You will already know someone at school!"

"And I'll probably see Lucas, the kid from the grocery store," Dillon remembers, perking up. "Hey, maybe the kids will want to sign my cast!"

"If there's room on it," Morgan responds. He has filled several spots on the cast with his drawings. My kids play well together and show each other love like this.

Maybe I haven't completely failed in the mom department.

"How's your hand, Mom?" Dillon asks. I've kept it in my lap while I drive to give it as much rest as possible before I begin working on the house.

"It's great. Getting better every day, honey." It's only a little lie. It still aches quite a bit when I use it too much or grip something too tightly, but I'm not about to tell him that.

The school is nestled in acres of farmland, giving it the feel of being part of the country. We find the neighbor boys in a heartbeat, with Cinda bouncing her baby by the line of kids waiting for their teachers to gather them.

The boys allow me to walk them to their lines instead of shrugging me off like they did at their last school. "You're going to have a great day," I say, allowing my arms to rest on their shoulders. It's the first time they've relied on me for comfort since they were toddlers.

"Hey there, neighbor," Cinda says with her ever-present smile. She's adorable in a pair of jean capris with a light blue flowery top. I return my smile, having connected with her and her parenting skills.

"Good morning."

"The boys seem settled already," she says, rocking the

baby girl strapped to her middle. She points her chin their way as all the kids mingle. She reminds me of how my hands were always full of baby bottles, toys, diapers, clothes, or the baby himself.

I'm reminded by how demanding Morgan was as a baby. He had colic for eight months and cried for hours every day. The crying stopped the minute he started crawling, but then he was literally climbing on everything, including the blinds! How will I complete any projects around the house when I'll have a baby to care for?

"Look at this cutie!" I use my index finger to tickle the little girl, who coos and wiggles. I can't tear my eyes away from her, remembering the wonderful feel of a squishy baby. It all seems easy for Cinda, even with four kids. It's yet another thing I want to steal from her. With Marge here and my parenting skills growing stronger, it's no wonder the boys have been easier to handle.

"The boys told me you got chicks."

"We did! They've been fun so far. The boys run outside every morning to feed them and make sure they're warm enough. It's been a great way to give them responsibility."

"Mine need that discipline, too. They'd get into trouble if they didn't have the farm," she laughs.

"I'm seeing a change for the better." It's a twist from my original thinking about this move. I hadn't thought about raising a family on a farm. We were just getting through the days before, trying to get everything checked off the list. Surviving. "This is my first day to myself in God-knows-how-long. Well, I guess with the boys playing outside most of the time, I've already gotten more alone time than in the last seven years combined."

"What's that like?" she asks with a laugh.

"It's weird, for sure. I've always thought of myself as clingy since I've hated how many hours Nick worked. I've barely noticed our time apart this last week. Maybe I needed more of my own thing to keep me occupied."

"I always believe that behind a successful relationship are two people who have their own interests," Cinda remarks lightly. "Look at Dillon showing that kid how to tie his shoes even with his broken arm. He sure is sweet."

I look at her with a pause, and she laughs. It's one of the only times someone has said this about Morgan and Dillon. "Sweet?"

"Yeah, they were good at our house the other day. They shoveled dinner in their mouths like there was no tomorrow, but Dillon was polite when asking for more."

"Dillon was?"

"Don't be so surprised," she laughs. "You're doing a great job, Mom." She touches my arm to drive the compliment home. It seems typical for her, but it nearly brings me to tears.

I hesitate with my next question, not wanting to sound like a loon. "I know this is off-topic, but have you, um, ever heard of the house we're in being haunted?"

"Haunted? No. Are you seeing something spooky?" she asks, as if on the edge of her seat.

"More like hearing something. I probably just need to get used to all the sounds this house makes. It's pretty old and rundown," I say, my voice brushing this off more than my insides can.

"Maybe you'll stumble on what it is with your renovations. Hey, have you thought more about doing a project for me? I found exactly what I'm after on Pinterest." I was going to work on the house today, but maybe doing something fun initially is a good place to start. "Here are the end tables. And I came across this ottoman with storage inside." She turns her phone to show me the picture.

"That's a great idea. Why waste all that hollow space?"

"Right?" I hesitate, not ready to tackle her request. It must read on my mind since she continues. "It's just a suggestion. Don't feel obligated at all."

I wince, hating my transparency. "It's not that, really. It's just that I haven't built anything in so long, especially for anyone else. I always make some kind of mistake, and..."

"Stop right there," she says with her hand in a stop sign position. "If you think I'm after perfection, you're dead wrong. Don't you remember the distressed look of my house? Please, make mistakes; it's kind of the theme in every Garden Valley home I've seen and is what I'm after!" she laughs.

This pep talk kicks my butt into gear. "I guess it won't hurt to take a stab at it." The boys wave goodbye, and my eyes tear up as if it's the first day of kindergarten. Cinda texts me her ottoman pictures before we part and wish each other a good day.

As I drive home, I feel a calling to work in the shop instead of diving into the house projects on my list. Marge is down by the barn with a weed whacker when I pull into the driveway. "Have at it," I say, looking at the house with a disconnected feel.

I stay in the car for a few moments, staring at the house with panic. It appears abandoned from the outside, with white chipped paint, missing roof tiles, and a front yard that consists mainly of mud. And that's after Marge and Phil have put hours in.

I exit the car without a positive word in sight. It's not a

'feel sorry for myself' thought as much as the dozen pages in my notebook with tasks to be completed.

I dodge the side door, heading for the back garage instead. It's a place I previously didn't want to visit, but I'm currently using it as a refuge.

I start gathering my supplies for Cinda's projects, hoping this will soothe my racing mind. I sketch out the pieces of furniture based on Cinda's pictures, taking my time with the measurements. I pick through the wood piles I brought home from Nick's work. There is almost enough for Cinda's design as long as the grubby pieces sand down into something beautiful.

I put my protective glasses on and start the planer to discover how much I can salvage. As soon as I put the wood in the planar, it shoots out of my hands and hits the back wall with a loud thud. I must not have my angle quite right.

"Okay, maybe that's not the best way to start," I say, vowing never to tell anyone about this rookie mistake. I measure and cut several pieces down to size, really getting into the project for a couple of hours.

I'm bopping to the music when I realize I've had the whole thing backward. The wood pieces that are supposed to be long are short, and my short ones will no longer work. "Darn it! What the heck is wrong with me?" It wasn't like this when I worked on my chair the other day.

After another hour, I hate everything I've put together for Cinda's project. It's the opposite of Midas' touch; everything I've touched has turned to rust. I look at my hands, wondering if someone has cursed them.

I keep trying, wiping my eyes throughout the day, barely giving myself time for lunch or bathroom breaks. I'm determined to have something to show from the work I've done. I can generally whip through a project and have progress to show at the end of a session.

Luckily, the logical side of my brain kicks in, and I step outside for a breather, thankful that Dahlia is here. Her presence alone is helping me skirt a mini-fit for my lack of skills.

A glance at the chicken coop brings back my irritation. It's one the biggest eye sores on the property. "That's it!" I say, hopping in the van twenty seconds later.

Within minutes, I'm at the home improvement store, a place that's like an amusement park for me. I stomp through the parking lot with a goal in mind when my eye catches on the various gravel choices piled on the pavement. This would look great in the area surrounding the coop.

I continue inside, passing a section of tarps. I could throw one down in the back of the van and put a load of gravel in there. A few minutes later I throw a shovel into the mix since I haven't seen one at the house. One thing leads to another, and I am soon on my way home, my van weighed down by a load of gravel. I smile at the windshield, my good hand gripping the wheel.

"I can do this!" Luckily, I didn't spend more than a couple of hours on Cinda's project before giving up. I have plenty of time to switch gears and make something of this day.

Marge isn't there when we get back, but I can see her progress. A sense of accomplishment overcomes me, fueling my ambition to shovel the gravel all on my own. The fenced-off muddy area around the chicken coop is about a thousand square feet. It's quite a big area to cover, one heaping wheelbarrow at a time.

"It's not nearly enough," I say to Dahlia when I see how

my first load barely covers the ground in the sizeable fenced-off area. "Didn't I see…" I run to the side of the back garage, laying eyes on a medium-sized trailer that will work perfectly for my next load.

I'm hooking the trailer up when I receive a text from Nick.

What do you say we have a dinner party for the people at work in a couple of weeks?

Seriously, this again?

I don't think it's a good idea. How about we wait at least six months? I answer via text. I wait a few moments, brooding on the possibility that Nick has made yet another decision without me. *What aren't you telling me?*

I might have invited everyone over on the thirtieth. Nick sends the message with that 'yikes' emoji, the one where the guy looks like he's in trouble, which he totally is!

"What the hell!" I yell, angrily kicking the ground and flinging several pieces of gravel across the yard. I hate that Nick has put this kind of pressure on me. What is he thinking, inviting people over to the house already?

"Hello?" hollers a voice from my driveway, interrupting my fit. I peek over the car's roof to find a familiar but unwanted face heading my way.

"Yes, I'm over here," I answer back.

"There you are." Alice walks towards me with an oversized purple dress flowing behind her. She was a bit pushy when I met her the first day we were here, and I remember her from the rally. She's all smiles, putting me on guard for a two-faced meeting. "Remember me? I'm Alice."

"Of course," I reply. I bite my lip, wondering if I should weave myself into the game she started. "I think you were part of the heckling squad at the hair salon."

"I'm sorry about that, Joanie. We aren't against newcomers, just new housing developments."

"Well, the boys were scared nonetheless." It's not like me to dish out bitterness, but she's the one who showed up holding her plate out for seconds.

"How is your family liking Garden Valley so far? Your husband works at the mill, right?" I stare in surprise, wondering if she also knows what we had for breakfast. I hesitate with my answer. Lumber mills aren't exactly loved by all, and I have no idea what her standing is amongst her group.

"He does. The town is growing on me," I say with a truthful nod. "I'm taking advantage of the nice weather. I hope to get a lot done," I say curtly, hustling the wheelbarrow to the back garage so I can get back to the hardware store for another load of gravel.

The black crow picks this time to join our conversation. He swoops down and confidently lands on Alice's shoulder. The woman doesn't share my flinched reaction.

"Walton?" the bird says in that throaty voice.

"Well, hello, Sheldon. Have you come to meet Joanie?" Alice asks, giving the bird a pat on his head. The bird turns his head this way and that to get the scratch in just the right spot. It's a sweet display, but his unblinking yellow eyes keep my guards up.

"Oh, we've met," I say between clenched lips.

"Of course you have. Sheldon likes to scour the neighborhood and keep watch over everyone."

I wonder where he got that from. I can't help but smile at the thought. Luckily, Sheldon flies away, taking his creepiness with him.

"How about a house tour?" she says, boldly starting for

the house. I run ahead, hoping to stop her before she reaches the doorknob.

"I'm sorry, Alice, it isn't a good time. I'm all geared up to go back to Daisey's for more gravel. Maybe you can come back once I have completed more of the inside. You understand…"

"Fine, I'll get out of your hair," she says, lifting her chin in judgment. "I'm sure your list is a mile long."

"Ten miles," I say with a smile to curtail my track to her bad side.

I wave Alice goodbye and hop in my van to return to the hardware store. I shake my arms out after the conversation that gave me the same kind of willies as Sheldon does. I'm hardly after starting a fight. Still, I don't see what's wrong with an innocent family moving to town and fixing up one of the rundown houses here.

I turn the music up in the car to drown out the thoughts that want to engulf me. My leisurely to-do list got hundreds of degrees hotter, with all the tasks demanding to be completed before the party.

"Stupid party," I mutter to my steering wheel. "Stupid Nick." I roll my shoulders, pretending I'm rolling with the punches instead of putting up a fight. This is usually my 'go-to,' and it's grown as old as the willow tree I pass.

"Running errands again, huh?" the man at the register asks when he rings up yet another load of gravel.

"Errands?" I ask. Of course, I know what he is referring to. My facetious side makes him squirm as he thinks through his remark.

"Oh, I figured you're getting another load of gravel for your husband," he says, flicking his eyes to the diamond on my left hand.

"Nah. My first load wasn't nearly enough, so I'm back for another."

"Getting your feet wet, huh?"

I laugh and shift my weight with my hand on my hip. "Sir, I'm so experienced with this that I'm drenched from head to toe."

"You're doing this yourself?" he asks in surprise, tipping his hat up. He resembles my grandpa with straight salt and pepper hair in a braid down his back. It makes me wonder if he can do as mean of a stomp dance as ol' gran papa.

"Yup." It's a one-word answer that I hope will make him realize that a woman can shovel gravel the same way a man can.

"That's awesome. Sorry, I mostly see men in this store. My wife is just like you and can outrun me any day of the week. Keep me posted about your progress, will ya, young lady?"

"I will," I reply, happy that he called himself out. I honestly don't mind when people make this type of comment, figuring it's an oversight on their part. Still, I'm the one doing the work, and I want the credit.

I load up and make my return trip home, picturing myself creating a rut in the road from these trips to the hardware store.

I can't wait another minute before talking to Nick about this ridiculous dinner idea. Instead of sending texts that sound as sweet as a love message, I click his name.

"Hi, honey," he answers in that sort of exaggerated happy voice that people do when they know they're in trouble.

"You better have that tone of voice," I snap. "What the heck? We are *not* ready for a party, Nick."

"I know!" Nick whispers as if he's trying to keep from being heard. "Joanie, I didn't bring it up. Everyone here is curious about our home and invited themselves over."

"Then tell them it's not happening!" I demand.

"Oh, it's happening. I don't think you understand the Garden Valley crowd."

"I understand that they want to be nosey and determine if we belong here. It's *our* house. Tell them they aren't invited."

"It's not like that. They want to give us a housewarming party to welcome us. They've been talking about coming over since before you and the boys got in town, but I've kept them at bay until this morning. They pulled up their calendars and coordinated it while I was in the back of the crowd, jumping up and down to get their attention. They say they'll bring all the food," Nick says as if this solves the problem.

"You aren't serious about this, are you?"

"I don't know what else we can do? Honey, I'm sorry, but my boss just got here, and I need to show him the progress of our new glue line machine. Sorry, Joanie, we'll talk about it later. Love you, bye."

Apparently, this housewarming party is a done deal. *What's the problem?*

"Everything!" I shout, using my sleeve to wipe the familiar tears as they streak down my face.

Chapter 17 The Tractor

I don't allow the failure of my first day alone derail me. The next couple of days, I quickly get into the swing of things, moving as quickly as I can. The ever-present pressure of the housewarming party builds like an Instant Pot in the background.

Putting my furniture-making ambitions on hold was a good decision, especially since I botched Cinda's project so badly. Instead, I've been unpacking and doing regular daily chores. The house finally shows progress, especially since I've scrubbed out that dusty smell.

I speed-walk to the garage to grab a screwdriver and pass the trailer full of gravel that I abandoned days ago. I pause, pondering whether or not I should allow myself this break from working inside. "Why not?" I say with determination, getting the wheelbarrow.

I shovel gravel in the coop in the sunshine until my muscles are sore. I find it amusing how interested the chicks are, pecking and following me around the yard.

"So much better!" I say with an elated tone. I'm returning the wheelbarrow when I spot the supplies for painting the coop. "Why not?" I repeat, making two trips to take everything outside. On my last trip in the garage, a blue tarp in the back corner catches my eye. I pull back the tarp and discover, "A tractor?" I say with amazement.

I pull out my phone and type a message to Nick.

Did you know that we have a tractor in the garage? Joanie

Yes! I completely forgot. That came with all the other stuff. Nick

Stuff? Joanie

Yes, that's my technical term. The guy who sold us the house said it needs a new fuel pump or something. Other than that, it should be good to go. I wonder if we can find someone to fix it. Nick adds a laughing emoji to his text.

I still have three hours until I pick the boys up today. And just like that, I'm derailed from my original plan of organizing the boxes upstairs and am sucked into the curiosity of the tractor, wondering how I missed this gem.

I scrounge around in the garage and let out a holler when I find a brand-new fuel pump. The person who previously lived here must have been a Jack of all trades like I am. "Joan of all trades," I say, copying what my brothers used to call me when they realized I had more of a knack for fixing things than they did.

Luckily, the side door is next to where the tractor was parked, and I use all my might to push it outside to work on it in the sunshine. I lug the tool chest next to me and throw a pad down to lie on. Dahlia joins me not a minute later and, in perfect cat fashion, pokes around in the tool chest, eventually lying between my knees. Her purrs are soothing, and I'm happy to have her company.

I'm deep into my project when I hear a loud noise that sounds like someone is throwing a brick in a bucket. I sit up straight, pointing my eyes towards the back of the house. Dahlia darts away and hides behind a bush, something I wish I could do.

"What in the heck was that?" I stand with my ears open, slowly removing my gloves as a stalling tactic. I don't want to check this out, but hearing the noise again has me jogging to the house. "Hey! Who are you?" I shout in my most stern voice, wondering if Marge is here again.

I turn the corner of the house only to see an empty pathway to the front door. While I've been wondering if these noises were in my imagination, this time, I'm certain I heard something. My ears even pricked up at the sound. "Did you hear that?" I ask Dahlia, trailing behind me. Her tail swishes, and I take this as her answer that she heard it, too.

After an inconclusive investigation, I return to the tractor with adrenaline coursing through my body. I tighten a few bolts and stand again. "There," I say, wiping my hands on my work pants. I turn the key and… nothing. I turn it again and get a little rumble. The third time is the trick, bringing the eighty-five horsepower tractor rumbles to life.

"There she is," I say with satisfaction and pride. I've told myself I've been falling short in many areas for years. I now wonder if it's because I gave up trying for them. It's not like someone was keeping me from doing my tinkering or woodworking. I just never added them to my schedule.

I allow the tractor to idle its way to familiar grounds as my eyes scan the field. Growing up, I hated working outside, except for mowing the field. Project after project awaits me inside, yet I'm craving the smell of freshly cut grass. "Stay here, Dahlia," I instruct.

This job will be a whiz, with this gem of a tractor gliding through the tall grass. A glance at my watch shows that I have over an hour before I need to pick the boys up. "Let's see how she does," I say, putting the green machine in gear.

This land initially scared me, yet the smell ignites happy memories from childhood. I take one deep breath after another, closing my eyes for a moment. I open them with delight shining through as I look over my land and house. For the first time, I feel a sense of panic that the house sale will fall through. I make a mental note to check on things with the bank.

After what seems like only a few minutes of mowing, my phone vibrates with a call from the school. "Hello?" I say after turning the tractor off.

"Hello, is this Joanie Nelson?" I try to gauge from the tone of the voice if all is well or if the entire school is already done with the boys.

"It is," I reply in a sinking voice.

"This is Principal Merrill. I'm sorry to report that Dillon has been running around the school most of the day. It took us almost an hour to get a hold of him. He acted like a wild animal locked in a cage for a while but has calmed down and is back in his classroom."

"I'm so sorry. You should have called me earlier."

"We really try to resolve these issues on our own. All is fine now, but I wanted to see if we can meet regarding Dillon and Morgan's behavior."

"Morgan, too?" I ask. It's not surprising that both my boys are causing problems at school.

"Unfortunately. Do you have time to come in today about a half hour before school gets out?"

***

I clean myself up with a familiar yet unwanted disappointment. It's embarrassing to send my boys to school to wreak havoc on others. And now I'm bringing baby number three into the world.

I look out over our half-mowed field on my way to the school. "Darn it!" I say, hating the reason for being interrupted. The behavior problems have followed us all the way to Garden Valley.

I've never been able to control the boys. I've tried to stick to punishments, but their personalities outweigh my own. They bulldoze their way over my wishes… just as Nick did with this move.

My phone buzzes with a message from Cinda. *I can't wait!* A few seconds later, she sends another text with a photograph of a fancy invitation to a dinner party at our house only two weeks from today.

"Two weeks?" I say as I check the calendar. Nick told me the date, but it has snuck up on me with my days of unpacking flying by.

The clock is ticking, and I've been messing around with tractors and chicks!

My worries are never-ending on my drive to the school. Sitting in the principal's office brings me back to the handful of times I've wound up here pleading my case about trying but failing to enforce the rules. The principal is nice enough to greet me with a smile, yet the list of Dillon's misdemeanors is similar to the one in Fargo.

"Can I offer a suggestion?" the principal asks, moments later when I'm in her office.

"It wouldn't hurt. I feel like I've tried everything," I say, throwing my hands up in defeat. Emotions well in my chest and I curl my lip into my mouth to hold the tears back.

She leans towards me for effect. "Try showing them your emotion."

My eyes widen, wondering if she can see through my tough exterior. "They know I'm upset. I've yelled, I've threatened, I've grounded them, I've taken away sugar."

"I mean, try crying."

"Crying?"

"I know it sounds manipulative, but that's what happened with me," she laughs. "My boys were *so* much like yours, pushing buttons, getting into trouble. I let them get away with it for years, so there were plenty of pent-up tears."

"I'm always on the verge of tears. Or, at least, I was before we moved here."

"Boys and men hate to see women cry. It's only a suggestion. Morgan and Dillon aren't bad, Joanie, but I wanted to let you know what's happening. We're strict at this school but work with the children and parents as much as possible."

"Thank you for that. This isn't a surprise, unfortunately. You've told me about Dillon. How is Morgan doing? He tends to be bossy."

"I'll say," the principal says with a laugh. "The first time I met him, he said we should put the garbage cans outside our classrooms at the end of the day to make it easier for the custodians."

"Oh my gosh. I'm sorry."

"Actually, it was a great idea! We've been doing it, and Harv, our custodian, says he has sped through that task now. His teacher, Mr. Horton, immediately caught on to this trait. He had the brilliant idea of putting Morgan in charge of a reading group."

"Really? Did that work?"

"It sure did. He's advanced with his reading, and he helps his peers. He has strong leadership qualities, Joanie. He just needs to have an outlet to direct them."

"I've been wondering if he's been like this because he

felt like he needed to take over the parental duties for Dillon. Nick and I worked so much that it probably felt natural for him to somewhat step into a parent role."

"People are who they are," she says softly. "Sometimes they come into the world as natural leaders. That's what I see in Morgan. You should have seen his eyes light up when we told him about the student senate. It was just this morning. He's already gathered all of the signatures needed in record time. He liked the idea of coming up with rules."

The sound of my laughter loosens my death grip on my purse strap. "I bet he does. It sounds like they are in good hands here. Please let me know if there's anything I can do." I was nervous to come in here, but having someone on my side instead of being scolded does wonders for my bruised parenting ego.

"We have a PTO meeting coming up soon if you're interested in joining," she offers. "Maybe your involvement in the school will be good for the boys."

"You're right." I nod, knowing I have time in my schedule. "I think I will."

I wait for the boys to get out of school, my disappointment mixing with a plan. Morgan waltzes out the front doors when the final bell rings. His two fingers are hooked into his jacket draped over his shoulder. "Bye, guys." He says casually to two friends.

"See ya, Morgan," they answer.

He has always been quick to make friends. His popularity from school spilled over into a boosted ego back home and has followed us here.

"I still have my beagle," he says, holding the dog in the air when he sees me. I nod but keep quiet. "We saw frogs on the playground," he starts. "It was really cool. The kids at my last school would have stomped on them, but everyone here saved them!"

Morgan's storytelling of his day, instead of grunting one-word answers, is world's different, but things still need to change. The three of us file into the car, with me wondering how this drive will go.

"Dillon, you stink! Are those Cheetos still in your cast?" Morgan asks.

"It's the perfect hiding spot! I can pull one out if I get hungry during the day. See?" Dillon boasts with a demonstration.

"Then you eat them from the bag, not the stuff you've put in your cast," Morgan instructs.

"Lunch was gross today! They had beans with yogurt on top!" Dillon yells in surprise. Neither boy has acknowledged that I have yet to say a word.

"You sure are a Dill. It was chili with sour cream," Morgan laughs, glancing at me to see if I'm joining him.

"No, it was yogurt. I had a sandwich and chocolate milk instead. It was okay." I glance in the rearview mirror and briefly connect my eyes with Morgan.

"Are you okay, Mom?" he asks.

I hesitate at first with the fear of crushing their bad moods from the day. Not long ago I would hardly get a three-word phrase from the boys about their day, now they are sharing small details with me.

I muster up the confidence to embark on this new technique. If I can fix up the house, I can fix our family.

It doesn't take much to tap into the years of pent-up frustration and feelings of failure. A single tear drifts down my face, paving the way for many to follow. The one tear quickly builds into a steady flow with real sobs. The boys look at each other behind me as I pull over on an unfamiliar street.

"I just don't know what else to do, boys. Morgan, you've continued your bossy ways even though we've asked you to stop being the one in charge. I'm glad you've found the student senate, but you need to work *with* the group, not be in charge of it, young man. And Dillon!"

I pause to blow my nose, the boys' eyes as big as saucers. I continue, now unable to stop my rant.

"I don't understand why you can't grow up a little! I'm not asking you to be an adult, but running around the school with your shoes and socks off? Really? You're not three anymore! You're more than twice that age and making the lives of the people around you hard. Is that how you want to be? Do you want to go back to preschool with all the little children running around, standing on desks, and acting like wild monkeys? I was in the principal's office today, just like in Fargo."

My voice chokes, putting my tongue lashing to a stop. I return to our route with the quietest van we've ever had. I don't like operating in a way to control others with shame. At the same time, this might be the missing link to get through to them if they know how they are affecting me.

I dash into the house before the boys can open the sliding door. I'm sure they think that I am thoroughly upset, but I have to pee something fierce!

"Mom, are you okay?" Morgan asks from my bedroom a moment later. Of course, it's Morgan. That kid isn't afraid to confront anyone about anything, even though he just got chewed out. I stay quiet, wash my hands, and find the boys playing on my bed. They stop the second they see me, their eyes glued to mine, no doubt observing the red puffiness that follows a good cry.

"I just want you to *try* not to cause problems. We're in a new town. We have a new start. Neither of you has to allow those bad behaviors to follow us here." I raise my arms and allow them to slap against my legs in near defeat.

I look at Dillon, hoping to get some kind of commitment to be a little better. He looks at Morgan first and then at me. "I'll try," he says weakly.

"That's all I'm asking for, not perfection."

The words look me straight in the face, demanding to be understood and applied to my life. Why on earth would I expect perfection out of my work? I know darned well that trying to be good enough is, well, good enough.

"Come here," I say, holding my arms out. To my surprise, the boys gently get off the bed and come in for a tight squeeze. I bend down, thread my forearms under their armpits, and swing them in a circle. The boys giggle, and a big portion of the hole they've dug over the years is filled.

"Hey, what's that green thing out in the yard?" Dillon asks, breaking the silence.

"It's a tractor, Dill-weed," Morgan laughs. "Can you believe this guy?" he says to me with a thumb pointed at his brother.

"Yes, I can believe it. Not everyone grew up on a farm like mom did."

"You grew up on a farm?" Dillon asks, sitting up on his knees.

"Yes, stupid, it was at Grandma and Grandpa's. Duh!" Morgan says with an eye-roll.

"Morgan, this is exactly what I was talking about in the car! I don't know where you learned to talk like that or why you think it's okay, but we don't do that in this house. Do you understand?" Morgan looks down at his hands. I bend to be at their level, needing them to try to understand. "I love your personality, but… it's just time to let some of the attitude go. Okay?"

Morgan nods solemnly and reaches his fist out to tap Dillon as an apology.

"Owe!" Dillon says jokingly with a huge smile.

"You little clown," I say, throwing my arms around my sons. I stand and wipe my remaining tears. "Let me show you what I did today!" I say, rushing from my room to the side door that brings us to the coop.

The boys follow, their eyes lighting up upon seeing the gravel by the coop. "That looks better," Morgan praises.

"Thank you! I finally got it done. I'm sure Marge and Phil will have more ideas to spruce it up."

"What's all this?" Dillon asks about the painting supplies on the ground.

"Looks like Mom left a mess, huh? I was going to paint the little building today but got side-tracked." The boys look up at me with disappointed eyes. "What?"

"You weren't going to wait for us?" Morgan asks. I look at Dillon, whose shoulders slouch in disappointment.

"Oh! We can do that together, sure!" I switch into high gear, showing them the paint colors to compensate for not including them. "I was thinking white with a yellow trim, but I wasn't sure about the color. What do you think?" I ask, showing them the top of the paint can with a blob of the color on it.

"Yellow, yuck," Dillon says with his tongue out.

"I was thinking red," Morgan adds genuinely.

"Me too!" Dillon says.

"Red is good!" I say, dramatically pushing the small yellow paint can over. The boys giggle at the gesture. "Maybe we can pick something out after school tomorrow. Anyway, you asked about the tractor in the yard. We can go see it after we feed the chicks!"

Dahlia trails behind us, joyfully jumping over the weeds and tall grass on our way to inspect the tractor. The boys gingerly approach the John Deere, and I laugh at how they stand next to it with disconnection.

"It's okay. You can't hurt it." I pull myself up, sit in the cushy seat, and bounce several times. The boys climb on the sides next to me with interest, pulling the wheel and asking questions.

"How does it start?" Dillon asks.

"Just like a car." I turn the key and bring it to life.

"How does it cut the grass?" Morgan shouts over the engine. I show them the blades while they continue pelting me with questions.

"Want a ride?" This shifts the boys from their state of wonder to excitement. They push and pull at each other, both wanting to be the first to have a ride.

"Do we need to wear a helmet?" Dillon asks. Morgan and I share yet another smile about his brother's funny questions. I shake my head and suggest a game to decide who gets to ride on the tractor first.

I rest my balled-up fist on my outstretched hand, and the boys look at me in confusion. "Rock, paper, scissors. Whoever wins gets a ride first. But don't worry, we have plenty of time for both of you."

"I know this game!" Dillon shouts, sticking his hand out first. Morgan wins, but Dillon is okay jogging energetically alongside.

They each take a turn, having a blast steering the wheel. "I was cutting the grass with it. See?" I point to my tracks in the field.

"I want to do that!" Morgan shouts.

I start the tractor again, resuming where I left off after shouting to Dillon to stay further away. I have quite a bit of the field left to mow. After over an hour of switching turns between the boys, I steer the tractor back to the garage.

"I had to fix this part," I say, showing them the old fuel pump. Morgan takes the part with fascination written on his face. "I can teach you to do that," I say with a smile. "Your dad will be home soon; let's wash up and make him those biscuits he likes. This morning, I started some dough with the sourdough starter."

It's a stretch to ask the boys to help, but they are on board. The long counter in the kitchen closest to the nook is perfect for us to work on both sides. I show them how to knead the dough and leave them to it while I make salads. After throwing everything together to make an easy spaghetti with meatballs recipe, I join the boys again.

Our nook in a dining area offers a great space to share stories about our day once Nick is home and cleaned up. I hold off throwing my questions regarding our impending dinner party. With the boys and I having bonded today, despite my fit, I don't want to ruin this with an argument.

"Mom mowed the front grass! She fixed the tractor and everything," Morgan boasts. He gives me a hesitant look, and I know he's wondering if I will rat them out. I mouth *it's okay*, figuring I'll tell Nick later about my trip to the principal's office.

"I thought I saw that when I pulled in. Your mom is quite amazing," Nick says, sliding his foot up my leg.

Easy, Nick, this is what got us into this pregnancy mess.

I sit up straight with the topic I've barely thought about

today. Would being pregnant be a mess? My mind wants to shout a firm yes while my motherly instincts crave the squishy, soft hugs only an infant can provide. Nick and I figured we'd stop at two kids, which was comfortable for us. Morgan and Dillon have provided as much energy as four kids.

"Working up quite an appetite being here, huh?" Nick comments with a chuckle as I heap on a second helping of spaghetti.

"Oh, yeah. I didn't have lunch," I lie.

Nick laughs. "Joanie, your eyebrow is up. I don't care how much you eat," he says, thinking I'm lying about my food.

"I'm joining the student senate!" Morgan boasts.

"You are?" Nick asks in surprise. "That'd be a good place for you."

"I'll vote for you," Dillon says, "if you give me your water gun." The boys run upstairs to figure out a fair trade a minute later, leaving Nick and I alone.

"The grass looks great," Nick says with a hug in the kitchen after the boys go upstairs. "I'll have to tell the guys at work."

"That's not all I did today." I flip the light switch by the side door, illuminating the light fixture I replaced, and point to the chicken coop visible from the kitchen windows.

"I thought we were going to do that together." Nick smiles and shakes his head. "This place will be shaped up faster than you thought."

"For the party, right?" I say through gritted teeth.

"Joanie, I'm sorry."

"What the heck?"

"It was like stopping a freight train, I swear! They were

all talking, and I couldn't get a word in. No one heard me," he laughs.

"I don't see what's so funny."

"They want to stop by, bring food, look around, and leave. It's okay if everything isn't done. Heck, that's what they are expecting. Most people I work with have done house projects like this in their homes. Old towns equal old homes. They were sharing memories as I jumped up and down, trying to get their attention."

"I guess I need to get used to this new Nick," I say with irritation.

"What's that supposed to mean?" Nick asks with a sincere, confused expression.

"You're kidding, right?" I take a steady breath, knowing the other side of me is coming undone. I rarely allow her out, the Joanie that speaks her mind. The last time I did, Robert fired me. "You have been bulldozing over me for the last three months. You kept the job from me. You put an offer on this house! You've made all the decisions about moving, and even though I'm here and you've gotten your way, you're still doing it with this party!"

It's freeing to let this out. Add that to the lecture I gave the boys, and I've advanced a couple of notches in trying to be in charge of this family. It's how it should be, and I'm not ashamed that I'm finally stepping into this quality.

Nick hangs his head slightly with a sheepish smile. "I have done that, haven't I?" I nod in a way that says, 'You think?' "Wow, I've really gotten carried away. I wanted this move so badly. It won't happen again." He kisses my forehead.

"I'm not trying to be mean," I say, my gentle side stepping forward again.

"No, no, you're just telling the truth. I'll help as much as I can before the party. I swear, it'll work out."

"Listen, I'm not upset about being here. I'm… actually happy." Nick seems choked up on his words before he hugs me, rocking me back and forth.

"Are you guys fighting?" Morgan asks, getting his beagle figurine from where he sat at dinner.

"No!" we answer in unison.

Nick rests his head on my shoulder as I sigh in relief that this little tiff is over. The guilt of keeping my pregnancy a secret weighs heavy in my core, fighting for room over the gallon of spaghetti I ate. Here, I chewed Nick out for his flaw while keeping this secret in a vault.

Two things are for sure, whether I like it or not, this party *and* this pregnancy are happening.

Chapter 18 All About the Farm

Rain keeps me indoors the next week, rooting me to work on the kitchen and living room floors. I've been running off my high vibes from nightly heart-to-heart conversations with Nick. Every night after the boys go to bed, Nick and I spend an hour talking. I show him the progress I've made, and we make plans together. I didn't want to hurt his feelings when I stuck up for myself, but opening up this wound allowed for much-needed healing.

Sanding takes me the longest with the floors. I rented a standing sander from a nice man who insisted on showing me how to use it, even though I'd spent hours with a machine just like it when I redid my brother's floor.

The machine cruises over the wood floors, sending vibrations through my arms that I'm sure I'll feel for a week after I'm done. A new layer of dust covers the entire house, but I'm still glad I put in some elbow grease to do a deep clean.

My hand is healing up nicely and just in time. We'll need one heck of a cleaning spree before the day of the housewarming party.

What was once a dark cherry stain has become a light, natural pine color. After using the hand sander in the corners, I sit back on my heels to admire my work. The light, natural color opens up the space even more, appealing to my visual sense.

It has been a love story like none other, me falling for this house. What started with what seemed like a hate-hate encounter turned to a simple appreciation. This has morphed into a high-school crush where I check the box next to the phrase 'I like you.' Lately, I can't wait until the next sunrise, jumping out of bed to spend time with my new passion.

With everything moved out of the living room, I can easily see it in its raw form. The exposed beams and visible balcony now go nicely with the floors that are no longer scratched and water-stained. I'm not surprised. After all, this is an old house, and these are signs of others who loved living here.

Light gray walls with white and light blue accents would suit the house well. No matter how many times I flip through the rainbow in my mind, I keep landing on this palette I've already deemed successful since I saw it at Cinda's house and again at the salon.

"You're next, buddy," I say to the fireplace, otherwise known as the biggest eyesore in the room.

I take a load off, plopping on the couch I've shoved against the wall. It looks miniature in here. Surprise, surprise, furniture shopping is on the ever-growing list.

I pull up different types of stone for the fireplace on my phone. I haven't done much rock work, but it's not much different than everything else I've been diving into. I text Phil, and he immediately responds that he'd be happy to help anytime.

"Ooh," I say a moment later, clicking on one of the images. "Honed marble brick joint mosaic sheet. Sure, why not?" I say with a chuckle.

Now, I just need the seal of approval from the party

guests. As much as I don't want the thought to derail the positivity I've built, it feels like the whole town is giving me this test. It's one I'm determined to pass with flying colors.

"Well, maybe not these colors," I say with a drab tone that matches my surroundings. I call Daisey's downtown to see if they have it, and to my luck, they do!

Tap, tap, tap.

The noise comes from the adjoined room to my left, throwing a wrench at my good mood. I jump up and stare into the wing of the house off the living room. It's one place we haven't used, mainly because...

Tap, tap, tap.

"Who's there?" I yell, wanting to acknowledge that I'm aware of their presence.

I turn my music off and stand my ground, playing a tug-of-war with being afraid and wanting to learn the source of the noise. I wait a full minute in near silence, with my shallow breathing and rain the only sounds. I return to my sanding project, my sore body rigid and on high alert.

"I don't mind if you're here, but can you keep quiet?" I holler, having heard that one can make friends with ghosts. I'm not thrilled about this, but I can't control whether a spirit is here or not. I continue to work on the floors, turning up my music to drown out any potential rap-a-tap-tapping.

The house is supposed to close in a week, and then it'll officially be ours. I've come to peace with living in a construction zone. At the rate I'm going, I'll accomplish my goals by the dates I've set out.

More like a due date.

I jump a foot off the ground when I hear a knock at the side door.

"Hello?" Cinda's voice sings. I release my breath before

running to the laundry room to let her in. It's surprising to see Nick's sister, Brooke, standing beside her. Instead of feeling the full excitement for seeing my sister-in-law, my anxiety kicks into full gear, hating that they will see the state I'm living in.

"Brooke, what are you doing here?" I ask, flinging my arms around her. "It's so good to see you! Did you two come together?" I ask in confusion, waving them in out of the rain. It's not our formal entrance to the house, but one used almost exclusively since the pathway to the front door needs to be redone.

"We happened to pull up at the same time. Cinda and I know each other from Glenbrook. Our kids go there together. I didn't think you'd hear us over your usual blaring music," Brooke answers in her speed-talking fashion.

"I hope I don't get kicked out of town for not listening to country. Don't tell *anyone* I don't own a pair of boots!" I say with a smile.

Brooke and Cinda laugh. "That's such a stereotype," Cinda says with a wave of her hand. "We're more country-meets-the-modern-world if there is such a thing. This place is amazing!" Cinda lets herself in the kitchen and looks around, slack-jawed.

"It looks loads better than when I first saw it. You're making progress before the big party date," Brooke says sneakily.

"How did you know?" I ask incredulously.

"The whole town has been invited," Brooke says with a wink.

"Don't remind me!" I say with a light smack to her arm. "It's nowhere close to being done. I'm only one person."

"It looks like you're a productive one!" Cinda comments.

"Oh, she's always been a 'do-er,'" Brooke chimes in.

"What does that mean?" I ask with a bashful smile.

"Oh, come on, Joanie. It's like your bandanas give you energy. I don't think you ever sleep. I remember how she would work through the night getting projects done," Brooke recounts for Cinda. "She would nail, hammer, chisel, and sand things, one after the other, without skipping a beat. It was always with this look," she says, sticking her tongue between her teeth. "How's it working out for you, Stickers?"

"Stickers?" Cinda asks with confusion.

Brooke laughs yet again, reminding me of her ever-present good mood. "She sticks her tongue out when she's woodworking. It's hilarious."

"Do you have anything you've built that I can look at?" Cinda asks with her eyebrows shooting towards her hairline.

"This one here is something she's made," Brooke shouts from the living room. "It looks like you've been playing Tetris in here with the furniture."

"I have," I say, tossing a pillow at her. "I've been sanding and…"

"She made this couch," Brooke interrupts. "You made the end tables in here, too, right?" she says, continuing to 'sell' my pieces.

"Don't look too close," I grumble. "Those are getting pretty beat up." I think back to our time in Fargo when the boys would jump off the end tables onto the couches. It feels like a lifetime ago when we were cramped in that little rental.

"You saw my house, Joanie. The main theme is 'distressed.' This would work for us perfectly, but maybe with a little more of a beat-up look." She goes through the specifications, and I pull out my small notebook from my tool belt and sketch her vision.

"Something like this?" I ask, showing her my drawing.

Cinda looks from the paper to me a couple of times before responding. "Are you in my head?" Brooke and I laugh in response, my insides swirling with delight. "This is exactly what I've been scouring the internet for! Can you really make something like this?"

"I sure can. It won't be a quick turnaround. As you can see, I have a lot of work to do around here."

"Yeah, but you'll need a break every now and then to do something fun," Brooke offers as advice.

"And I'll pay you!" Cinda says, grabbing my forearm. "Just wait until the ladies at the things you've made! Keep track of your hours whenever you do get started. You'd make quite a business with this skill. We have markets with furniture, but we have to go to Eugene if we want anything more customized. My book club would go nuts over having something custom-made right here in town."

"News like this spreads like wildfire around here," Brooke says with a wink. "Looks like you'll fit in just fine, sis. How do you like it here?" I think of my answer, not wanting to disappoint the two broad smiles pointing back at me. I know people are fiercely guarded of their towns, and I'm not about to poke holes in theirs.

"It's a big change, but I do like it. Even though I've been hearing all those weird noises in that room," I say, throwing my head toward the extra room.

"Is that where the ghost is?" Cinda asks in a whisper.

"What ghost?" Brooke asks with twinkling eyes that match Nick's.

"I don't know what it is!" I say quickly, trying to match their energy. "I've looked for signs of mice or birds and haven't seen anything."

"Who are you, Cinderella?" Brooke teases.

With company by my side, I feel the courage to spring into action. I fling the door open with a yell, only to find emptiness waiting. "Great, now I look crazy."

"That was one of the funniest things I've ever seen," Cinda says, clutching her stomach. "I thought we would have to fight a werewolf or something."

After sharing a good laugh at my expense, the three of us get cozy with a pot of tea and homemade carrot and zucchini muffins from Cinda. We chat through various topics as if we've been friends since grade school. I'm grateful for the reprieve from my work list.

"Nick seems to think this party is a good idea. Look at this place! We're not ready at all."

"I think I saw a flyer downtown. It's this Saturday, right?" Brooke teases with a big gulp of tea.

"Haha," I reply, stuffing the last of my muffin in. "I don't even want the two of you to see my house in its state."

"It's really not that bad, Joanie. I can see that you've already done a lot with the place," Cinda says, looking around. "It's clean and obvious that you're working on it."

"You say that, but compared to yours, this house looks like a warzone," I say convincingly. "I have a list as long as a tape measure."

"You need to ease up, sis. She always does this. She takes on too much, burns herself out when she doesn't get through everything in two days, and then wants to give up. I know you're freaking out, but I put a little spin on it. What *can* you do in the next week so you're proud?" Brooke suggests.

My lips cinch tight with this thought, having not crossed my path. "I'd feel better if the moldings and baseboards were in, the kitchen cabinets were stained and finished, and everything down here had a fresh coat of paint. I think that'd be doable, actually. I have the moldings already. I just need to cut them all to size."

"Is that all, honey?" Cinda says before slurping her tea, wide eyes and mystified. This is entirely doable for me, especially since the clock is my boss, constantly reminding me my time is limited. "Let me know if you want help decorating. I'm good at that part."

"I'm going to take you up on that!" I say, snatching another muffin. Brooke eyes me suspiciously since this is my third one in less than five minutes. "I'm so glad you brought these, Cinda. I haven't eaten yet today," I lie.

We talk about the approaching summer, with them detailing their vacation plans and clueing me in on all the activities in town.

"Between the three of us, we have nine kids!" Brooke says, holding up her fingers.

Almost ten, I think, with a flurry of butterflies in my stomach. As badly as I would love to share my news with the girls, Nick needs to be the first to know. Hopefully that will be soon! With everything he's been throwing at me lately, I've hardly had time to think of a special way to tell him, let alone digest the fact that we'll have a new addition to the Nelson family.

We set another tea date at Cinda's for next week. Between the two of them and Alice stopping by, I've already had more visitors here than I ever did at our old shoe box rental.

I wave goodbye with the warmth only friendship can provide. Brooke's vote of confidence in my skills has me wanting to spend the rest of the day in the shop. "My shop!" I say, finally, with an enthusiasm that matches the ladies who were just here.

I look around the house and visualize what it will look like when it's done. While I wasn't sure about this move, I have a hunch that this is our forever home, even if it does have a ghost.

Despite the square footage, the house is cozy and welcoming. The high ceilings and upstairs balcony exposed in this room will make for a spectacular entrance. The kitchen is set up to be a state-of-the-art chef's dream. There's room for the boys to run and play while Nick and I have our own area with our master suite.

I stretch my arms, squeezing the pop of muscles I've grown since being here. It's a welcomed surprise to feel and see my body get into shape.

Soon, that shape will be round.

I look down at my stomach, remembering how I loved being pregnant.

"What do you think?" I ask Dahlia after I stuff a pillow under my shirt. "I know," I sigh, "it wasn't in the plan! How in the world am I going to do all of these projects with a baby? We still have the barn and a garden, not to mention the hours I'll have to spend mowing…"

I have an urge for fresh air and flee from the house with Dahlia in tow. I take a lap down our path around our yard, which I've done every morning before the boys get up and have clocked at fifteen minutes.

The movement and scenery help me control my emotions before I spiral out of control.

"I do like it here," I say to Dahlia, "but how am I going to keep all of this up? And what if the guests don't like the house?"

Cinda's encouraging words come to mind. She has more

kids, land, and animals than I do, and still, she totes her little one around with a 'can-do' attitude. If she can do it, I surely can too. It's not like I'm the only one with kids and a farm.

What if I have a baby girl like Cinda has?

This thought slows my feet as I swoon at the possibility of adding pastel colors to my life. A jolt of excitement rushes through me. Growing up, it was only my brothers and me. I never played with Barbies or did my hair or makeup, something I've carried into adulthood. There wasn't one bit of me that was girly. The thought of adding pink ribbons and dolls to my life is exciting. I worry that the boys won't take well to this change, having claimed this space as their own. It's inevitable though, something I cannot control now.

The path leads me back to the house in lighter spirits and in time to see a red pickup with a trailer rolling up my driveway. I can't place a noise until I recognize the bleating of a goat in the trailer. "Hello again!" the man says, jumping out of his truck and straightening his red flannel.

"It's Fred, right?"

"Yup," he says with a tip of his hat. "This might be strange, but I've been asking everyone if they want to take this goat off my hands. Her name is Glenda, and she hasn't been happy since we kept her kid. It sounds funny, but sometimes they just don't get along. She's a sweet girl, but she's been wandering off a lot lately, which isn't like her."

"A goat, huh?" I scrunch my eyes against the sun and peek at the trailer. The brown and white goat repeatedly bleats while turning in circles.

"She's normally not this noisy. She never has been very flexible with change." I snap my eyes to Fred, having described myself this way.

"I can understand," I say with a pause before looking at

the fenced-in space for the chickens. "There's plenty of room there for them to have a friend. I've cared for goats before, but that was in the past. As in, way, way in the past," I say, indicating this with a swish of my arms.

"Not much has changed in regards to their care and upkeep. They still either want to eat everything under the sun or climb on it. That area right there would be perfect for her," he says, pointing to the two empty horse stalls in the pasture. "It looks like a few place might need mending in your fence, but I hear you're quite the fixer-upper. I'm not trying to be pushy. It's up to you."

I glance at my watch to see I have a half-hour before picking the boys up. I should ask Nick about making this decision. However, he has been talking about adding more animals to our brood as time passes. I hold my hands up before letting them fall on my thighs. "Well, let's get her out and see what she does."

"I can throw some hay into the deal since we grow it," Fred continues as he opens the gate to his trailer. "My wife grows a garden, and this one loves all types of vegetables. We can send some your way when it gets to be harvest time."

His mention of a garden sparks my interest again. I spent most of my childhood watching the sprigs grow and eventually form into food. It's exciting to think that my boys could experience the same!

The goat allows me to put a rope around her neck before she quickly jumps out of the trailer. "She rarely does that," Fred says with delight.

Glenda circles around before walking over to give me a sniff. "Hello, girl. I hear you're not happy," I say with a pat on her scalp. She lifts her head, leaning into my scratch. "You like that, huh?" I laugh, digging in behind her ears before moving under her chin. Her back leg pounds on the ground several times, making me laugh.

Fred straightens as if in surprise. "She's never done that with me. In fact, this one here doesn't like to be petted." He allows the silence to grow between us as I think about what owning a goat would mean. The boys certainly would love it. And I'd love to surprise Nick!

Dahlia eases forward until the two animals touch noses. They back away from each other but circle around as if sizing each other up.

"Well, look at that!"

"I'll take her," I say, no longer with hesitation. "How much are you asking?"

"She's free to a good home!" Fred says with a smile. Glenda will add to my list of chores. But this is the way of country living, isn't it, to add more animals and vegetation? The boys have been wonderfully responsible with the chicks. I'm sure they'll love to help care for Glenda, too. And with their summer break coming up, they might even take on some of the chores I'm doing now.

"I'll help you lead her to her stall." Fred blesses the area Glenda will live in with a compliment about the stream that runs through the pasture. "This has always been a great area. You've already made a lot of progress, I can see. Looks like Glenda will have plenty to graze on, but you might want to add a few things for her to climb on. Goats are curious in nature."

"I remember that growing up. We would find our goats on the tractor and on my parents' cars. My dad loved that," I say sarcastically, removing the bandana from my head and tying it around Glenda's neck. It's silly, but I've rekindled my love of animals since being here, and something I didn't know was missing.

"Even a pile of wood will help with her urge to climb. I've found Glenda in a tree more than once. They like to be social with chickens, so opening the gate to the chicken coop sometimes will do her good."

Once Fred leaves, I skip to the car to pick the boys up, feeling the excitement of the surprise that awaits them.

I keep quiet about Glenda when I see the boys. We walk quickly back to the car with my hands on their backs. The boys tell me about their day on the way home, with me soaking up Morgan's exciting news about becoming Vice President.

As soon as I stop in the driveway, I quickly turn to them in the backseat. "I have a surprise!" I shout. I don't wait for them to respond before jumping out of the car and running to where Glenda is in her new stall.

The boys tear out of the car and sprint after me in a whirlwind of anticipated glee. Dillon stops when Glenda lets out a loud bleat from her stall. "What was that?"

"A goat! No way!" Morgan shouts.

"Yes!" Dillon says with a fist pump from his good arm.

I don't have to tell them to be gentle. They hesitate and inch forward once I open the gate. Glenda rushes up to greet them and turns this way and that so they can scratch every inch of her black and white patchy fur. Fred said she doesn't typically like this attention, but it's like she's been craving it.

"I love her ears!" Morgan says with a little laugh as he toggles them back and forth.

We spend the afternoon in the backyard with our animals. The boys listen as I read articles out loud about how to care for a goat. They plan to get up early every morning to let the chickens out and feed Glenda. Their interest in taking care of animals is starting to shape my two rambunctious boys for the better.

"I can't wait for a few months to go by so we can use the eggs," I say. I pause with the talk about months going by. Guilt takes over me, for I've been ignoring my own offspring.

As much as I'm in denial, in just a few short months, we will have yet another family member to add to our growing bunch… and I'm the only one who knows.

∗∗∗

"You okay? You look a little pale," Nick observes.

"Yeah, I'm fine. It's just…"

"What's up?"

"I've been swamped today," I say with a sigh full of lies, willing my eyebrows to stay in place. "I reached ten thousand steps by noon!"

"Wow, that explains it," he says with an arm around my waist. Even with the extra calories, my pear-shaped butt and thighs have been shrinking. It's the perfect time to share the baby news with him, but I need it to settle in with me first. Is that so bad? "Maybe you need some goat's milk," Nick laughs. "Do goats give enough milk to drink or make cheese?"

"Yes, but they have to have a baby first." My face heats up at the correlation to my secret. "She's had a kid. Fred said she didn't get along with it. We could try to milk her and see what we get."

"It's fun, this farm thing," he says with his hands on his hips as he watches the boys. It's become our new hobby to simply wander around out back after dinner and enjoy the outdoors before Nick digs into the landscaping. It's a stark difference to how our nights used to be. "What do they eat?"

"Anything really. Kind of like you guys," I say, tickling his side. I move behind him and thread my arms around his stocky, strong waist. I lay my head on his upper back and close my eyes.

"That feels nice," he says, rubbing my arms. He puffs his chest up and holds his chin high. "Farmer Nick."

My laugh turns into a yawn. "Fred said she likes all kinds of vegetables," I say in a sleepy voice. "Yet another reason to have a garden this summer."

"Where will we find room for something like that?" Nick proudly spreads his arms out wide over his domain.

"Down to the left of the barn will be perfect. There isn't anything there, and the sun will hit it just right."

"I'll help you put some beds in if you'd like. Based on your track record, I'll come home one day, and you'll have it all set up." We share a chuckle before he proceeds. "I wonder if we should get a mate for Glenda."

"It doesn't sound like she likes other goats."

"You never know," Nick says with a shrug. "We'd have little baby goats. Because you know what happens when a male and female get together…" He turns and pokes my sides.

Little does he know how I'm experiencing this miracle of life right now.

Chapter 19 Morning Routine

It's been over a month since we moved to Garden Valley, and I have pushed myself to my limit every day. Today is no exception, as I've started staining the kitchen cabinets. I'm well into the groove when…

Bang!

I jump a foot when the noise startles me, but anger comes rather than fright. "Alright, let's settle this once and for all." I throw my rag down and stomp to the laundry room to grab the boys' bat before stomping back. This haunted room could be eliminated from the house for all I care.

As I get close, I hear the same tapping noises I've listened to this whole time. My stomach flops as my feet slow to a stop outside the room.

Tap, tap, tap.

There's definitely something in there. I've been aching to find out the source of these disturbances. The mystery will be solved if my hand can just… twist… the… doorknob.

Tap, tap, tap.

Hello, I'm here, and no one is paying attention to me.

I look down at my stomach wide-eyed, knowing where the thought came from. I've done my best to ignore this room of terror, just as I've been ignoring the human being inside me and the slight bump he or she is creating.

With everything I have, I fling the door open,

anticipating my answers waiting for me on the other side. I'll figure out how to tell Nick, and he won't be upset that I've kept it a secret. I'll wake up one day, and upon some miracle, the house will be done, or better yet, the stupid dinner party will be canceled so I can blissfully work through each room without the demanding date screaming at me from my shoulder.

In a rush of adrenaline, I storm into the room with my bat in hand to find…

"Glenda! Dahlia! What in the world?"

Finding our new goat in this room with the cat who adopted us is an unexpected surprise. I'm unsure what I expected, but it wasn't this. Of course, seeing a goat in one's house is probably always odd.

"Are you the one making all the racket in here?" I ask when she comes over for a pat. Her hooves on the floor make the familiar tapping sound, and in a second, my worries ease.

I think back to what Fred said about Glenda escaping his yard and know it's been her scaring me all along. I look at Fred's plot of land right across the dirt road. The fence is wide enough for her to squeeze through, and I already know how good of an escape artist she is, for I've had to guide her back to her pen dozens of times. Glenda merely bawhs at me and goes back to exploring the room.

I sink to the ground, allowing the adrenaline to dwindle. The door to the outside sways gently in the breeze, allowing the fresh Garden Valley scent to waft in.

Glenda butts her head against my shoulder while Dahlia rubs against my side, each begging for attention. I happily stroke their fur, allowing the anxiety caused by these last few weeks to flood out of me.

A flapping noise joins us before Alice's bird lands in the doorway, twisting his head this way and that to get a good look at us. "Walton?" he says. I can't help but laugh now that the whole situation has been resolved. The entire scene is so strange that I doubt anyone would believe me if I repeated it.

It's a relief to have this mystery solved. One hairy situation down, a couple more to go.

After calling Nick and getting another laugh about the ordeal, I lead Glenda back to her stall. I follow the fence line around her pen to inspect where she wiggled her way out, finding the weak spot she's been squeezing through.

"Glenda, you're an outside pet, girl." I grab wire to cinch it together and head back inside.

I fill the time before I need to be at school by downloading a pregnancy app on my phone. I sit by an open window in the nook, enjoying the fresh, damp smell with the familiar hint of lilac, which indicates rain is approaching. I breathe a deep breath in, closing my eyes and saying a thanks for the new baby. So far, the worry of breaking the news to my family has overshadowed the joy that should be here.

The app helps to pinpoint how far along I am, saying the baby is six weeks today! According to my calculation, I'm due in early December. A Christmas baby!

A vision flashes before my eyes of me holding a baby in white and pink with a cute little headband around her head. The boys, Nick, and I are somewhere in town with a sign that says 'The Polar Express' behind us.

"That was weird."

I bite my lip, my mind filling with comfort and acceptance. The winter would be a perfect time to have a baby. I already know how I want to spend the summer months with the boys. They will be in school in the fall and winter as I prepare a nursery, but then we will have the winter break so the five of us can be together as a family.

"Always the planner," I say with a chuckle, my fingers itching to wrap around a pen and scrawl in a new frilly notebook. My phone chimes with a reminder of the PTO meeting I've been looking forward to. I feel elated that I can participate in the school activities for my two kids.

Soon to be three!

On my way to my room, I peek into the extra bedroom to the left. My eyes land on the wooden chair I made for Morgan when he was one. Dillon added scratches and dints when he took it on as his own. In it rests my bunny, Annabelle.

"Aww, Belle, Belle." I lift my childhood bunny and hold her tight to my stomach. Either the boys or Nick set her on the chair in here. Whoever did this has given me a sign that everything will be okay, even if the news will be spread a few weeks late.

The oversized room is painted white, but my mind bursts with color combinations for a nursery. I've always wanted to use pastels to paint each wall and even the ceiling a different color. A large window overlooks the rolling hills, making this area perfect for a rocking chair. I remember the days of laying back in the recliner and nursing the boys. They never clung to me, and it seemed like they wanted to separate from me as soon as they could crawl. Yes, they are slowly bonding with me, but maybe this is my chance to get that baby love I missed out on.

The only sounds in the house are from my footsteps as I walk around the newly stained floors. I find myself standing in my favorite spot in the living room that overlooks the valley. Dark clouds roll towards us, the telltale sign of rain in the distance. I've been learning how to predict the weather here, making it one of my favorite pastimes.

I circle my hand around my stomach, which hasn't changed much. Nick loved having babies and was one of those dads running around with his kids at the park, whenever we had time to go. I take a deep breath as anxiousness surrounds the idea of sharing the news with my family. No matter how long I stall, I know a month or two of time will reveal my secret for me.

***

It's out of my comfort zone to join a group where I'm a newbie. I meant to show up right as the PTO meeting started to avoid chit-chatting with strangers, but it doesn't look like anyone is ready to start the meeting. I flip through the appropriate small talk topics in my mind while my stomach calls me to the oatmeal cookies on the refreshments table.

"Joanie? I'm so happy to see you here!"

"Monica, thank goodness!" I yelp, self-consciously looking around. "I don't know anyone here," I whisper.

"I can remedy that." She introduces me to a few people in the room, which is solely made up of women attendees. Cinda hugs me, making me feel more settled about being here. I'm greeted with warm welcomes from the women, who easily accept me into their group.

All except one.

"Joan, hi. Do you remember me from the pharmacy?" I ask with my pleasant voice. It already feels like an eternity since Dillon whacked my hand.

"Oh, yes, I remember," she says smugly. There isn't a

pleasantry in sight. Her eyes flick to my hand, but she doesn't ask how I'm doing. In fact, she purposely shifts her body away from me and walks away, her short brown hair nearly brushing against my face with the snub.

"Joanie, hi!" It's another familiar face, Annette, from the grocery store. She saves me from saying something stupid to Joan, the outlier here who has already taken her seat, and glares at everyone with her arms crossed.

"Annette, it's good to see you again."

We chat about the boys being in the same class until a woman in a long flowery skirt and a pale pink blouse stands in front of the group and asks us to take our seats so we can start in a few minutes. The group obliges, and I find myself sitting between Cinda and a woman with a head of curly dark hair.

She moves her hands around, and I see that she's crocheting. "I'm Lisa. I hear you're new in town?"

"Yes, I'm Joanie." I look from her face to her fingers working away at her crochet project. "How in the world do you do that so quickly?"

"It's kind of my thing. I'm making a stuffed elephant for Melissa over there."

"That's amazing. I can definitely see it's an elephant. It would look like a bunch of jumbled knots if I were doing it. Mind if I…?" I reach out to feel the beautiful gray and pink yarn.

"Of course, feel away!" The colors and design start my mind spinning on how I will decorate the nursery. "I have about a hundred more animals at home." Lisa giggles, pushes her long curly black hair out of the way, and reaches into her bag to pull out a herd of elephants in different sizes.

"These are adorable! How do you come up with ideas?"

"I mostly get requests on how to do stuff from my subscribers." The confusion on my face causes her to explain further. "I have a YouTube channel called Coping With Yarn! I just started it, so I only have about a hundred subscribers. It's a fun little community, and something I hope will take off."

"*Only* one hundred? I'd be super intimidated if I knew a hundred people were watching me. I'm impressed. That sounds like a fun hobby," I say with a grin.

"It's one of my hobbies. I'm also a part of the Yakama tribe here in town. You look like a fellow Indian sister. Are you a part of a tribe?"

"No, I'm not too much into my heritage. My family is more. I've thought of it, but…"

"You should check it out sometime. If you're interested, you can get a hold of me."

"I'll think about it," I say with a friendly nod.

A slender woman named Jennifer officially starts the meeting by banging a gavel several times at the front of the room. The wooden podium could fall over with the next stroke of the gavel, giving me the idea of building a new one for the group.

"It seems as though introductions are in order today," she says with her gaze on me.

Oh no.

I pat my hair, quickly checking for a stray piece of straw or granules of dirt. "Joanie, I'm not going to be swayed by that terrified expression." The room of a dozen women responds with laughter, with all eyes on me. Lisa motions with her crochet hook, encouraging me to stand. Before I know what's happening, I'm introducing myself in front of the group.

Jennifer stands aside at the podium as I awkwardly side-step to her previous spot. "Hi, um, I'm Joanie. My family and I just moved here from North Dakota. My two boys go to this school, so if you've heard of one new boy who is bossy and one who is causing problems, those are mine." The group of women laugh. Even Joan's face slips into a brief smile before it returns to stone.

"Maybe they'll take mine out of the running for the worst-behaved children in the school," one woman in a light blue dress says with a humorously hopeful expression.

"I thought they were doing better, Mellissa," Annette says in the seat beside her.

"I did too, but Principal Merrill says she's had both of them in her office this week from pulling your daughter's hair," she says, leaning over and looking at another woman. "Sorry, Angela."

"Is your son's name Dillon?" Melissa asks me.

Oh no.

My face must show the anxiety that's running through my body because the room of women laugh again.

"Don't worry. I think it was Dillon who helped my son yesterday. He fell on the playground and said a new boy helped get him to the office."

"And I swear that name came up when Chelsea said she needed help tying her shoes," another woman says.

I bite my tongue and dig my fingernails into my skin to keep from shedding tears in front of this group.

"Alright, we can discuss tactics at our next parenting meeting," Jennifer says, bringing the meeting back to order. A parenting meeting? Now, that is something I could benefit from.

"Where do you live?" asks a woman in the audience. It

would seem odd, but maybe this is common knowledge for small-town folk. She's sitting next to Joan, and both have matching glares.

"She's up by me on Tranquility Hill. In the old Darnell house," Cinda replies for me. Murmurs around the room indicate that everyone knows exactly which house we are living in.

"That's quite a fixer-upper," Joan comments with a smirk. Her long fingers tap her face as her chin rests in her palm.

"Don't I know it!" I agree.

"I went in there once. The house is literally falling down," Joan continues. "I honestly thought they would knock it down when Glen moved. The kitchen was quite literally rotting away."

"It's not rotting away," I say with an odd laugh. "The kitchen actually is shaping up quite nicely. In fact, my first Garden Valley sourdough loaf is rising as we speak," I retort without another thought. The women in the room let out a little cheer in response.

It's the open embrace I've been looking for in life, this feeling of being included and accepted by moms like me.

"You should see what Joanie has done with the place already," Cinda says, coming to my rescue. "She's quite the carpenter. She has brought all the floors back to life. Look at this coffee table she's making for me!" Cinda brings up the crude photo of my sketch on her phone and shows it to the women beside her.

I'm soon being asked questions about how extensive my skills are and whether I know how to make bed frames, end tables, and shelves. I stand in front of the group, filled with more anxiety than I came here with.

"What's your story with woodworking, Joanie?" Monica asks with an easy smile as if she's trying to help settle my stomach.

"I've always been a bit of a tinkerer, just without cotton balls on my toes," I say quietly, unsure about opening up about this topic with this group. I continue, figuring that all but one or two people in the group seem genuinely interested in my story.

And there she is, sinking in her seat with her arms crossed. I've dealt with women like Joan before. I assume her angst against me is because I am good at something they've tried and failed at in their own lives. We are all like this to a certain degree. It's called jealousy.

"When I think about it, it's probably my fault that I manifested a house that desperately needs my help." The sound of giggles helps to ease my public speaking anxiety.

The women keep me in front of the group for fifteen minutes until I've answered all their questions. "I'll do all your projects if you just let me sit back down!" I say to yet another round of laughter.

Lisa gives me a wink as I sit next to her. "Seems like you have a fan club of your own now," she whispers.

I take a deep breath with acceptance replacing the nervousness. Not only have I found my town, but I've also found my community of friends.

Chapter 20 Sense of Accomplishment

The boys run off and play with Glenda and the chicks the second we get home from the PTO meeting. 'When we get home.' The phrase startles me. I've been looking forward to getting home since I left to pick the boys up. My thoughts have shifted, with this place morphing into my sanctuary. It's my green light to head straight for the shop to start on the door frames for the kitchen. I'm not alone; I have Dahlia to keep me company.

Are you in the shop? Nick asks via text when he gets home.

Yup! Joanie

I'm not surprised that two hours have flown by in the blink of an eye. Time seems to speed up when I'm deep in a project. The world can spin around me, and I'm as happy as can be in my shop. It's different now that I have the added responsibilities of a family, but I feel like the scales are balanced.

A few minutes later, the side door to the garage opens. Nick steps in with his once crisp, black button-up shirt, now untucked, and dark jeans that never get old. His brown hair is tousled now instead of combed nicely as it is in the morning.

"You're at it again, huh?" he says as he looks over my progress.

"I am," I return, keeping my eyes on the tape measure. I've stopped by Nick's work three times in the last couple of days to pick through their wood pile. It's fun to see him in the middle of the day, even if it is just for a few minutes. I've met some people he works with who know me by name. "You might want to plug your ears," I say, laying the wood flat on the table saw. It's a bit overkill for this three-inch piece, but I'm having fun with all the machines. Nick plugs his ears as I zip through my cut.

"You make it look easy, hon," he says, pulling his fingers from his ears. "Door frames, huh?"

"These, sir, are interior door casings," I correct with an English accent.

"Excuse me," he says with a shake of his head. "What are these pieces?" he asks, picking one up.

"That's part of the whole design. It's not simple either."

"Why would you make it easy on yourself?" he teases.

"I have a vision for the house. With the high ceilings and extra space, I think a fancier design is needed. I feel like it was plain once upon a time. The exposed beams and balcony in the living room, plus the huge windows everywhere, make me lean toward these casings, which will add the extra sophistication I'm after. This is how they will look once they are up." I lay out the pieces like a puzzle to give him a visual.

"That looks amazing," he says, wrapping me in a hug that pulls my feet from the ground. "I have a hankering for burgers tonight, so I've fired up the grill. Keep on with your casings," he says with a crooked smile.

To my surprise, Nick and the boys work diligently to make our dinner. I don't know why I've always labeled myself as the only one who could cook and do the chores. The boys are thriving with some of these responsibilities.

The boys flow in and out of the shop with interest in my project. I show off my work, wondering if they have noticed that none of the doors in the house are done and framed. Everyone, including me, carries on with their own thing in their own definitely of happiness.

"And I don't have to feel guilty," I say, thinking back to every time I wanted to do this activity but couldn't because the call of responsibilities was louder than my hushed passion.

I don't think my previous stress had anything to do with where we were living or my strict dinner schedule. The busy schedule was my own doing and something I created myself. The Garden Valley breeze has blown away the fogginess that previously clouded my vision.

I sit back and enjoy the chatter from my three guys during dinner. It's what I've always wanted, this free-flowing conversation full of excitement and respect. We stay in the nook and talk long after cleaning our plates. I allow them to get their words out before I fill them in on the PTO meeting.

"It sounds like we aren't the only parents in town with spirited children," I say, letting them know what the other moms said. "They have a parenting club where they all get together and figure out the best ways to punish the kids."

Nick and I laugh when the boys look at each other with worry-filled eyes before darting from the table.

"I'm happy at how much the boys have changed since we've been here," I say in a small voice.

"I've noticed." We share a knowing expression, one filled with relief and a knowing that this area of our lives is improving. Maybe the days of not knowing what to do with the boys are over. "Sounds like you're making a few friends," Nick says as we put everything away after dinner.

"I have, but there's one woman I've encountered a couple of times who can't stand me. She and her small friend group glared at me the whole meeting."

"That's kind of strange. We haven't been here long enough to make enemies."

"I thought it was strange, too. I tried to make a joke about us having similar names. Hers is Joan, so I said, 'Just add an 'E,' and you've got me.' I know it was cheesy, but…"

"Mmm, Joan. That sounds familiar. I work with a guy whose wife is named Joan."

"Oh? Is he a jerk to you, too?" I ask with a laugh.

Nick stands straight as if he has a revelation. "Actually, um, I think he tried for the Assistant Plant Manager job."

"Your job?" I ask with surprise. Nick nods with that 'sorry' type of smile. "I guess that explains it. "Oh well. As long as she doesn't come to the party, we'll be good."

"Yeah, I guess we'll see."

"Wait, is she coming to the party?" I ask with a whine.

"Probably," Nick says with a smile.

"Wonderful. All the reason to get back to work." I kiss Nick and head back out to the garage, grateful that daylight stays around longer every day.

I paint four door frames next, knowing the bright white is a good choice against the neutral gray I envision for the rest of the walls. As they dry, I get started on the moldings for the living room.

The boys bring a few of their action figures into the chicken coop area while Nick gets to work on weeding the backyard near the garage. I've kept the garage and side doors open to keep tabs on all of them. "I think I could pull weeds for a month straight," he says loud enough for me to hear.

"It'll be on the revolving list that never stops. Laundry,

cleaning, dinners, mowing, and weeds."

"We should give that meal service that Cinda was talking about a try," Nick suggests.

"Yeah, like we can afford something like that," I say, voicing my financial worry. Nick stops his work and saunters over to join me.

"You don't need to worry about money, Joanie," he says, circling my waist from behind while I paint the moldings. "Our mortgage here is less than our rent in Fargo."

"We still have all these projects and farms to take care of. None of it is cheap." Even as I say it, I can feel the flow of money coming to me from selling my furniture. It's a weird thought, but something to consider.

"We're doing good. I've only been here a few weeks, and my boss has mentioned when I'll take over for him."

"Is he ready to retire or something?" I ask.

"He's a couple of years away. He's said he wanted to ensure a solid succession plan before retiring. Now that I'm here, he says he already feels more comfortable."

"It's so nice that you're finally in a place that appreciates you."

"And the leftover money from my sign-on bonus and moving expenses went straight to savings. So, relax," he says, giving me more of a squeeze. "These projects are slimming you down more than I like."

Soon enough, I won't be able to hide my basketball-sized stomach. It's the ideal time to tell Nick, but just as I open my mouth to break the news, the boys burst into the garage to show us something funny that Glenda is doing.

"Silly goat." We all laugh at Glenda standing on top of the chicken coop. "I'd like to continue on my moldings, but the boys need to get to bed," I say with disappointment.

"I can put the boys to bed," Nick offers, patting my bottom on his way out. "Don't work yourself too hard, now."

"I wouldn't, but my husband insists on having a dinner party, so I need to get the house prepared," I say with a playful tone. Nick stops, returning my smile.

"You don't have to do the whole house. You don't have to do any of it!"

"I'm planning on getting as much done as possible! I can get most of the downstairs ready. Well, except for the laundry room, our room, the formal dining room, and that room off the living room." My shoulders sink forward in defeat. "So, basically, the kitchen and living room will mostly be ready. Or, the floors will be good. Your dad is doing the kitchen cabinets, so…"

Nick takes a few steps toward me and cups my nervous hands with one of his. "It would be fine if everyone sees our house as it is now."

"Yeah, right!"

"Who cares what *our* home looks like?"

"Um, I do," I say in defense.

"Joanie, we are the ones who live here, not them. I've already told them it's a fixer-upper. They keep saying they want to see the before version anyway."

"I'm telling myself that the party is a good deadline for completing some things, not *all the* things."

"That's a good approach. I really appreciate everything you've done for our family and me. Joanie, I'm happy here." He gives me a kiss that mimics the ones he gave me when we were first together. I can't help but swoon at the energy that passes between us, even if this romantic time is interrupted by the shadow of the secret growing in my belly.

***

With some queasiness-killing crackers in tow, I start directly on the first door casing after taking the boys to school. It takes me an hour to get everything laid out on the freshly stained living room floor. I stand back, trying to not pick apart anything that doesn't align perfectly.

"Keep going," I mutter, knowing that even one-sixteenth inch of imperfection is enough to derail my progress.

The casings go up quickly, and my nail gun and music speed up my efforts.

"Instantly, a new house!" I happily stand back to admire my two hours of work. Ideally, I'd like to paint the walls before these went up, but I can't decide on a color. "You're next," I warn at the large entrance between the kitchen and living room. I walk through the lime green laundry room to return to the garage, still hating the color scheme. The size alone lends itself to something as grand as the foyer at the front of the house. It's not rundown; it just needs a new coat of paint and a theme to decorate. I've gotten lost on Pinterest trying to find suitable designs.

There's a chill in the air that feels good after all the work I've done this morning. I set my Wonderboom speaker on a workbench and am blissfully lost in measuring, cutting, and painting. I get the next three-door casings nailed in by noon, surprised by how quickly it's all coming together. I still have loads of these to do throughout the house, but this satisfies some of the itch. Nick's dad has been taking a few kitchen cabinets home at a time, giving me daily updates on his own sanding adventures. With his first round of half a dozen cabinet doors already in place, we're rockin' and rollin'.

Each improvement I make in the house is an extension of me. It's why disappointment hits so hard when a mess-up arises. It's not just a piece of wood; this passion of mine brings my creations to life like a painter weaves colors into a masterpiece or a sculptor into a statue.

Still, even though I'm doing my best, it doesn't feel like I have enough time to finish what I'd like before the party. Panic knocks at my door, with people arriving in only five days. It's inevitable. Time is going by no matter how hard I've been wanting to stomp on the breaks. Maybe I can do what I do best: plan.

I fix myself a proper lunch, throwing a few chicken pieces to Dahlia before relaxing in the nook with my notebook. From this place, I have a view of the kitchen, the living room, and the beautiful staircase. I look out over the house, feeling content over how far it has come just today. It's sorely missing decorations. I still only have color ideas, and I've seen nothing of the layers of beautifully decorated houses on Pinterest.

What I need is a decorator.

With my belly growing and the party on the horizon, I no longer have time to sit around giving myself pep talks. If I'm going to have this house done, I need to kick it into gear. I might not be cut out to do the decorating thing, but I know a group of ladies who might help.

Chapter 21 The Decorations

Stopping by the salon after I pick up the boys is a long shot. I mean, these problems are my own. Why would someone want to take time out of their busy schedules to help me decorate?

My stomach erupts in butterflies when I open the salon door. I can't tell if I'm nervous about asking for help or, worse, scared that Leslie will say yes and see the state our house is in.

"Hey there, Joanie," Leslie greets, laying her pen on her planner and coming our way. The boys fly by her to the kids' station, nearly knocking her over. "Whoa!" Leslie says, flinging her arms up with a laugh.

"Looks like you're stocked with the good toys," I chuckle.

"Hello, I'm back here too!" Monica hollers from her office.

"Hey, Monica," I say with a shaky voice.

"Do you need to schedule an appointment?"

"Actually, I'm here for something else. I, uh, was wondering if you'd be interested in helping me decorate my house. You and Monica offered, but I wasn't sure if you were serious."

"You bet I was serious! When were you thinking?" Leslie says, resting her hands on her hips and widening her stance as if ready. Her luscious brown hair swings from side to side in a perfect ponytail. It only adds to her adorable persona and peppy attitude.

I wince before breaking the news that might derail my whole plan. "I don't need the whole house done yet; I just need a couple of rooms to start. My husband invited his coworkers over on Saturday, and my house is nowhere near ready."

"This Saturday?" I nod and bite my lower lip, hoping she won't back out of the challenge. "I'm up for that!" she says, her eyes widening with the challenge.

"Really?" I sigh in relief.

"Don't leave me out!" Monica shouts, coming to join us. "I'm one of those weirdos who likes to paint, and I'm good at it. I have some wedding planning, but it's a pretty light week around here."

"I'm done for the day and can do a walk-through now if you want," Leslie offers.

I've never encountered this type of generosity before. "That would be great! Come on, boys, let's go home," I say with a spring in my step.

Leslie follows us home while I mentally imagine every lousy scenario possible. The predominant fear is an image of Leslie running from our house screaming.

"Are you okay, Mom?" Morgan asks while doing that annoying hand thing with Dillon.

"Yeah, why?"

"It looks like you're trying to strangle the steering wheel," Morgan laughs.

"Oh, I guess I am. I'm nervous about what Leslie will think of our house," I admit.

"Why? Our house is great!" Dillon says. The boys have

barely noticed all the work that needs to be done. It's an innocence I wish I shared.

"It is," I say with a higher voice. "I was hoping it would be a little more house-like before people came over, though. I'd be happy if we could land on a paint color and get a couple of coats on."

Leslie pulls in behind us after making the trip down our gravel driveway. I've become accustomed to how everything looks outside, but now that we have a guest, I'm hyper-focused on all its dinginess. "We have a plan for painting the outside," I say the second I open my car door. "Not before this Saturday, I'm afraid." I guide her to the side of the house, where we take our shoes off by the laundry room. "Keep in mind that it isn't done yet!" I fret, but need to explain. "My mother-in-law said she'll spruce up the walkway and front. She's already done so much."

"Joanie, stop worrying. I'm not an expert," she says, giving me a warning of her own. "I've remodeled houses with my brothers from the frame up. Nothing you have here will shock me."

I take comfort in her smile, hoping she's telling the truth. The boys check on Glenda and the chicks, allowing us some quiet time inside. "This is the laundry room, obviously. I took the shelving down, but it needs more work."

"This room would look great with wainscoting. You know, with the boards on the wall?"

"Yes, I could do that pretty easily."

"That's right, you're a woodworker," she says with a bat of her hand as if to say this is easy. "We could work well together in this trade. As for the room, we could set Monica loose in here with a bucket of paint, and it would make a world of difference."

I can't help but beam a smile with some of my worries melting away. "I like your wainscoting idea. We use this room as somewhat of an entrance to the house, so I'd like it to be more grandiose than it is."

"We'll think through that then. Maybe we can put some sort of divider to cover the washer and dryer. Otherwise, we can add a fresh coat of paint and some fun decorations here. Wow, this kitchen is a chef's dream!" she says, peeking through the laundry room door before bursting into the house.

"My father-in-law has been helping to sand and re-stain the cabinets. He offered, and I couldn't turn him down. I would do all of this myself, but the looming party has me working around the clock. We are getting there, see?" I point to a few that Phil and I have finished.

"Those look great. And the door casings add a fancy touch."

"I just finished the casings this morning," I say with pride.

"You're kidding? You did these?" she says, reaching up and inspecting my work. "These add an elegant touch."

"Thank you. Ignore the ding I made by the floor and the gap in the corner," I say with embarrassment.

"I can see you're hard on yourself like I am. Sometimes, these tiny flaws show we're lovingly doing the work ourselves instead of an assembly line on the other side of the world. You know?" she says, gleaming some light on my mistakes.

"Doesn't that have some truth in it?"

"Is this the pantry?" Leslie reaches for the door and helps herself in.

"It was bright red, so I slathered two coats of primer to cover it before landing on this gray."

"It's like a mini-mart in here! This color was a good choice. Where to next?"

"I just redid the floors, and it made a huge impact. Except for the bay window and maybe adding a pot rack, I don't think there's much we can decorate in the kitchen," I say, flowing through the kitchen and peeking at the boys outside. "My main goal before the party is to decorate this nook and the living room."

"This is a nook?" Leslie says with a laugh, standing in the spacious area.

"I said the same thing to Nick on our first night here."

"I love this table," Leslie says, touching the smooth finish.

"Thanks. I made that quite a while ago. Of course, at the time, I had no idea it would end up here."

"Really impressive. Let me look at the living room before I give suggestions. This place is roomy! Look at these windows! And the view!" Leslie stands in my favorite place, which has yet to hold the chaise lounge of my dreams. "I like the couches in here."

"Thank you. We finally just got these. I didn't know what color to get, but I knew I should go with the oversized theme."

"Gray is always a good choice; it'll go well with the floor. We can do two tones of gray, too, with a main color on top, so to speak, and a darker shade on the bottom. We can add accents with pillows, blankets, chairs, and a different wall color here and there. I like the gray in the pantry if you're open to making that the main color on the walls."

I nod, giving her space and time to look around and think before she gives me more suggestions. She praises everything, even the dirty, extra space where Glenda snuck in.

Leslie loves the story of me solving the haunting of the Tranquility Hill House. A piece of my negativity breaks away with every positive word she speaks.

"The way your stairs and railing are exposed in the living room is…" she kisses the tips of her fingers with a smacking noise. "This is a gem of a house. It's so exciting that you've started from the ground up with everything. You can customize it to your liking."

"I get that now," I sigh. "I just kept thinking what a burden all these tasks are that I have to do."

"Oh gosh, no. Could you imagine stripping everything down to begin with? Or having to deal with someone else's old wallpaper or dirty carpet. They've done all that by getting it ready for your special touch."

"Well, the boys and I pulled up the carpet when we arrived."

"Wow, you got these wood floors in fast. Haven't you only been here for a month?"

"Yes, but I did these floors. I mean, they were here, but I sanded them down and stained them. Didn't they turn out nice?" Was that a compliment I just gave myself?

Leslie looks at me with admiration. "I rarely find another woman who is as handy as I am. You've done an amazing job. I can see your style with the few things you have out here. Mind if I go through what I have planned?"

"Please do!"

"I'm thinking of a dressed-up modern style with a touch of farm themes here and there. Nothing too rustic like distressed wood unless you like that look. This room would look great with long gray drapes on these tall windows and pillows that match." Leslie uses her hands to showcase her vision, getting into it and bouncing around the room. "Your couches are here, but I think they would look great in a different layout."

She asks for a piece of paper and quickly sketches our living room. I'm instantly sold on her ideas of rugs, plush pillows, throws, paint colors, and a small sitting arrangement by the window.

"Now, the trick will be to get all this stuff at the store," I say, without mentioning my worry that this will throw our bank account in the red.

"We have a store downtown with tons of accessories, and the prices are reasonable. We can meet after I'm off work tomorrow if you want. I have Wednesday off, and I don't go in until two on Thursday. What do you say?"

I take a deep breath of relief and face Leslie, my eyes blazing in anticipation. "Let's do it!"

Chapter 22 Friends and Color

Every day this week, Leslie, Monica, and Bailey have come over to help. Monica is the office manager and has approved rearranging a few appointments for her crew to spend half days at my house. The outpouring of generosity feels like an induction to this town if I've ever felt one.

Six gallons of paint and one full day of painting later, Leslie, Monica, and I have covered most of the downstairs. We flew through the living room with Monica on accent wall duty, and Leslie and I painting the rest of the walls. It flows perfectly with a dusty blue in the foyer and a soft green in the nook. We got started on the wainscotting yesterday, which transforms the room instantly.

Adding paint is a quick show of progress, especially when three people are involved. Every day, when the boys and Nick get home, they say it's like walking into a new house. With freshly stained floors, a nearly completed kitchen, and even the outdoor space shaping up from the hours Nick has put in, I have a newfound appreciation for my surroundings.

Today, Leslie, Brooke, and Cinda are finally adding the decorations they've been buying, undoubtedly draining my bank account. Nick gave them an endless limit, but they said they'd be more than conscious of prices while heckling the best deals possible.

I've been working into the late hours of the night, making shelves for the living room, and finishing the end tables that have been uncompleted for years. My motivation feels endless and stems from the thought of judgmental eyes that will soon land on my creations. This mental space isn't a great way to live, but the extra push is resulting in leaps of progress.

You'd think there was a celebration at my house with our blaring music and the energy we share. Everyone is engrossed in her own task when I bring in my end table. This piece I started ten years ago was one of the only things light enough to carry. I've given my permission to finish these pieces that had only been ninety-five percent completed.

"Whoa, I don't remember buying that!" Monica exclaims upon seeing the craftsman style, a favorite of mine.

"That turned out nice, Joanie!" Leslie praises. "I love the spindles."

"Thank you, that's what drew me to this piece."

Cinda and Monica drop what they are doing to take a closer look.

"Holy cow, Joanie, you did this yourself?" Monica asks, rubbing her hand across the smooth surface.

"I want one!" Cinda says, which I've learned is her usual when it comes to anything I've made. I can't help but smile.

"I messed up on this spindle right here. I drilled the hole a little crooked, so it's not perfectly straight," I admit.

"Oh, who cares?" Monica blurts. "I never would have noticed that. This looks like something you'd find at a high-end store."

"Didn't you tell me this is part of a set, Joanie?" Leslie asks, leading the way out the front door to the shop.

"Yeah, I've been working on the set for a while. This

couple has been together ten years." The ladies don't hear my joke as they flee to the shop on our new cobblestone walkway that Nick and his parents put in over the weekend. Even before I get to the shop, the ladies have scattered, making themselves comfortable.

"This chair would look amazing on my back porch," Cinda says, taking a seat.

"Please tell me these shelves are for the living room. I know exactly how we should place them," Bailey says excitedly.

Leslie nods enthusiastically in answer. "These would be perfect on the wall across from the large windows. We could put three on either side of that big painting and add books, little potted plants, and figurines."

"Bingo!" Cinda says.

"It's going to be a hit; you just wait and see," Monica says with a side hug. The women are crazier than a corkscrew, and I love it.

"So, when we're done here, you're going to make us each a few things, right?" Cinda laughs through her teasing, but it would be a great way to thank them. Their praises hammer home, giving my confidence a boost. I couldn't put this hobby back on the shelf if I wanted to, and I don't mind a bit.

***

Saturday morning arrives whether I want it to or not, and soon, my house is bustling with people. We have one more full day until the party, and my stomach is full of knots from not getting everything done. The swell of worry has taken over, blurring my thoughts into thinking the worst is waiting for me around the corner when it's judgment time.

While Monica, Brooke, and Bailey finish the second coat of paint in the living room, Leslie helps me nail the rest of the white wainscotting in the foyer. It's nearly the grand entrance I was after, only I can't take the time to enjoy it. Cinda moves this and that from shelf to end table, making sure everything flows, all while babbling phrases to herself like: "Does it look better here?" or "I think it looked best over there."

Nick and the boys take advantage of the sunny weather and make more of a dent in the landscaping with Marge while Phil and I finish the fireplace.

A part of me wishes I could do everything myself to take pride in saying I've done it all. That is, until I remember I'm hardly close to the finish line. I still have the upstairs, my bedroom, the dining room, the haunted goat room, not to mention the nursery! I'll have plenty of time to 'prove' myself, something I admit shouldn't be a factor.

Exhaustion is knocking at my door, but luckily, I've been known to get a second and even third wind. "I'm wired and tired," I say to Leslie as we get another shelf perfectly aligned on the wall.

"I bet. I can feel your stress," she observes, not knowing the real reason for my sleepy eyes. "But look, we're getting so much done."

It's true. This living room once had dirty carpet, dingy walls, and no color. We all worked together to install a grand silver chandelier that was big enough to match the grandiose space. With the pleated drapes tied back and framing each window, the fireplace stones cemented in place, and the furniture placed to ensure feng shui, we are cruising toward the finish line.

I'm far from being out of the weeds of judgment, but looking back over these last few weeks, I don't think I would have changed a thing. I've put gallons of elbow grease in, spawning a bond between me and these walls. With so much of the house being done and livable, the pressure has been lifted to finish the other rooms *right now*.

Just when I think I can pull this whole thing off, a crashing sound in the kitchen rings through the house. "What in the world?" I ask, starting in that direction. As I round the corner, a baseball rolls through the kitchen and bounces lightly against my foot. It doesn't take long to notice the gaping hole in the middle of the large window by the kitchen sink. "Boys!"

I run to the window to inspect the damage, instantly seeing it's hopeless. "It's shattered! It's supposed to be cold tonight. The guests are going to be cold."

"Oh, they will not," Monica says nonchalantly. "Even if we have a party in the winter, I literally turn the heater off. With the extra bodies in the house and the slow cookers you have planned, it'll stay plenty warm."

Dillon and Morgan show up with their heads down. I take a breath, ready to let them have it, when Cinda rests a hand on my shoulder.

"Remember, you're not in the business of throwing parties," she says quickly. "This happens at least once a year at my house. I have a window guy who can probably come out next week."

I understand her advice perfectly and turn back to the boys with more forgiving eyes. "Come here," I say, waving them in. They bury their sorrow-filled faces in my slightly pooched stomach. Seeing their reaction is all I need to calm down. A few months ago, this kind of misdemeanor wouldn't have fazed them. Having them care shows how much they've grown since we've been here.

"We'll get it fixed," I say, kneeling to their level with an ease that matches Cinda's. They follow my calm nature, agreeing to clean up the mess. "You can use the shop vac."

"All right! Come on, Dill!" Morgan says, leading the way to the garage.

"Perfectly handled," Cinda sings. It's a verbal badge of honor I've needed. I'm not perfect and am still figuring this parenting thing out, but I no longer feel alone. "A pot rack would look great above this island."

"I thought the same thing!"

"Walton?"

My lips pursed at the sound of his voice. The bird is perched on the empty planter box, poking his head through the fresh hole in the window. "You aren't on the guest list, so get lost!" I swear the bird shrugs before flying off. I turn to witness the ladies staring at me like I'm crazy. "That bird gives me the creeps!"

"Um, Joanie," Phil interrupts, "I hate to break it to you, but we don't quite have enough stone to finish the fireplace?"

"What?" I ask, my voice switching to panic mode.

I stomp to the fireplace in Sasquatch fashion. All eyes are on me, the performer of this show, but I don't care.

"That's definitely noticeable," I blurt. "We should have started at the front and worked our way back."

"It wouldn't have worked that way with the layout of the stones we chose," Phil chimes. "I called the store the moment I noticed, and they won't be getting another shipment of this stone until next week," Phil says.

"Of course, they won't," I whine.

"This isn't a big deal," Leslie says, coming into the room

without a worry. "We'll just put a plant right here. See, it easily covers up the blunder." The other women agree, all talking at once about how they actually like the new placement of the plant better.

"Hey, what's in here?" Bailey interrupts, peeking into the dining room once we've put a band-aid across this crisis.

"That room is hopeless if you ask me," I frown.

"Nothing's hopeless when you have a set of hands like yours, honey," Leslie says, squeezing my hand.

"As long as one hand doesn't get hit by a hammer," I laugh, happy that my leftie has healed.

"Oh my gosh, it's a huge dining room!" Bailey yells from beyond the swinging door. I sigh when the rest of the women follow her voice into the room I've dreaded most.

"How did we miss this room? I thought the backyard was beyond that wall, not a dining room. I love how there's one entrance from the nook and another through to the hallway outside your bedroom," Bailey says on our way to the dining room.

"We missed this room too. Look at the view," Monica says, peering into the soon-to-be nursery.

"Yeah, it's nice," I say softly, leaning against the doorframe.

"What's that look for?" Brooke asks sneakily after spying on us.

"What look?" I ask quickly.

"That 'I've got a secret' look that I know so well," Brooke says with a bump to my side.

"It's nothing. I just have plans for this room," I say now that we're standing in the nursery.

"Oh? Like what?" Leslie asks. I know her well enough to assume that her mind is more focused on decorating this room than gossiping.

"I don't know. Maybe an office or something," I babble.

Monica gives Cinda a sideways glance before digging her claws into me. "It'd be perfect for a baby's room. This room is right next to yours." The comment causes the other two women to snap their heads in my direction. There's something about the word 'baby' that comes across as if spoken into a megaphone.

"Ha! Good one," I say, trying to escape. Monica steps before me, flashing a perfectly aligned, white smile. I know her type. She's nice enough but is someone I want on my team instead of as an opponent.

"You're young enough to have more kids, right?" Monica asks, close enough now to wrap her arms around me for a hug. Is she squeezing my muffin tops?

"She's still in her fertile thirties. Plenty of time," Brooke chimes, beaming beside Monica.

I look from one woman to another, shock indeed registering on my face. "I'm not having more kids."

"Then why do you look like we've caught you with your hand in the cookie jar?" Brooke asks, her one eyebrow an inch higher than the other.

"I don't have a specific look! I'm mega stressed from planning this party, that's all." I sweep past them to join Bailey in the dining room, hoping to close the door on the subject that is solely my own.

"Joanie, this room is great!" Bailey exclaims, still stuck on the dining room.

I follow her gaze. "This room?"

"What do you have planned in here?" she asks, hands on her hips, awaiting my command.

"I was planning on nailing the doors shut during the

party to keep people out of here," I respond in exasperation.

"Oh my gosh, why? This room is huge and perfect for people to gather in."

"This room?" I ask again.

"Damn straight, this room," Monica says, agreeing with Bailey as she peeks out the window.

"It looks like a dumpster," I say, not understanding what they are seeing.

"We still have a half a day," Leslie says by the windows. She throws the older-than-dirt drapes aside, sending about two inches of dust flying through the room. We each share a cough before she continues. "All we really have to do is get rid of these hideous drapes. We'll throw a coat or two of paint on the walls, maybe add wainscotting to match the rest of the house, and do some general cleaning."

"More wainscotting?" I ask, suddenly wanting to nap and give them the freedom to take over.

"Let's do it!" Bailey says. It's all the blessing these women need to go gangbusters in the formal dining room.

With Cinda putting the finishing touches on the living room, the rest of us blow through the dining room, touching every inch like cats in a new space. Luckily, there are just enough scraps for Leslie and me to nail up the wainscotting. At the same time, Monica and Bailey decide to use the leftover dusty blue accent color on one of the walls.

I touch the soft yellow wall between the staircase and the kitchen to learn it's already dry. I'm surprised this burst of color looks as good as it does.

"It looks like sunshine and the blue sky have taken up residence in here," I say as a compliment. I push my hands on my lower back and stretch backward with a groan. "At this rate, I won't be able to mingle with the party guests without a cane," I say as the others laugh.

Leslie and I continue to work as the sun moves to the other side of the sky. With every window and door open, the spring air blows through the house, perfect for drying the walls and airing out the dust and paint fumes, replacing them with that sweet lilac smell I love.

"I feel like we're chain-working, going from task to task," I observe.

"It's why we're here, friend," Leslie says, wiping the old dining room table down and placing a vase of freshly cut lilacs at its center. "The guests will have no idea how much we whipped together at the last minute."

"I owe you all the world. The table here doesn't look that bad," I observe, running my hand across the rough surface. "It just needs to be sanded and re-stained. Not today, though!"

The ladies stay until the sun goes down. They work tirelessly, with me barely keeping up. I've made all the promises I can give, all having to do with some kind of furniture or shelves.

"It'll take me five years to pay off my debt to them," I tell Nick as the women chatter on their way to their cars. "Look at them. They've been working all day and still have a ton of energy." Brooke plays tag with Morgan, and Bailey and Cinda discuss what they're bringing to the party tomorrow. "Thank you!" I shout to the ladies as they duck into their cars. "You're all amazing!"

Monica rounds her way back to me, not stopping until she enters my bubble again. The unmistakable sparkle in her emerald eyes sends a jolt to my stomach.

"Now that we have the house ready... have you thought about how you're going to do your makeup tomorrow?"

Chapter 23 The Party

The day of judgment has arrived. I don't recall a more stressful morning, even counting the chunk of my life when I worked for Robert. I'm still on the fence if I can pull this off. Only time will tell. The downstairs looks excellent, but a keen eye could spot the missing kitchen cabinets, touchups needed in freshly painted areas, the unfinished fireplace, and the gaping hole in the kitchen window. Plus, what if the guests want to see the rest of the house?

I'm grateful that Monica and Bailey spent so much time in the foyer and living room. At least the guest's first impressions of the house will be good before their opinions come crashing down. And why wouldn't they? The way Nick has talked me up, they probably think they'll be entering a house that should be on 'Cribs.'

Nick shares none of my dreaded anticipation of our guests arriving this evening. I've gone through nearly all of my outfits, and nothing works. Everything I own shows my tiny baby bump. Even over the last two days, I swear the baby has doubled in size, wanting to make his or her own grand appearance at the party.

"Joanie, you're fine," Monica soothes. "You haven't even tried on the outfits I brought."

'This needs to work. Otherwise, Nick's coworkers will have much to discuss over the water cooler. *Did you see Nick's house in shambles? How about his wife's frumpy outfit?"*

"They're going to talk after being here anyway."

"I have a hundred things to do, and the party starts in an hour!"

She grabs my arm as I walk by. "Tell me why you're so nervous. What's going on?"

"It's just," I sigh, "I've never felt accepted. Like ever. It's mostly my fault. I've been too busy to get involved in anything. It took me a while to accept this move, but now that we're here… I don't want to be an outsider anymore."

"That makes sense," Monica says firmly with a tug of my arm. "Sit down. Let me finish your makeup." I plop in her chair in defeat, wishing this whole thing was over. "This is your house, it's your domain. Whatever they think, you need to own it. You've put in a lot of work here in a short amount of time and you need to be proud."

I ease into her words, closing my eyes as she brushes on makeup. Only when she's done does she allow me to see myself.

"Oh, Monica. I look kind of pretty," I say quietly, allowing the compliment to flow from my mouth, lined perfectly with dark pink lipstick.

"No, you look stunning. You sure clean up nice, Joanie," Monica says with a wink, grabbing my shaky hands. "Stop being so nervous."

"Um, hello!" I say, holding my hand out to my disastrous bedroom. More than one outfit was thrown across the room before Monica got here.

"They're not going to come in here," Monica chuckles. "People are coming to get to know their boss's family better. They're not going to criticize your home."

"Yeah, right," I say with a chuckle. "People love to pick

others apart."

"Maybe in other places. Some of that happens in Garden Valley, sure. Like that club of gossipers who have been chanting outside the salon. They're mostly harmless, though. They put their hour in and then go get pastries. We have a good community." Monica pats my shoulders and continues to shower me with praises. "Your party can't be worse than Joan's bachelorette party was."

"Joan's?" I ask with interest.

"She decided to have it in a barn, which wouldn't be so bad, but all the animals were still there. Somehow, the pigs and sheep got out, and we spent the whole party corralling them back. Some people fell in the mud, others in cow pies. We all had hay stuck in our hair by the time we left." I laugh, the imagery somewhat easing my stress. "Go try on that dress Amy is lending you. I bet it'll be perfect."

Monica's sister, Amy, lent me a blue and white sundress that comically matches my new living room. Knowing Monica, I doubt this is a coincidence.

"I doubt this will fit my weird shape. I don't know if you've noticed, but I'm a pear," I shout from the bathroom.

"And I'm shaped like a teenage boy," Monica quips. It always surprises me to hear how even the skinniest of women have issues with their bodies.

To my delight, the dress fits perfectly and barely shows my pooch. After I give her a twirl, she gives me a two-thumbs-up rating.

"Enough primping! If you want me to stay, you'll have to chain me to the vanity!" I say, heading for the door.

"Sounds kinky," Monica says behind me.

I speed-walk to the kitchen after my makeover and find a pleasant surprise. "Cinda! What are you doing here?" I ask with exasperation. I can't stop myself from giving her a hug full of relief.

"Joanie, you look nice! I figured you could use the help today, and I needed an excuse to get out of the house," she says with a full mouth while stirring a slow cooker filled with teriyaki meatballs.

I'd worry about feeding all our guests, except Cinda made a colossal-sized lasagna, Monica brought a king-sized Caesar salad, and Brooke and Bailey each brought a side and a dessert. It's more than I could have asked to have these near-strangers agreeing to give up their week for me and bring food!

"You have no idea how much I appreciate you!" I say, pulling out the vegetable and cheese trays I woke up at five this morning to assemble before nailing up the rest of the wainscotting. I know people are supposed to bring food, but I couldn't help myself.

Every appliance and slow cooker I own is filled with my favorite appetizers. They are replacing the dusty, paint-filled smells with the wonderful aroma that reminds me of when we used to have holiday feasts when we were all together in Fargo. Monica was right; with the oven and slow cookers, the house is plenty warm, even with the afternoon breeze blowing through the hole in the window.

The boys run through the laundry room, spreading mud on the floor. "Whoa, whoa! Take your shoes off." I catch Morgan just in time before he tracks mud through the house. I add tickles to their tummies to lighten all our moods. "You two need to wash up and change, okay? Put your clothes in the laundry basket." I use my voice of authority, but the boys aren't listening.

"There's chocolate cake in it for you," Cinda says,

holding a cake she must have made. The boys freeze, having been quickly won over by the sugary treat. "As long as your mom says it's okay." They look to me for an answer, but I'm not bending that easily.

"It depends on how clean they get."

"I'll be squeaky!" After dropping their shoes off outside, Morgan tears through the house with Dillon in tow.

"There's nothing wrong with a little bribe," Cinda says, revealing another parenting secret. "Besides, this dessert uses applesauce and zucchini in place of half the sugar. It's so good they won't know the difference."

"More tricks I need to steal from you," I say, shaking my head.

"You're doing great, Joanie. What's in the oven? It smells like heaven," Cinda says, bending down.

I sneak a peek at the tiny bump that harbors my own bun in the oven before quickly giving an answer. "Bacon-wrapped figs. It sounds weird, but…"

"They look amazing! You have all these slow cookers full, the coolers are full of drinks, and you have this amazing punch," she says, spooning another ladle full into her glass. "This is going to be a great party, Joanie," she assures.

"Thanks to you guys, I only had to make two dishes. As long as people stay close to the food in this vicinity and don't go snooping through the house, we'll be fine," I say with a shaky voice.

The doorbell rings, cutting Cinda off from what I'm sure is a speech of reassurance that mirrors Monica's.

"What? They're a half hour early," I sulk, removing my apron and smoothing my dress.

"Go ahead; I'll take care of what's in here. You'll be great," Cinda says, turning me around and shoving me out of the kitchen.

Nick and I meet in the common area by the stairs on our way to the door. He sucks in a breath and flashes a smile that warms me from the inside out. He would smile at me like this even if the house was falling down. "Somehow, Monica made you look even more beautiful." He's wearing a shade of blue that matches my dress.

"I don't need any help getting warmer," I say, fanning myself. "I don't think I've ever been this nervous."

Nick rests his arms around my shoulder, walking me slowly to the door. "This place looks great. I hope you can relax and have a good time. I'm sorry it's been so stressful. I'll make it up to you."

"It hasn't been easy. But… it did push me to get these rooms done." I look around at my house, feeling like I've been on a decorating show where they wave a wand and turn a room into something as impressive as I'm witnessing firsthand.

"Just a quick bite to eat, and then we'll kick everyone out!" Nick says, trotting the rest of the way to the door. I hold back, allowing him to greet the mysterious guests.

They exchange the usual greetings while I look on in high analysis mode. A couple and their two boys enter the foyer, their eyes roaming over every inch of the place. And why wouldn't they? This is the reason they're here, after all, isn't it? Bitterness fills my mood, wondering if this is a typical Garden Valley initiation.

"This is my wife, Joanie," Nick says, ushering the family of four into the living room.

The man instantly engages Nick in a topic about work while the woman looks me in the eyes and hands me a casserole.

"I'm Carrie, and this is my prized egg and meat casserole. Your house looks lovely," she says with an easy smile. Why wouldn't she be relaxed? She's not the one on the chopping block. To my surprise, she chose casual jeans and a simple white shirt for the occasion. Even with my sundress, I feared I'd be underdressed.

I want to disagree with her compliment but stop before the words form. "Thank you," I say, turning as I hear the boys barreling downstairs. They've cleaned up in record time and are dressed in button-up shirts. "Your kids can play with mine upstairs or outside if they want."

The four children strike an instant friendship as I look on. I blink a few times with a thought hitting home. I need to change this automatic thought of envy. I've made friends easily in this town. I already have more friends here after a month than I ever have.

Carrie looks around the living room as Nick opens the door for more early arrivals. Ready or not, here they come!

***

Forty-five minutes pass before I slip from the room to join Cinda again in the kitchen. I've stretched my face into a smile for long enough, and it needs a break.

"How's it going out there?" she asks as she plates more bacon treats.

"One thing's for sure: I suck at being a hostess," I say, plopping on one of the bar stools that arrived yesterday. "Small talk never has been my strong suit."

"Judging by the level of talk and laughter, it seems everyone is having a great time. And these are amazing,"

Cinda says, popping a bacon-wrapped fig in her mouth. "I've had five already."

"I wonder if Joan and Alice will agree," I say, spying on the two critics in the living room.

"So that's what's causing you so much tension."

"How could it not?" I bark. "Neither woman has wanted us here. Alice made it clear that we weren't welcome."

"She does that to anyone new in town. She walked up to my place two weeks ago and told me our blue house trim was off-putting," Cinda says with a snort. "Let me ask, do either of those women live here with you?" Confused, I shake my head. "Do you think you'll have them over often?"

"Goodness, no."

"Then what's the problem?" I gasp at the statement again that has the effect of calming my every nerve from head to toe.

"Everything's ready here whenever people want to load their plates."

"Okay, great," I say, liking the natural progression of moving on to the food and away from focusing solely on the house. "They sure brought a lot of food, didn't they?"

"And some housewarming presents," Cinda says, pointing to presents on the table.

"Oh! I certainly wasn't expecting anything like this," I say in surprise. Cinda gives me a knowing look that doesn't require an explanation. This crowd isn't as stuffy as I thought they'd be.

I sink in disappointment in myself. I've let my nasty interactions with Joan and the protestors typecast the Nick's coworkers instead of giving them a chance.

I whisper to Nick that the food is ready, and he taps his wedding ring on his glass to get everyone's attention.

"Thanks to my wife and her friend, Cinda, you can eat to your heart's content." Several guests let out a small hoot as a few shout jokes such as 'We won't fire you then,' or 'We're only here for the food.' "And a big thank you to everyone who brought a dish or gift. Here's to hoping no one gets food poisoning!" He raises his glass to the chuckles around the room.

Some guests form a line to the kitchen while Joan stays pointed on the couch. Despite what Cinda said, seeing her makes me shrink an inch. It's not like I can ignore her attitude. It only takes one bad apple to spoil the whole bunch.

"How do you like the town?" an older woman next to me asks. I'm embarrassed that I didn't see her, with my eyes focused on the two Negative Nellies.

"Oh, it's good," I say with a nod. I haven't thought much about how I would respond to questions like this. The woman stares up at me, awaiting more of an answer. Her silver bob shimmers slightly as she talks. Her sweet face reminds me of my mother, easing me into her presence. "I really like the weather here."

"It's rainy this time of year, but April showers, you know?" she says sweetly. "You have a nice place here," she says with a pat on my clenched hands.

She moves on to the line when Nick comes out of the kitchen, holding a plate of food for me. "I got your favorites," he says, shining his smile. He's in his element with being the host of the party, and acts as if he knows nothing of my inner turmoil. While I'm grateful that he's spent every free moment getting the house ready after work, I still wonder if we had to have this party so soon after moving in. Why couldn't he have put his foot down and at least delayed this a few months?

"Thank you," I say, barely able to look him in the eye as I take the plate. I've allowed my resentment to grow toward him. He has caused me so much stress in the last few months. Based on how tightly I hold my plate, I'll have to revisit this topic with him later.

And that's when it hits me amongst this crowd in my house; I've barely shared my feelings with him aside from that one time during dinner. I've taken his apologies, but I haven't shared how I've truly felt about this whole thing. I've kept my head down, jumping into every project and not allowing myself time to digest this move.

An honesty settles in that I'm forced to acknowledge, surrounded by all these strangers. Maybe I didn't share this with Nick because I've been enjoying myself in Garden Valley. I've been having fun with the boys and have felt fulfilled with accomplishing these projects. With a Cinda-like fashion, I deem these feelings to be enough.

I now gaze at my husband with a softer attitude as he carries Dillon around, proudly introducing him to his new friends. He meets my eyes and gives me a wink, which still sends a pleasing jolt to my chest. I take a deep breath, finally feeling more at ease with this party and our situation.

"Just look at this ding," a woman's voice rings out. Hers is amongst the general murmur in the room, but I can hear the critique as loudly as if she were to scream it in a bullhorn. "I can't believe the shoddy craftsmanship that is plaguing this town. So much for 'progress,'" she says with air quotes.

To my horror, a few people gather around my obvious blunder in the wainscotting, touching it and telling stories about workers' mistakes in their homes.

"It's because of all the new housing developments they're putting in," Alice chimes. "We only have so many contractors in town; they must be spread too thin."

"I saw a bigger ding over in the other corner, too. Joanie, you should ask for your money back or at least a discount." It's another wife of a man Nick works with. The dozen or so people all turn to look at me, awaiting my response.

My eyes flicker to Joan, and I witness her first smile. Figures. It shouldn't matter what their opinion is, but it does. I want their approval. I want to belong, to have a community of support and love from my family. I want to follow my purpose and feel accomplished. I want it all.

My hyper-sensitivity to my flaws kicks into full gear, my vision of fears playing out in real time. Guests across the room inspect every inch, pointing at God knows what other mistakes I've made. I had some help with these renovations, but we were in a rush. None of that matters. I'm the ring leader of this operation. This rests solely on my shoulders.

The room begins to spin around me, and I'm convinced that every laugh and conversation is now about my faults. Nick even runs his hand against the wall where the chair rail meets the fresh light blue paint where a small gap is. He's pointing out my mistakes, too!

"My mom did that!" I turn to look, astonished to see Morgan speaking out. Every person turns to look at my boy, who limply holds his plate of food. "She's been working really hard on our home every day since we got here." Everyone looks back and forth between Morgan and me.

"Morgan, honey, it's okay," I say, taking his plate before it spills to the floor. My heart is hit with his enduring words as he defends me. "I know my work is flawed. It's why I didn't want y'all in my house," I snicker. The guests laugh, thankfully understanding my joke.

"I bet none of the other girls here could do this,"

Morgan continues. "Heck, maybe even some of the guys too." This makes the group emit an embarrassing chuckle. I put my arm across his shoulders and give him a loving squeeze before he can continue.

The woman who started the domino-critiquing effect stares at me, her face changing to sympathy. "Wait a minute. I saw this house a few months ago, and it was in shambles. Joanie, did you do all of this?"

I nod, now unable to find my voice. It's my worst nightmare living in plain daylight.

"She did," Morgan answers for me with clutched hands. "She's a carpenter, and I want to be one when I grow up." His words bring a chuckle from the crowd and tears to my eyes. It's worth it to endure this criticism to hear him stand up for me.

Suddenly, none of it matters. The grumbles dissemble and fly out of the window with the afternoon breeze. The knots in my stomach unravel. Morgan will never again need to get me a Mother's Day gift, for this moment will forever be soldered in my memory.

What's the problem?

The phrase that has pushed me along is helping me yet again to shed the fear I've had for this very scenario. Sure, I've made a few mistakes while getting the house prepped for this party, but look what has happened: Morgan and Dillon have been noticing my hard work. Morgan is even proud enough to stand up for me and wants to follow in my footsteps.

The woman touches the ding again and looks at me with glossy eyes. "Well, that makes this tiny ding something special, then." We nod together, this moment forming a bond between us. "I can't believe you did all this yourself."

"I did," I confirm with confidence. "Or, I tried to. And I even had time to feed my sourdough starter!" The group laughs in response in only a way that the Garden Valley residents would understand.

"I've told you guys that my wife is a fixer-upper," Nick interjects with an arm around me. He lightly squeezes my side, and I wonder if he notices the extra cushion that joined me this week. "She literally took this place from studs to this. I have a slideshow to prove it," he says with a finger in the air. "I have a little surprise for everyone, especially you," Nick says, throwing a wink my way.

He jogs upstairs, returning a few seconds later with an old projector. I glance at Joan and Alice, whispering in the corner like they're the head of the high school gossip club. If they want to be miserable, let them!

Nick points the projector at an empty wall, which is now hard to find now that we have decorations. He plugs his laptop into the projector and starts commenting.

"Joanie and guests, this is the transformation of our house thus far."

I smile sheepishly, looking around at unfamiliar faces, wishing I could run to my room and hide. Cinda comes in as soon as the lights dim down. I grab her the second she gets closer to my side, whispering into her ear.

"Did you know about this?" I ask forcefully.

"I had no idea," she says with a head shake.

"Sorry for the slideshow, but you are intruders in my home," Nick jokes.

"More like a shitshow," I mumble. The people around me chuckle in response, loosening me up as Nick continues.

"This is before we moved in," Nick says, running through a few pictures. A photo of Nick with an exaggerated frown starts the show with the caption *Alone in Garden Valley*. "And then, this started to happen."

Nick first shows pictures of the muddy chicken coop and then of me and the boys working together to paint the small building. He has captured photos of me in my dingy clothes, woodworking, pulling those dreaded weeds, and showing the boys how to use measuring tape.

"As you can see, my wife works tirelessly. This is the before picture of this room. This was before Joanie got a hold of it."

The picture changes to the living room when it still had the dusty brown carpet. The crowd makes an audible gasp, commenting on how good it looks now.

"I don't believe it!" the woman beside me says, with a friendly nudge to my arm. And yet, Joan still clenches her crossed arms. The differences in personalities throw me for a loop. All of the people I've met are rounding out my experience here like a joiner does to a piece of wood.

"Joanie has spent every waking moment working on this house. And look, there's my little 'Stickers,'" he says, showing a less-than-flattering picture of me in the shop with my tongue sticking out as I measured a piece of wood.

"Oh, Nick!" I say, allowing my face to fall into my hands. The slideshow continues, with each before-and-after picture gaining more approval.

"Can she come to do my house next?" a woman asks as her husband frowns next to her.

"Not before she comes to mine," someone else says.

"And here's the ghost goat named *Glenda*," Nick says, giving me his sideways glance. He urges me to tell everyone how Glenda gave me quite the scare when we moved in. Everyone eats up the story, with people roaring in laughter once I recount the climax of the situation with the bird and cat. I even see Joan smile again.

The slideshow comes to the final days with pictures of me and all the girls painting away. Photos of Dillon balancing a chick on his head and Morgan holding weeds out to the camera keep the group entertained while they eat. A shot of Nick and the boys bleating with Glenda is one I'll have to frame.

"If it weren't for my wife, her friends, and our two boys, this place would still be in the dumps," Nick says.

"Hey, don't forget us!" Nick's dad says with a raise of his glass as my mother-in-law pats him on the shoulder.

"Of course not!" Nick replies with a smile to his dad. "Thank you to everyone who has helped, and thank you, Joanie. You have made this house into our home."

The slideshow ends, and the room erupts in a friendly cheer. My eyes move to Joan and Alice again when the light flicks on. Alice shakes her head before doing something I hadn't expected: she claps. Joan nods several times as they whisper and soon joins in the clapping. Our eyes meet, and she nods with the tiniest of smiles.

"And just like that, you've won them over," Cinda says with a comforting squeeze.

Chapter 24 Dropping the Bomb

With the party in the rearview mirror, we're on to more house projects, taking them at a much slower pace. Today, we are painting the ghosty goat room. I've decided to remove the door and some of the wall, opening this closed-off space to the living room with a large framed entrance.

"I want to do it, Mommy," Dillon says, taking a paintbrush from me, eager to help. I've given them a tutorial about how to paint with an extra reminder to be more careful since this isn't the same as painting the coop outside.

"Thank you," I say, touching his shoulder. We share a smile, mine full of pride and his full of admiration.

"Your hand is all better," he says sweetly, brushing his fingertips against the squishy part of my left hand that is back to its normal color.

"It sure is, one hundred percent!" I say truthfully.

It's funny; we've lived together for their whole lives, but we've only really gotten to know one another here in Garden Valley. Every day, I learn something new about my kids and them about me. They think I'm a master electrician and carpenter when doing something easy, like changing one of the flickering lights in their bathroom. They love my dorky jokes, which has allowed me to tap into my inner child every chance I can to make them laugh.

I love my position as a stay-at-home mom and fixer-upper. It feels good to breathe life back into this old house. I imagine the walls are happy to have laughter bouncing off them and little feet again pad across the floor.

"I love you, house," I say, stretching my arms out wide to give the wall a hug. The boys laugh and say I'm goofy. "Hey, come here a minute," I whisper into Morgan's ear when Dillon and Nick run an errand to the back garage. I've interrupted his painting on the ladder with his ever-present beagle on the first rung, but something tells me he won't mind.

He follows me to my room, where we can be alone. I unclip my knife from my belt and hold it in my hands. I kneel to one knee as my dad did with this informal ceremony.

"You've proven to me over the last few weeks that you are worthy of wielding this knife. I would be honored if you carry on the family tradition."

Morgan gingerly takes the knife from me, his face stuck in a serious stare as he traces my maiden name engraved on the blade. "My name is on here."

"That's right," I nod. "I don't think you knew that my last name before I married your dad was Morgan."

"I didn't," he says, shaking his head lightly. "What about Dillon?"

"I have another one for him when the time comes," I answer, proud that Morgan is concerned about his brother. I pat him on the shoulder, but his watery eyes show he needs more. I engulf him in a hug, tearing up myself.

"I won't lose it!" he promises.

"I know you'll take good care of it." Morgan clips the knife onto his pants at his waist and holds his chin high.

"You have to be responsible with this one," I say with seriousness. Morgan's lips form a firm line as he gives me one big nod. This alone shows how much he's grown since we've been here. "Good. I have to go to the bathroom, and then I'll meet you back in Glenda's room."

"Okay!" Morgan says, running from my room.

Our room will be renovated last. I took the time to wash the carpet in the bathroom, so at least some of the 'ick factor' is gone. It'll need blinds, decorations, and possibly new furniture one day. Along with the rest of the house, my mind has switched these tasks from worrisome to enjoyable.

I look forward to tackling the different parts of our home. Everything I touch transforms into something beautiful. It blooms before my eyes, like the lilacs of Garden Valley that I love so much.

I pass by the room next to ours, the one for our mysterious guest taking residency in my womb. This time, it feels different than when I was pregnant with the boys. They pooched out early, sharing my news with the world whether I wanted to or not. With me being busy around the farm, I still only have a small bump. Even Nick doesn't seem to notice when we are alone at night. Of course, I have been taking advantage of the lack of street or city light glow in the late hours, hiding in the darkness.

I saw Dr. Thompson yesterday, and she said the baby and I are healthy. I'll be finding out the gender next week!

I have no idea how my boys will react, Nick included. It feels like we've always been a family of four. I hope it doesn't damper the bonding we've been sharing with this whole move.

My boys are hard at work when I join them in Glenda's room. "Remember, Dillon, just put the tip of your brush in, don't dunk the whole thing," I instruct while climbing the ladder. Yes, I'm pregnant and on a ladder. It's probably not my best idea, but it's not like I'm incapable of being safe, with my stomach still small enough to allow me to be nimble.

"Got it," Dillon replies.

It's common for us all to be together like this on the weekend. Nick wired the house with a new speaker system and has queued up a playlist for us to paint by. "See, I can do stuff, too," he says with a friendly pat to my butt.

We've been spending hours talking while doing these projects together at night. Nick and I walk around the property while the boys play, discussing our dreams and visions for the house and yard. Being here has opened up a whole highway of communication that we've never had before, taking our relationship to the next level.

We fly through the room with him on the roller and me on the trim. The second coat overwhelms my senses, even though I got the less smelly paint. My head buzzes to the point of me getting of the ladder and sitting in my favorite spot, now complete with a chaise lounge.

"Are you okay, Mom?" Morgan asks. He has been in tune with me more than ever lately, asking why I'm eating so much and taking a nap some days for a few minutes after I pick them up from school. I've been making the excuse of working like a horse around here.

"I'm fine. I just need a whiff of fresh air." I step outside and press my hands on my lower back while taking deep breaths to clear the smell. "It's all normal and okay," I say with a touch of worry.

"Walton?"

"Ugh, go away, Sheldon!" I look up to the sky as if begging it to strike this bird with a bolt of lightning.

The bird shifts his head around to look at me from all angles with those creepy red eyes.

"Joanie?"

My name from his mouth stuns me. I break my grouchy stance with him and laugh.

"You okay?" Nick asks, standing by the door.

"He just called me Joanie," I say, pointing at the blackbird. Nick and I share a laugh until sprinkles dot our heads. I find the sensation refreshing and tilt my face up to gather the drops.

"It's raining out here," he says with his hand out to collect a few crops.

"It's just sprinkling. It doesn't bother me," I say, taking another deep breath. Nick squints his eyes and turns his head with a smile. "The paint fumes got to me for a second."

"Huh. I didn't notice since you got the non-smelly kind," Nick says suspiciously. Is today the day that I tell him? I'll be damned if he makes another decision for me by guessing. I can't exactly show up one day with a baby in my arms. "Hey, how about lunch?" he shouts to the boys. "Maybe hot dogs and sauerkraut?" he says in a lower tone meant just for me.

Oh no. This was the one meal I ate and threw up when I was pregnant with Morgan and then again with Dillon. It's a test! Hot dogs and sauerkraut is one of my favorite meals, except when I'm pregnant.

Nick is on to me.

"Sounds good," I reply with a smugness that rivals Monica's.

"Okay," Nick responds with his chin up. "I'll fire up the grill," he says, leading the way to the bar-b-que.

"I need to work on a back porch," I say, hoping to change the subject. "I've sketched out furniture plans."

"Maybe later this summer. It's supposed to be a hot one," he says with a glance my way.

Yup, he's speculative. I was pregnant with both boys during the summer months. It was a killer for me to be out in the sun. Even five minutes was too much. I constantly drank water and ducked under an umbrella or tree to stave off the plague of being light-headed.

"That's what I hear." I pretend to brush this off with a swipe of my hand across his back as I pass by.

We sit down for lunch twenty minutes later with apples, chips, and the God-awful-looking hotdog. I've opted for mine without sauerkraut, which I don't mind adding to my meals occasionally when I'm not pregnant.

"Mommy, how about some kraut for your dog?" Nick asks.

"Ehh, I don't feel like it today," I answered lightly.

"Come on, I know you like it," Nick pushes while plopping a scoop smack in the center of my bun.

Even the sight brings the memory of nausea that now fills my stomach. Oh no, don't tell me I'm going to throw up in front of everyone!

"Excuse me," I say as I rush to my bathroom. Why is this house so darn big? It feels like it takes me ten minutes to get to my toilet, which I've scrubbed clean due to the time I've spent secretly kneeling in this very spot.

I return to my seat with three sets of eyes glued to my every move. And there's the hot dog with sauerkraut. Nope, I can't do it. I push the plate away and pop out of my chair to make a peanut butter and jelly sandwich.

"Morgan, you can have my hot dog. I know how much you love them. It just doesn't sound good today," I say, taking the food out of the remaining cabinets without doors.

Finishing the rest of the cabinet doors is number twenty-eight now on my list instead of thirty-nine. See, I'm getting there. "Yeah, right!" I say, nearly slamming the refrigerator door.

"What's that?" Nick asks from the table.

"Oh, nothing. I'm just wondering when I'll get around to putting the cabinet doors in here."

"There's no rush, right?"

"Sure, of course not." The boys look at Nick with question marks in their eyes, as I'm sure they are suspicious of something brewing. Nick keeps his usual calmness.

No, not calm, *amused*.

I glance over to see that he's resting his chin on his fingers laced together. I sit down moments later and angrily take a bite of my sandwich, knowing the stuff is hitting the fan and hating how I can't stop it. It's not like I wasn't going to tell them; I'm worried how this will change the good thing we now have.

"How about a mimosa to help chill you out, hon? It's been a long day."

And there's the drink I threw up when I was pregnant with Morgan. There I was at a baby shower for a friend, not knowing I was pregnant, and up came the mimosa right in front of everyone.

"Oh, okay!" I say, dropping my sandwich on my plate. I sit back and lock eyes with my husband, who appears to be fighting against the smile on his face.

"What's going on?" Morgan asks with curiosity. I'm sure his intuition is sounding all kinds of alarms.

"Boys, I have news," I say, looking at each of my children. Nick sports a grin with a slight nod. "Okay, here goes," I whisper while straightening the napkin on my lap. "Your father and I love you very much…"

"Ewww," the boys say in unison, shoving each other in play.

"I'm serious now," I shout over their noises. "We've moved here, and we have really come together. It's the loving family I've always wanted." Again, they respond with the eww that has crept under my skin. Of course, this can't be serious. Why would I expect anything different from them? And there's Nick, not helping me one bit as the boys start making that high-pitched noise I hate while messing with each other's hair.

"I can't do this right now! Thanks for the help, Nick!" My voice is choked with tears as I push myself away from the table and flee to the safety of our room. I know they are just having fun, but this is precisely why I haven't been able to share my news with them. I pace the room a few times before I plop down on the bed with my bunny.

"Are you okay?" Nick asks, crawling next to me a few minutes later.

I slump over, not sure how he's going to react. Nick loves babies, but we thought we were done with this life stage. "Nick, I'm pregnant, but I think you already know that."

He tilts his head, his smile remaining. "No, I didn't know. I've only suspected and just now put a few puzzle pieces together. You got all skinny like you were at the beginning of your pregnancy with the boys. You've been pale for weeks, and then today was the clencher." I stare at him, tears flooding my face, awaiting his answer. "Joanie, I'm thrilled!" he says, his voice raising an octave.

"You are?" I screech.

"Of course!" He leans forward to rest his forehead on mine. My eyes close with the feeling of his touch. "I was honestly going to talk to you about this a few weeks ago, about having another baby. I didn't want to put more on your plate though, and I definitely wasn't going to overstep your boundary of me not making any decisions."

"Oh goodness, that's not what I meant," I say.

"I know," he says, playfully tickling my side.

"I was going to tell you a few weeks ago. I'm sorry; I just needed to settle in with it. You brought us here, and the house was practically falling apart. And then we had that dinner party, which turned out to be okay. I need to be included in big decisions!" I cry.

"Like having a baby," Nick throws back. He's not looking for a fight. His wide smile shows the playfulness in his voice.

"It's not like I planned this. I didn't know how to tell you. I guess we're even," I sigh. "I'm hoping the life-changing news will be put aside for a while."

"This is the best news of all. We'll be a family of five!"

"What?" Morgan asks from the door.

"What does that mean?" Dillon asks Morgan.

"I think Mom's having a baby," Morgan whispers to his brother.

"She sure is!" Nick shouts.

They freeze, and neither one of them makes a peep. Worry fills me in the silence.

They're not happy!

My eyes fill with tears for how good it feels to finally get this out. The boys look between Nick and me as I dab at my eyes. And then, something unexpected happens: Nick stands, throws a fist in the air, and yells.

"We're having another baby! Woohoo!"

The boys join him, probably not out of their own

excitement but because they want to follow anything their dad does. It's a wonderful feeling to be celebrated and to have my family excited. The three of them run around the room while I stay with my fingers in my ears.

Nick lifts me from the bed and holds me up with one arm. "We're having a baby! We're having a baby!" they chant with me in the center, taking in every bit of the loving attention.

Chapter 25 Epilogue–One Year Later

It turns out that my instincts were right; I had a baby girl! Nick wanted to name the baby after himself, with a Nichole or Nicoletta-type name. With my brothers calling me Jon most of my childhood, there is no way I will have my one and only girl named after a boy.

It was quite fun to name her, with the boys playing a big part. We followed the same routine as we did to name the chickens, making it a tournament of sorts. Morgan's names all started with an 'M,' such as Max and Marley, and resembled more of a dog name. Dillon picked names of girls from his classroom, such as Hannah and Katie, which I loved.

All in all, we now have a six-month-old beautiful and healthy baby girl, Adalynn, which was my name choice that won. With a new summer approaching, I can't wait to be home with my three kids. We've been here for over a year, and I can't imagine life being different.

The boys bounce out of bed early every day to feed the chickens and goats. They take Glenda out daily so she can be free to roam about and chase after them. My sons have proven to be such a great help that I decided to rescue a dairy cow. If someone had said two years ago that I would give my husband a cow for his birthday, I would have told them they were crazy. Fresh milk and eggs are part of our diet, and the boys and I have been learning how to make butter and ice cream.

I've realized how much I've contributed to pulling my family together again, and it didn't have anything to do with how much I worked at a traditional job.

Adalynn comes with me just about everywhere. Now that she can sit independently, I have a covered outdoor playpen for her on nice days, which are more often than not. She's a fantastic baby who is a mama's girl through and through. She loves to watch me work and laugh at her brothers, and they love to be silly to make her giggle.

It all flows with love and fun. The boys are excited to plant an even bigger garden than last year for their summer project. It was ultra-satisfying for them to pick peppers and cucumbers and eat them or feed Glenda, who is a good role model of eating vegetables.

I've been slowly building a playground with help from the boys. I started with a simple swing set last summer and have been adding on ever since. It's something I never expected to give them, the freedom to roam and play out in nature. I've settled in a peaceful place with my own childhood. Watching the boys play outside and spending their time on our acreage has aided in healing my past fears.

Cinda's ottoman was a big hit. I made a sturdy podium for the PTO, which has resulted in more requests than I can keep up with. At night, Nick takes over a lot of parenting duties for an hour or more to allow me to do the woodwork, all with Dahlia by my side, swishing her tail in glee. It's not a ton of time to work on my craft, but I'm a fast worker. While the boys are at school and Adalynn naps, I work on the house or my furniture designs that are slowly flourishing into a business.

I took Lisa's advice and joined the tribal group in town. We meet monthly, and I've already been accepted into the group. My parents were so proud that they came down to visit and meet the group.

Nick has proven himself worthy several times over at the mill. With his help, they caught up on their orders and expanded their production area, adding fifty new jobs. Yes, he works many hours but has a lot of vacation time and has already been granted a raise. We can now sit more comfortably financially than we ever have. He prioritized staying home with me for an entire month after Adalynn was born, which brought our relationship back fully to the solid ground it once was on. We even have a trip planned for the end of the summer!

I'm living my dream life, located over the horizon in a town called Garden Valley. It's one I didn't even know was out there for me. Dreams that had nearly been forgotten have come true. It took flexibility on my part to step out of my comfort zone. What was waiting for me in Garden Valley was as cathartic as rebuilding a piece of furniture: pure bliss.

What's the problem? Absolutely nothing.

Thank you for reading Welcome to Garden Valley! I would sincerely appreciate if you would give me a review.

Want to read more about the people in Garden Valley? Sign up for my newsletter at www.jeanshelbybooks.com to get a FREE story, Winter in July, featuring your favorite Garden Valley characters, as well as some who will be featured in future books.

Stay tuned for my next book release, Coping With Yarn, coming this November!

I have *many* new books planned for 2025 and beyond. Join my newsletter and become a Jeanie!

Jean Shelby lives in Oregon with her family. Her daily life of being a mom, having a career, being an avid exerciser, and chasing her dreams makes for heartwarming stories of motherhood and friendship. She enjoys family time, writing, exercising, camping, and pounding out a tune on her 125 year old piano.

Connect with Jean on Instagram or on her website at: https://jeanshelbybooks.com